the

second

book

of

job(s)

I0638491

a novel by
ROLAND VERFAILLIE

Purple Onion Press

Published by Purple Onion press
Miami, Florida

Designed and produced by Sigmund Rich, Purple
Onion Press
versessa@comcast.net

Other works by Roland Verfaillie published by
Purple Onion Press:
The Ashley Dancers
The Lie (screenplay)
the book of job(s)

Writers Guild of America, East, Inc.
Registration Number: 1222598
Date Registered, November 25, 2010

the second book of job(s)
ISBN 978-0-9787085-2-8

All work and no play makes Jack a dull boy.
All work and no play makes Jack a dull boy.
All work and no play makes Jack a dull boy.
All work and no play makes Jack a dull boy.
All work and no play makes Jack a dull boy.
All work and no play makes Jack a dull boy.
All work and no play makes Jack a dull boy.
All work and no play makes Jack a dull boy.
All work and no play makes Jack a dull boy.
All work and no play makes Jack a dull boy.
All work and no play makes Jack a dull boy.
All work and no play makes Jack a dull boy.
All work and no play makes Jack a dull boy.
All work and no play makes Jack a dull boy.
All work and no play makes Jack a dull boy.
All work and no play makes Jack a dull boy.
All work and no play makes Jack a dull boy.
All work and no play makes Jack a dull boy.
All work and no play makes Jack a dull boy.
All work and no play makes Jack a dull boy.
All work and no play makes Jack a dull boy.
All work and no play makes Jack a dull boy.
All work and no play makes Jack a dull boy.
All work and no play makes Jack a dull boy.
All work and no play makes Jack a dull boy.
All work and no play makes Jack a dull boy.
All work and no play makes Jack a dull boy.
All work and no play makes Jack a dull boy.
All work and no play makes Jack a dull boy.

bildungsroman (bil'dungz-ro-mon") n. A novel which details the psychological development and moral education of the principle character.

Introduction

You should read <u>the [first] book of job(s)</u>. Although this novel is a sequel, it can stand alone. The first Book of Job(s) chronicles the job experiences of Jack Mc Kane throughout his early career. It is the auto-biographic journey of a young man in search of a good job that doesn't require a lot of hard work. Jack's early job experiences shaped his world view. Others might say, distorted it. His seemingly deliberate choice of menial employments didn't discourage him in the least from posturing as a career advisor. Jack would of course disagree; and argue that such an assessment of his outlook on jobs is a bourgeois attack on his sympathies for the working man. He perceives the plight of the working man as dreadful; not having evolved significantly from indentured servants of the eighteenth century. Jack tends to take an extremist viewpoint when the topic of big business is introduced. He's not invited to fund raisers for the National Institute of Mental Health and the like because he is an outspoken contrarian to its policy on soliciting corporations for donations. This perplexes the Institute. You would think that an opportunity to milk a fat cow Fortune 500 Company through a funding campaign would even the score for Jack. But no, Jack has principles he will not compromise. His principles, so to speak, may surprise his readers because Jack rarely stands on principle when debating his politics. Opinions and biases, yes. Principles, morality or any of the Ten Commandments, no. However he is probably right about the worker being unfairly compensated; even exploited for corporate profits that are shamefully disproportionate to the workers'. He decries: that to become a slave to a menial, shitty paying occupation is the ultimate sell out. He advocates that the job hunter seek out a job that he can exploit for its benefits. In effect, strip-mine it of every advantage. I submit that his unorthodox methods are by and large unfair to the company and not always considerate of others on the job. He proposes that a good job is a con job. And having lofty aspirations to impressive-sounding occupations is fine. But let's be up front about it. The honest to god motivation driving such pursuits is the piggish hunger for a lot of money and social advantage. I have heard Jack say that his own not-so-successful negotiations through a maze of meaningless, piss poor jobs made him the stronger and the wiser for it. But then Jack is the eternal optimist. I believe he's just one of those people who over compensate for a deeply rooted pessimism. But, then I'm sounding like him with all this psychobabble. I can hardly speak for someone else's experience. Now Jack, he'll jump right in there and dissect another man's experience… without ever having met him. Jack is ballsy. I'll give him that. He has the audacity to relate his employment experiences to the universal world of jobs. He is the "every man," of the worker. Each and every job – and there have been many – about which Jack writes is carried off with the enthusiasm of the cub reporter for the Daily Planet. It's like reading a breaking news event. The event is typically about one of his past forays into some job or other he was convinced would lead him to his ideal occupation. The one embodying his entire work ethic: little effort; high pay; and generous benefits. In effect, the 'Golden Fleece' of career accomplishment. He'll absolutely deny that these are his motivations for scaling the heap of jobs he's added to his resume. Maybe it isn't fair to reduce another man's work to the scatological word pile. Remarkably, Jack Mc Kane, the self appointed career guru, has attracted a following. But madmen throughout history have succeeded in rallying fanatics to their cause. His sutra is that all jobs have value. Or, again, truth be told, opportunities to exploit. And if he condescends to admit that there are some 'menial' occupations consigned to idiots, he'll elevate the fools to welfare artists. Men and women who plot their habitual unemployment and display their paltry skills as a ruse to milk the system in order to finance a perpetual vacation. And don't be deceived by professional monikers like MBA, M.D., PhD, ad homonym, ad nauseam. Even Jack will admit to the power of the alphabet, when it comes to titles denoting elitism. America purged itself of royal titles in the aftermath of the American Revolution. However, American's have replaced the earls, dukes and duchesses of the former empire with the educated aristocracy. And don't confuse the highly educated with the filthy rich. There is hardly any correlation between the two. You see, Jack matriculated through the gauntlet of higher education and earned the vaunted PhD in psychology. For all his tedious studies and reckless self-experimentation (you'll have to read his first book), he ended up earning less than the local plumber. He enjoys being called Doctor Jack because it gives him an edge when it comes to convincing people that he knows what he's talking about. His thinly veiled humility is echoed in his pedestrian use of his first name following his academic moniker: "Doctor Jack." I think it's kind of catchy. It has a nice ring to it. Sort of a hybrid persona of one of his former summer occupations as a commercial fisherman, and his present work with the unscrupulous court referrals and the mentally ill (with whom I think he too closely identifies). Captain Jack Sparrow of the psychology profession springs to mind. I say these things about Dr. Jack Mc Kane without forethought of malice. I don't agree entirely with his theories. I do, however, applaud his courage. His formerly heretic pro-labor credo is laudable in these difficult economic times. His Working Man's manifesto may get him on some Big Brother, government Watch List if he isn't more careful. He should consider employing political correctness in his writing. Exercising restraint would be wise when criticizing the government, because Freedom of Speech has been constitutionally modified since 9/11. But I don't think Jack will.

The second book of job(s) will surely entertain and depress you - as only a psychologist could combine in a single work. I read it and grew more fearful and disconsolate about life. I was glad to have finished it so I could return happily to my ordinary life. This may not sound like an endorsement to Jack's book, but it is. Read it. You'll come to understand the paradox. For the time being, suspend your disbelief. With a beguiler like Jack that's not difficult to manage. Doctor Jack's true life escapades are as genuine as reality TV. Through his odd assortment of jobs and a series of relationship blunders he has discovered the antidote to boredom. And, perhaps, even an unassailable resistance against suffering the awareness of life's impermanence that infects the majority of late middle age men.

On this last passage, I take particular note...

Dr. Jack Mc Kane's Biographer

Preface

I wish I had begun this book earlier. In my introduction to the first Book of Job(s), I had remarked on my age. Being fifty was a monumental occasion. After all, it was the half-a-century anniversary of my life. The pensive half-life, self-reflective time when a man takes his inventory. Where looking ahead is a crap shoot on surviving the next decade. Looking back twenty, thirty years is depressing. Looking in the mirror confirms it. However, I refuse to let age deter me. I am a baby-boomer; denying creeping old age and its infirmities. I take vitamins (very special ones that I order off the internet) and work out religiously in spite of low back pain and neck spasms. I look forward to the next job, and the next adventure with unbounded enthusiasm. I look forward to the next prostate exam and colonoscopy with dread. I prefer to focus on the positive: I'm still alive, and I'm still married to the same woman. The latter is a real plus because my first wife divorced me. For reasons that I'd rather not repeat in the sequel. I don't have the same job (the one I worked at for 16 years). I recently felt it was time for a change. After all, that's what this book is all about. It's what the first book was about. Since work defines so many people, I decided to write about work throughout the life span. Mine. The first Book of Job(s) established me as the expert on jobs, and since I have a PhD, I can expound on employment with credibility. My employment credo for those seeking coveted jobs unfortunately invokes anathema to some orthodox management geeks like Alex Drucker and the entire Japanese culture. It doesn't matter that my degree isn't in human resources or business administration. In my opinion these specialties are nothing more than arranged marriages between graduates holding dubious academic degrees and the old establishment. These graduates trade classrooms and graduation gowns for conference rooms and custom tailored suits. They become wedded to management when the rest of us are union members engaged in the cupidity of having one job after the other. My PhD is in social psychology, which makes me a friend to Hispanic farm workers and a socialist. Consider me your career guru. Or consider me your marriage counselor. You never know when you'll need one or both. Employment head hunters and head shrinks are closely related occupations. I profess, along with having impeccable credentials, to be a guru to the job seeker in search of sublime employment. Of course the ultimate job is managing your lottery winnings. Short of that, doing a job for which you have a passion is your best option. This is a lofty way of saying: you absolutely love your job, and it doesn't matter what you make. If you are as unlucky as most and have a boring, mindless job at least strive to earn a good wage so you can afford extra- curricular activities which compensate your piss-poor job. Besides, by the time you're my age you're dream job has vanished. Gone. Like the twenty-one year old athletic stud in the photograph you hardly resemble. The dream job. What was it: successfully self-employed; owner of an internet search engine; financial derivatives broker? Oh, yes, be careful what you dream.

...And from the look on his face I could see
he was one of the lucky ones, one of those
people who like doing what they're good at.
Locomotive, one of the most beautiful engines
ever devised. It was magnificent — big and
heavy and it made me think of a giant laid
over sleeping. Ever since I was a boy I'd
thought running a train'd be the most amazing
thing ever — especially out in the open
countryside with the throttle screaming wide
open, the whole world split by those two rails
*you're hurtling down. I could **feel** it- even in*

that cold dead engine – I could feel exactly
what that would be like. And when I leaned out
into the rain, and the engineer told me about
the sparks flying and he showed me his face,
all I could think about was all the mud in the
pasture, what cranky bitches the cows were going
to be in the morning if they didn't get to
pasture. And whether the mow roof was leaking.
Now, if that isn't a curse, the man said,
what is?

...

Edgar Sawtelle upon meeting an old farmer who
shared his passion about wanting to be a train
engineer when he was a young man.

Well, you get the point. All that remains at
this time in your life is the phantom dreams of
your youth that play hide-and-seek with you. You
come to realize that dreams don't just hide.
Eventually they vanish behind the hoop and webs of
the *dream catcher.* Depressed yet? It's not as bad
as you think. Put the book down and take a moment
or two to grieve the loss.......... Believe me, change is
good. And the best time to make a job change is
when you're on top of your game. Not when you've
been laid off. Don't wait for your job to burn you
out. Even a great job has a finite life span. So,
there is no such thing as a great job. Maybe a
dream occupation, but not a dream job or a great
job. Don't be influenced by the worker drones
whose sole reward is collecting a measly pay
check. They are fatuous lackeys who bow to their
employer's generosity: a pay check; a health
insurance plan; a two-week vacation; and a 401.
Look, I'm not against working. I oppose being a
slave to work. It might seem a contradiction to my
admonition not to let yourself become mindlessly
conditioned to a life of work, considering that
I've had a job since I was thirteen. I wasn't
assembling Nikes in Honduras. I sold snow cones.
For a kid, I made a lot of money. Moreover, news
of my good fortune spread throughout the
neighborhood. That's when the competition arose.
It is also when the politics of the work place
invaded my peace...and profit. The pleasure of
pulling my Red Flyer wagon along, ringing my bell,
shaving ice, pouring syrups and collecting
coin...happily...ended...not so...happily! I was
instigated into entering the snow-cone wars. My
neighborhood rivals, Ron Carr, and David
("weasel") Nickerson painted their wagons for war,
and competed fiercely. They tried under-selling
me, pulling ahead of me; cutting off a prospective
sale, ramming me. Our war wagons finally collided,
and all our businesses failed right there and then
in a flurry of fists, ice missiles and broken
bottles of syrup. Syrup ran the gutters like the
blood of battle. Our great enterprises were
consigned to the scrap heap, the trash pile, and

boxes of Band-Aids. This was my initiation to the free enterprise system and ruthless capitalism. The experience would mark me for the rest of my life.

Management consultants, corporate head-hunters, job placement counselors and Monster Job Search promise to guide the applicant to career nirvana. They depict a market-place of employment opportunities where you get to imagine being the sole shopper. You get to pretend that all the job merchants are competing for your talents. Even though we are now in the deepest recession since 1949 – the year in which I was born! For the gentrified boomer: your dream job is the promise; what you settle for is your personal recession.

For a time during my pre-teen years I aspired to become a rocket scientist. Pun intended, my high and mighty ambitions culminated in the unsuccessful launch of a home-made missile. Although spectacular in its explosive fury, my rocket dreams fizzled. My future building Atlas boosters evaporated that day in a mushroom cloud of blinding smoke. Though my hearing loss was temporary, my father's flashbacks were slower to resolve. I will never forget that scene as it plays over in my memory. Of my father, running for his life down the gravel pit road. In his mind…I supposed he was running for his life at Normandy beach while the staccato of machine guns and the pounding of German mortar rounds echoed in his head. He eventually slowed and came to a halt at Main Street, arms raised in surrender and babbling his name, rank and serial number in English with a bad German accent. Mom and I coaxed him into the Rambler station wagon and drove him home. He spoke and resumed his normal activities by the next day. He never said a word, ever, about that day. And I never again shared the dream inspired by a German by the name of Werner Von Braun. I learned the rule of: "the unspoken understanding."

Another unspoken understanding is the absolute

certainty that we will all die. I dare say this
because death and work are inextricably connected.
In fact, work may be the leading cause of death –
ahead of old age and disease. Bar none: work is
the deadliest occupational hazard. Classic is the
story of a man who shortly after retiring plays a
few rounds of golf or gracefully casts his hand-
tied fly over a pearling stream…and…drops dead of
a stroke. Was the cardio vascular event the cause
of death? Or was the cardio vascular event caused
by work and triggered by the shock of relaxation?
You follow, right? And, no doubt, you agree. So
why don't you do something to prevent it? Because
you're afraid. Afraid of losing your job and a
regular paycheck. But I know you're more afraid of
dying. You wager that you'll die in your sleep at
ninety after a dinner of sirloin and cabernet and
wild love making with someone without the sag and
wrinkles of a sharpie. You want to know something?
The odds of having such a blissful death,
according to the life insurance actuarial, aren't
favorable (except for me). Hold your water. Hope
floats.

Tips for Staying Positive at Work, that don't Work

I don't want to alienate "Yahoo!Hotjobs," because
Yahoo has the decency and good taste to list my
books on their web site. But…although they have
given me advertising and allowed me the freedom to
express my ideas, I don't think they fully support
my work philosophy. Otherwise, the book of job(s)
wouldn't have been relegated to the Humor
category. That's not a problem, because in our
society even bad and patently wrong advice is
given equal freedom of expression. Make no
mistake, wrong is never right no matter what the
spin. The slave merchants think its right to keep
the slaves in irons. Feeding them and supplying
them with the tools of their labor do not make
slave owners humanitarians. To the point: the
current propaganda aimed at prettifying menial

jobs to make them appear other than the piss poor jobs they really are is an unmitigated lie. Take for example - the many examples - presented in a recent article reading very similar to the one introducing this paragraph. So as not to be outright stupid and invite litigation, let's say there are, oh, about five or six suggestions for keeping a positive attitude at work. First of all, the rise in the number of such media generated recommendations strongly implies a mass hysteria of job insecurity and dissatisfaction. The social mandate is: if you have a job that sucks, be grateful you have a job at all. And pretend you are happy and like it. Fake it like a sex worker fakes an orgasm. Here is the foreplay, so to speak, that causes us to posture contentment in order to conceal the monotony of a boring job we don't love.

Embrace Gratitude?

Embracing gratitude is like visualizing peace. New age prophets who pander this slick solipsism have aged like old hippies. Not well. You, my peace loving friend go ahead and visualize all the peace and employment bliss your inner guru desires. We are advised to focus on the positive within the work place: value your colleague; your boss; not having to drive very far to work. Be satisfied with a few table scraps when you're starving? In my opinion it's better to hate your job and everybody and everything associated with it. Because anger can be motivating. Just so long as you don't go postal and take everyone out. Just get out. Preferably with the prospect of another job. A greater danger waits if you pretend satisfaction. Your delusion could become your reality. Worse you could end up dating the colleague you pretend to value. Most likely another malcontent who's also pretending - to value you. Any marriage counselor would tell you, if he could step aside from being gratuitously professional, that the circumstances surrounding your relationship was inauspicious from the start. Now there are kids, a mortgage, divorce, child support - and the job you have to keep in order to pay for it all.

Commit Random Acts of Kindness?

Sonja Lyubomirsky recommends doing things to help your co-workers without being prompted. Sonja is a faculty member at the University of California. She heads the *Positive Psychology Laboratory*. I believe it consists of convincing people to behave like two-legged Humboldt rats that have been neutered and lobotomized into being happy all the god damned time. Whenever work research from a laboratory is introduced into raw society Homeland Security should raise the threat level to red. When social scientists speak of the architecture of a concept, expect a social re-education program comparable to the Patet Lao's. The Work Laboratory is another Killing Field for the worker who justifiably seeks to avoid unpaid overtime and complains about low wages. It is wrong to inject happiness into the workplace where it doesn't belong. Here are the precepts of this system of making happiness happen:

The Architecture of Sustainable Happiness

- Mechanisms of Sustainable Change in Long-Term Positive Affect

- Mediators and Moderators of the Effects of Activity-Based Happiness-Increasing Interventions

- Pursuing Sustainable Happiness Through Practicing

- Gratitude, Kindness, Optimism, and Savoring

- Adaptation to Positive Experience as Barrier to Sustainable Happiness: Mechanisms and Interventions

I would prefer to have a root canal than be trained in happiness intervention. Come to think of it, why not just pipe nitrous oxide through the office AC system. Professor Lyubomirsky prompts us to: give a colleague a ride to the airport; offer up one of your sick days to someone who doesn't have any left. She'd have you believe that you'll get points in job heaven if you commit such acts of kindness at work. It's okay to drive someone to the airport, when that someone's a back-stabbing co-worker, after he's been sedated and you've bought him a one-way ticket to Bagdad. As for the person with no sick leave left? You be the one who's used all his sick leave. Praise the philanthropy of the do-gooders. Specifically target a Lutheran. Their ticket to heaven is paid for in "good works". The favor will be reciprocal. Enjoy the day off. Don't wait until you're sick.

The professor and I may be at odds in our behavioral prescriptions. We are not so different when it comes to recognizing the benefits these acts create. She points out that the benefits of committing these acts are good for both parties: "It's a good thing to do - and it also makes you happier in the process." I couldn't agree more. 'Was it good for you honey?'

I won't enumerate all of the jobs you could do for a living (no pun intended). My suggestions for jobs-of-the-future are expounded upon in the first Book of Job(s). In the first book, I drew heavily on market research. In other words I worked a lot of jobs and wrote about them. I certainly worked enough meaningless jobs to know *what not to do* for a living. Conversely, I was able to distill the

scads of occupations listed in the Dictionary of
Occupational Titles down to the few precious gems
that pay well and require very little effort. My
experiences in the work world have made me an
expert on employment. I have become intimately
familiar with the liabilities and benefits

associated with many occupations. However, if you
are past your prime; meaning you have no future,
read on. Young or old, it won't hurt to read
further. Who doesn't want having his future
foretold? Scrooge didn't, but it helped him. It
redeemed him. And it gave his employee a day off.

The Second Book of Job(s) is, to borrow another
book's title, a Course in Miracles. It will take
no small miracle to have a good death - painless;
following food, wine and sex - after having worked
enough years to retire young. The second book of
job(s) will reveal how you can work and live
happily until the day you die. Hopefully later
than sooner. And lastly (I promise), this is not
some curmudgeon's memoir. I've heard enough about
the virtues of work, so I won't repeat the lies. I
have no philosophy of work or of life to impart to
the young, so I won't create a, "Philosophy of
Life and Work for Idiots." There are enough of
those - philosophies of life and idiots - already.
However, it is unnecessarily time consuming trying
to figure it out on your own. Nevertheless, it's
the mistakes you make and the corrective actions
you take that shape your life. It is true that,
"what doesn't kill you, makes you…," well, gives
you another chance. Or makes you wish it did. I
recently tasted the bitter platitude espoused by a
retired, military double dipper. He bragged, "When
you get old you can be ruthlessly honest. You can
finally tell it like it is." He had been sharing
his shameless opinions about others' misfortunes.
About how the problems others experienced were
self induced. That the self-defeated had no cause
to bitch. He opined, "What do they expect? They
signed on for the job. They should just suck it
up." Rather than empathize, he sought to
euthanize. He judged the working man a drone

deserving of being devoured by the more powerful of the hive. The old man believed he had nothing to lose by being insensitive. Remember what happened to Scrooge. And he was old. The moral of the story - and the thesis of this book (sounds scientifically grounded) - is: Keep a fucking low profile if you have a good scam going. Don't poke your head out of the gopher hole when the gamers' got a mallet. And, for Christ's sake, warn the worker drones that the queen is a hungry bitch with a voracious appetite. And it's best to beat feet - or wings - and leave the hive before your sorry dead ass belongs to her.

Chapter 1

The Unemployed Professional

What do you do when you have neither the state licensure nor the investment capital to start a private psychology practice? This was my dilemma when I returned to the United States. I had been an expatriate for nine years. I had worked for the feds for nearly a decade of my life; having divided the time more or less equally between facilitating the mental health of soldiers whose primary role was training to become human killing machines, and developing services on military bases throughout Europe to comfortably sustain them while they prepared to annihilate the Russians. As you can imagine my job was, well, challenging. I found satisfaction in cultivating the, "warrior within." Within myself primarily. I was never really one to take the "peace and love" mantra of the 60s to the masculine-neutered extreme. I am loath to admit that I failed at peace; my avoidance of conflict with guys bigger and stronger than me might have been mistaken for pacifism. Love was my strong suit. Although my misfortunes in romance might suggest otherwise, my failures at marriage have had less to do with love or commitment. My problem was mate selection. In deference to my ex's, their problem was the same. Our different personalities, religions, politics, world views, education and life goals were mutually shared differences. In one instance our mistranslation of our foreign marriage license and its commensurate obligations led us down the aisle to extinction. Although, in the short term, these differences in a couple don't matter that much. Had I been wiser and fluent in a particular foreign language I might have been a better example to my patients. Like practicing what one preaches? However, I felt that I did those patients more of a service by making many of the same mistakes that they had sought me out to treat. I've digressed.

Putting all that's gone before aside, I left government service under protest. Donna, my wife of nine years by then, and mother of our two children, delivered the ultimatum: "Choose: Your career or your family."

"Having to choose either, "a" or "b" is poor test design," I told her.

"Then how about, "c," alimony, and "d," child support." Donna was a hard bargainer. She didn't cheat at cards because she didn't have to in order to win. I, on the other hand, always hid an ace up my sleeve. When I palmed the card and laid it down in this game, I exposed the Joker. And Donna and I had always removed them from the deck before we played a hand. So how did it get there? And how did we arrive at this juncture in our marriage after our nine year sabbatical in Europe? I could no longer stack the deck in my favor. I had just run out of luck. And there I go with those cheesy metaphors on life. Life doesn't need metaphors to explain its quirkiness. It has the world with its gravity bearing down on us, and the friction of its nine-hundred and sixty miles per hour revolutions to wear us down. One little jiggy-wiggle of the earth's momentum while buckled into seats aboard a Lufthansa 747 Donna, and I and our two young kids were deposited in the USA. I was spilled into that vast nation of endless highways, Mac Donald's drive-thrus and weak beer. I vowed to remain an ex-patriot, speak German and move to Wisconsin. Like most promises people make in crisis and soon after recant, I too reverted to the local customs. It happened embarrassingly, seemingly, overnight. Nevertheless, my pride remained intact and I bitched constantly about everything for months afterward. It was Donna's god damned logic and her immutable reality fixation that deflated my bitching and moaning about Wisconsin and all things domestic. Although it was June, she rebuffed, the temperature in Wisconsin was thirty-eight degrees. And to hell with me, and my disregard for what was practical; she wasn't moving any place where it snowed in summer. And so, the argument over before I could say a word, we ended up in Florida living with her parents. It was to be a temporary arrangement until we got on our feet. Meaning that in Donna's plan for my future, I would hire on as city manager of Palm Beach Gardens within a month or two. Why the city manager of Palm Beach Gardens? I supposed it was because it would be a short commute to work, and I could ride her nephew's bicycle. "Why," I asked her, "did you suggest the city manager job?"

"Because they are interviewing for a new city manager, and isn't that sort of what you did with the Army?"

"Donna, I have no experience with the kind of corruption the job demands. I was a government bureaucrat. I rose through the ranks on merit, not on favors and pay-offs."

"You have no idea what potential you have." And she left it at that, with me asking myself what the hell she meant.

Two weeks later...

"How do I look"? Does the suit make me look managerial?

"Yes," said Donna to her soon to be city manager husband. "You look very professional. You'll do well in the interview. I just know you will."

And that's how it went. There's something to be said for the American Dream, and the promise that you can achieve whatever it is you set your mind to become. It's a crock. A mythical American trope. The exaggerated expectations of your mother or your spouse are not a source of confidence you should bank on. Nevertheless, I would oblige my well wishers.

Part II

"Tomorrow's Jobs"

(From the Occupational Outlook Handbook)

Executive, administrative, and managerial... occupations are projected to increase by 16%, or 2.4 million, over the 1998-2008 period. Workers in this group establish policies, make plans, determine staffing requirements, and direct the activities of businesses, government agencies, and other organizations.

Significant Points

- General managers and top executives are among the highest paid workers; however, long hours and considerable travel are often required.

- Competition for top managerial jobs should remain intense due to the large number of qualified applicants and relatively low turnover.

My interview with the city's hiring committee was at 10:30. In fact, I was notified by official correspondence the week before that I was among the three finalists selected to be interviewed. The process of selection was no less a long drawn out affair than what passes for alacrity in government service. A month had passed since I had applied, and the contest had yet to be decided by yet another round of interrogations. I had been tested and evaluated by the best, and I knew from experience as an experimental psych post-graduate student how to behave like a trained hamster. I was confident that I'd negotiate this hamster Habit-Trail with expertise.

I arrived at city hall for my interview fifteen minutes early. I didn't want to appear too eager for the job by showing up any earlier. Being on time, mimicking the precision of German transportation, was an ingrained habit. Arriving fashionably late like an Argentine dinner guest was not an option. Although I had considered hurrying to the reception desk at 10: 45 and apologizing for being late, explaining that I had been called upon to render CPR to a choking restaurant customer where I had left my coffee to grow cold and my bagel half eaten. Heroics would be unfair to the competition. I was still the first to arrive. I took this as a good sign. I figured the other two finalists had dropped out of the competition. Maybe one had taken a lesser job saving her the embarrassment of entering the swim suit round of this competition. And the other? I could only hope that he had been struck by lightning on his way here. I had the job.

Ms. Shalanski, the receptionist, burst my bubble. She informed me that I was first up to be interviewed. We were scheduled an hour apart. What, were they afraid we'd pool our answers or fight each other to the death for the job? I wouldn't have objected to either method. In my opinion, the corporate world had grown soft since Machiavelli. It wasn't beneath me to play dirty. I figured being adept at dirty politics was a prerequisite. However, I didn't rule out that Ms.

Shalanski might be a spy, whose observations of the prospective candidates would be delivered to the committee in a thumbs-up, thumbs-down shorthand gesture behind our backs. I remained on guard; self-conscious about crossing and uncrossing my legs as I sat impatiently waiting to be called. I caught myself drooping one leg over the other and slouching all girlie like. I noticed Ms. Shalanski looking at me quizzically. Her thoughts I imagined running along the lines of, "Do we want a gay man running the city?" I grunted in compensation while pulling my leg up to my groin nearly rupturing my hernia and strangling a testicle. I rearranged my fitful appendages and sat stock still in the rupestrian pose of Rodin's "Thinker." I was on the verge of passing out from unconscious breath-holding, when Ms. Shalanski's intercom buzzer snapped my out of my hypoxic coma. I heard the muted voice of a woman who sounded like a Burger King drive-thru clerk informing Ms. Shalanski that, "Dimcomddiiiistweddeesee - mursterrmigkannn." I'd ordered enough Whoppers to understand that that the committee was ready to see Mr. Mc Kane in the flame broiler. Ms. Shalanski rose slowly off her chair, an act of great effort, since I observed that this woman packed a heavy trunk. We must have resembled a Native totem pole with my head and shoulders attached to Ms. Shalanski's torso. My lower half was lost behind the woman's copious ass. She opened the door - fortunately double doors - and demurely waved me ahead. I had to illegally pass her on the right, and shimmy a bit sideways to enter. The committee chairman motioned me in, and directed me toward the empty chair at the conference table. Ms. Shalanski backed out, drawing both doors closed as she maneuvered her bustle in reverse. The doors closed, and the sound

they produced was like a vapor lock. I half
expected to hear… *hiss*, *poof*… and feel the lick of
blue flames from a rack of propane jets. I was
having an anxiety attack. My sick imagination was

interfering with my characteristic calm. I had to
pull myself together. It didn't help that I was
sweating, and the perspiration from my armpits was
trickling down my sides. I engaged in therapeutic
self talk since it's not a bad idea to practice
what I preached to the nervous wrecks I've
counseled. 'Look.' I told myself. 'This is just
an interview. You're the best qualified for the
job. If you aren't selected, it's their loss.
Donna will stick by me…until the divorce is
final…and my in-laws evict me.' It wasn't helping.
The chairman, a Mr. Porter, gave me a withering
look. He had asked me a question while I was lost
in my tortured reverie. He had mouthed some words
but he might just as well have been a deaf
interpreter. Suspense hung in the air. He
repeated, "Tell us Dr. Mc Kane why you believe you
are best qualified for the job." My thought? 'Dumb
Question.' But I fought the urge. My answer
required a well crafted humility. One powerful
enough to restrain my ego from having me reach
over to the intercom and buzz Ms. Shalanski to
have maintenance gold leaf my name on the door of
the City manager's office.

"Because I am your best qualified applicant."

"Would you be so kind as to elaborate upon
your qualifications," piped up the woman on the
panel, who'd introduced herself as the city
attorney. She was fiftyish, a dyed brunette. She
wore a stylish, androgynous suit with black pin-
striped pants and a matching unbuttoned jacket
exposing a crypto-mammary cream colored blouse.
She looked inviting but displayed the stalking
behavior of a predatory cat. I was about to be
cross examined.

"Well, Ma'am, I…"

"Ms. Goldblum, please, Dr. Mc Kane."

"Ah, yes…Ms. Goldblum." Well, as I was about to say, I have considerable executive management experience, very possibly more than the other city manager candidates, and as such, I understand what is needed to effectively manage a large scale city government like North Palm Beach."

"But, Dr. Mc Kane, as I read your resume, it indicates that you worked for the federal government. Overseas I might add. How does working for a federal bureaucracy *operating in a foreign country* qualify you for city management?" The sweat was beginning to leave salt rings the size of the Nevada Salt Flats under my arm pits. The fucking bitch was a Republican. I was her enemy. A former fed threatening a take-over of city government. Her eyes were the crimson color of a bad photograph. She must be fuming over imagined widespread unemployment and bankruptcy under my socialist pogrom. I had to ease her suspicions. After all, I had lots of experience with deescalating paranoid sociopaths. She was a lawyer. Same thing.

"The government work I did demanded superior business acumen. The departments whose performance I managed have their counterparts in city and state governmental agencies. Take finance for example. I was the responsible fund manager for an eighteen million dollar budget. That budget included over a thousand line entries to include businesses, personnel, infra-structure support and ancillary services necessary to the operation of a large scale military installation." I felt myself swelling with pride, and about to stand up at full attention and snap a salute. Fortunately, I restrained myself. Learning from Dr. Strangelove the pitfalls associated with misplaced patriotic zeal. Particularly while confined to this conference room which felt like Hitler's Berlin bunker. I realized that positioning myself as an outsider, and worse, a democrat-subversive wasn't in my best interest as a job candidate. I'd have to win the panel over, and to do so I'd have to make an ally of Ms. Goldblum.

"So, Doctor Mc Kane...and I believe (*she squints over her bi-focals at my resume*) ...yes, you're a doctor of...psychology. Not economics, government, management? But not to dismiss your credentials as incompatible or insinuate that you might be unqualified to manage a growing city government; after all you are an expert on human behavior. Yes?"

"Well, yes..."

"Then I shall pose a psychological question: If you had to describe the City of North Palm Beach to a stranger in one sentence, what would you say?" I was wondering whether the stranger was a vagrant, a Japanese tourist who no speaky English or whatever. I was probably walking into her trap by over thinking the stranger angle. In Ms. Goldblum's mind the stranger is most likely a potential real estate investor or construction company chairman from New York or Chicago or at the least a retired GM worker and his wife from Michigan.

To the astute body language interpreter, my posture and eye roll up and to the left was screaming, 'What the hell can I contrive that'll sound civil other then the weather here isn't thirty degrees Fahrenheit in July and you can build high rises in the everglades and sell every unit to the unlimited supply of suckers who flock here every winter with the seasonal migration.' If the truth will set you free, then a lie will allow one to walk on bail. So, to buy time, I sat stroking my beard trying to appear pensive. Nothing came to mind. Nothing at all! Mind a blank. Not a thought...zero, nada. I am aware of how quiet the room has become. Of how the committee members suddenly resembled devilish Awaji puppets with gaping mouths and huge, wooden eyes rolling in their sockets. I realize I'm not breathing. I know that oxygen deprivation isn't very conducive to thinking, so I take a deep breath. And with a suddenness that sends a shock wave through me...answers to the question I didn't know I knew gushed out like storm water through a broken damn.

I let go without forethought. You know the feeling. The thrill in the pit of your stomach, the screaming in your head when the car brakes fail and you're accelerating downhill toward the cliff where the road ends. I am wide-eyed like a biblical prophet, filled with inspiration the source of which could have been my higher power (at the moment I forget I'm an atheist), I exclaim: "North Palm Beach is Florida's best kept secret. It straddles two cultures – the town and the city – where a family can grill out in the back yard in the month of December, and have at their disposal all the amenities of luxury shopping, excellent schools and local employment opportunities. It is a residential comfort zone that is within easy commuting distance to the major industrial and high tech employment centers. Its near-by beaches, parks and water attractions offer year round recreation. It is a town beloved by its residents for its hometown feeling and sense of historic community (*Amen*)." I slide into home, breathless; trying to remember exactly what it was I said. So, like a devotee of back woods religion having spoken in tongues, I awaited their welcome-home-to-Jesus embrace and pats on the back.

The panel of three, including a guy who'd introduced himself as councilman, a meek looking guy who I took for a clergyman or the city's medical examiner, looked at one another with a look of… well, a look I was having a hard time reading. Either they had unanimously pegged me as a big bull shit artist, in which case I had the job or a nut who just cracked under the pressure and painted much too pretty of a picture of their lackluster town. If the latter was their consensus I'd be hired to run the chamber of commerce. Either way I'd be happy. My neural juices not yet depleted, I sat poised in that high strung sort of way, and waited for the next question.

Silence. I swear I can hear the quartz works of the wall clock ticking (no, not oscillating) like the Telltale Heart. Ms. Goldblum pours water into

her glass from a sweating pitcher, takes a
delicate sip and swallows, Mr. Porter thumb clicks
his cross ballpoint pen like he's sending Morse
code, and the creepy guy rests his folded hands on
his protruding belly like he's greeting mourners
at a wake.

After what seemed like forever (exactly two
hundred and eleven atomic oscillations of the wall
clock), Ms. Goldblum says, "Thank you, Dr. Mc
Kane." *That's it?* Thank you she says, as if I had
picked her pencil up off the floor, and she was
acknowledging my good manners. She looks down at a
stack of papers in front of her and begins
shuffling through them like she's scanning sale
items at Macys.

Mr. Porter, the chairman, took this as his
cue to continue the interview. Ms. Goldblum had in
effect exited the stage, and now Mr. Porter,
deeply inhaled and swelled to the size of a
ninety-five pound buffo toad. He bellowed, in a
timbre that startled me. For a man who moments
before sat rigid as a bean pole and looked as
insubstantial as one, expanded exponentially and
bellowed: **"DOCTOR MC KANE, AS YOU MAY BE AWARE, WE
HAVE A AH...RATHER LARGE MINORITY POPULATION. SO...AS
THE DEMOGRAPHICS OF THE CITY CHANGES, WHAT
PROBLEMS DO YOU THINK WE FACE IN THE FUTURE"?**

Large minority. An oxymoron, like being the
tallest kid in a family of dwarves. Was he making
reference to fat black people? Was he asking me
to re-invent the Final Solution? Should I answer
like a social activist and propose programs and
services that would expose me as a socialist
candidate? Over thinking again...

"Well, the demographic trends are the growth
of a more affluent, older population, *and* the
increase of disadvantaged and immigrant
populations. I perceive a vanishing middle class,
which means fewer middle income families taking up
residence in the city..."

"And just how is the city manager going to bridge this divide, Doctor Mc Kane?" The challenge came from the mealy little worm that had yet to introduce himself.

"Mr….I didn't get your name…? To which he replied with a dead stare…"This divide, how do propose to overcome this impediment to our social and economic stability? This guy was eager for someone to suggest something awful like genocide, but I didn't want to risk it this soon into taking office. I was beginning to imagine that I had been invited to the Eagles Nest for a chat with the furor's henchmen. Here I am sitting at the table with Eva Braun, Heinrich Himmler and Joseph Goebbels. In the interview, I am being drawn into a plot to rid the city of its undesirables. Or maybe 'Mr. Mealy Worm' wasn't the Grand Wizard or a Neo-Nazi. Was he conceding that the races could be seamlessly integrated? And it was up to me to reconcile the class divide. Well, there was no straddling the barbed wire fence on this one. I'd ere on the side of equal rights… "These shifting trends are going to require a city manager who has the ability to identify the programs and the public relations initiatives that will facilitate bridging the gap between rich and poor…er…as well as attracting and retaining our middle class families."

"Eloquent equivocation, Dr., but, are you proposing that the city concoct a public relations snow job to fool people into believing that the… ah, blighted areas of our city are undergoing a renaissance of beautification…an illusion that would require a dozy of a snow job. This is Florida, Doctor Mc Kane. We haven't seen a snow storm since the last ice age," he chortled.

"No. Not only a public relations campaign. I believe I can develop solutions to the problems we're up against. I will propose solutions based upon my work managing the housing for military families; a population not unlike the city's. I am accustomed to working with people of diverse racial and socioeconomic backgrounds. I've successfully resolved the deep conflicts associated with mistrust and fear on both sides of the class divide."

"And you will approach these rather entrenched attitudes how, Dr. Mc Kane?"

"Through action, 'Mr. Smith,'…

"The name's Cuthperson, Dr.. So go on."

"As I was saying, through action. By taking a decisive stand that will communicate more forcefully the city's intentions. For example, I have read in the papers that the city's affordable housing program has reached an impasse over a land dispute with the county. It seems to me that it should be a priority to partner with the county and move this project forward."

"Yes, and indeed a huge challenge to our next city manager. Thank you, Doctor Mc Kane. I have no further questions."

Mr. Porter had zoned out and was transfixed on some mental image I supposed because he was smiling from ear to ear while staring out the window. There was nothing I could see out there that was even mildly pleasant. Just the dumpsters behind the Circle K, and the Pakistani clerk smoking a cigarette. Perhaps Mr. Porter was looking benevolently upon the "large minority" representative, and was considering offering him an interview for the City Manager job.

 An 'Humph!" from Ms. Goldblum carried the effect of showing the red queen to the Manchurian candidate….

"Ah yessiree Dr. Kinsey… maybe *Mr. Porter was back from some other place than I had imagined…* Oh, beg your pardon, Dr. Mc Kane. You are indeed a…ah… good candidate for the job. My only concern is that you have no city government experience.

Nevertheless, you present yourself well and articulate the city's issues very knowledgeably. As you know we have other applicants to interview before any decision will be made. So, we will evaluate all of our applicants, and make a decision within the next two weeks."

And with that, and the forced weak smiles and limp handshakes…the interview had ended. Now, I'd have to wait while they completed the obligatory interviews of the remaining applicants. Politics is fixated on perfunctory procedures while being unwillingly obedient to rules of fair play. They could have saved themselves the time and trouble - and the other applicants their inevitable disappointment - by handing me the job right there and then. But I suppose they had to go through the motions of giving everyone a fair chance and the experience of torture-by-committee.

I left the interview with an air of self-confidence. I stopped for a coke slushy at the Circle K. I thought it wise to support local small business while being seen doing so from the windows of the town hall conference room. I didn't hurt either to become friendly with the minority refugees that had taken over the city. I felt like I was on the job already. Donna and my in-laws would be proud. They'd be on the phone talking to this person and that telling them about her husband and their son-in-law, the city manager. Donna and I could now start looking for a nice bungalow to rent. Someplace close to city hall. Why wait for the official word that I had the job. We'd start looking for a place tomorrow. I also needed a new suit. I was thinking, Brooks Brothers. No, Louis Vouton.

Two weeks later...returning from the mail box at Wabash Drive.

Dr. Jack Kinsey
2550 Wabash Drive,
North Palm Beach, FL

Dear Dr. Kinsey:

Thank you for the opportunity to meet with you and discuss your qualifications for the position of City Manager of North Palm Beach.

While we were impressed with your background and experience, we have concluded that another candidate's qualifications more closely match our requirements. We sincerely regret that we cannot offer you employment with our organization at this time.

You have our best wishes for success in locating the career opportunity you deserve. We appreciate your interest and the time you have invested in interviewing with the City of North Palm Beach.

Very truly yours,

Mr. Henry Porter,

Chairman, City Governing Council

"Failure is only the opportunity to begin again,

this time more wisely."

Unknown

No wonder, he is unknown. To fail — SUCKS!

And to know this is wise.

The Author

Dr. Jack Kinsey
2550 Wabash Drive,
North Palm Beach, FL

Dear Dr. Kinsey:

Thank you for the opportunity to meet with you and discuss your qualifications for the position of City Manager of North Palm Beach.

While we were impressed with your background and experience, we have concluded that another candidate's qualifications more closely match our requirements. We sincerely regret that we cannot offer you employment with our organization at this time.

You have our best wishes for success in locating the career opportunity you deserve. We appreciate your interest and the time you have invested in interviewing with the City of North Palm Beach.

Very truly yours,

Mr. Henry Porter,
Chairman, City Governing Council

DOCKORFUCK'NKINSEY….No pun intended. Perhaps they had interviewed the enviable doctor of human sexuality studies and thought it best that he not be city manager. So he could continue his valiant work on perfecting the orgasm. But who was I kidding? It was absolutely humiliating that I left such an impression on the committee as to have them misspell my name. And a boiler plate letter. No wonder the city was in trouble they had a template for everything. The bastards wanted a clone for the job; just another city manager identical to the roughly twenty-five thousand, three hundred and seventy-five thousand places in which there might be a town or city manager in the more precisely three thousand counties comprising the whole god damn United States. Well, Dr. Kinsey and I would have to ply our indispensible professions apart from politics. And as for Donna - cruel for having falsely inspired confidence in a husband fearful of having to live with his in-laws until social security benefits would produce an income - should gladly share my fate. I would show her my, rather Dr. Kinsey's, rejection letter (after I ironed it) and say nothing. Let my silence envelope her like a poisonous Bhopal fog, watch her blanch in a gesture of empathic disappointment, and then turn on a well worn Birkenstock sandal and walk away. Show her my back without the pathetic slouch. Rejected, yet still noble and impervious. Just Like that.

I threw the letter way. I decided to lie by omission and just let the whole matter go away. If in a week she asks, 'Geez, haven't you heard from the city yet? They should have called you about the job by now.' And those were her words exactly, when she asked the question three days later. To which I replied…with a shrug and walked away...with a slightly pathetic slouch.

"I don't want to talk about it."

"Didn't they give a reason? Who did they hire? Are they hiring for assistant city manager? Maybe you should have called a few times before they sent out the letters, and told them how interested you were. What are you going to do now?"

"I don't want to talk about it."

Chapter 2

'Jack 'of all Trades

I didn't talk about it. I'm still mad at everybody: Donna for encouraging me against such staggering odds; my in-laws for their wisdom - knowing I wasn't going to get the job and not interfering by stating the truth; and with myself for going along with the whole charade and trying to please everybody. I'm really pissed because, for a while there, I started believing I had the job. Being a psychologist didn't do me any good. I could be just as gullible and delusional as the certified lunatic. You see the difference is that I was aware that I was being stupid. And admitting it exonerates me. Now, if I were to do the same thing, say a month from now, then I should be given a psychiatric diagnosis of some sort. I know the virtue of learning from bad experience. If for no other reason than to spare myself the same disappointing outcome that was the result of the first unsuccessful effort. To my credit I didn't apply for assistant city manager. Even though I would have had a damn good shot at it.

When there is no plan B, you should be spontaneous and create one. I did. I accepted an offer to do lawn maintenance for the condominium association that my mother-in law works for. She, being a realist, saw a future for me in this fortuitous opportunity. See, she was managing the business affairs of the company that owned the condos. And, as you no doubt realize, these virtual city states are comparable to national corporations. Or at least feisty little Banana Republics. She was positioned to hire a temporary lawn service when no reputable business would bid on a contract designed to enslave illegals who'd work for guano. She added that I could double dip as night watchman for the condo to supplement my income. Marion missed her calling. She should have been born a hundred years earlier as the over-seer of a Mississippi plantation. To her credit, she saw me as a young buck that could handle menial labor with the mandatory shuck and grin. She had me by the balls. If I refused I would be homeless.

Although I'd whimpered below the threshold of hearing I accepted the offer.

Donna admired me for my grit. For my willingness to work far below my station. To continue to support us, no matter the cost to my ego. It goes to show that female biology is still hard wired to swoon in response to the primitive male attributes of muscles contracting under servile labor, and the pheromone scent of failed underarm deodorant. I would be irresistibly sexy to my wife, but too exhausted to perform.

Part II

Lawn Service Occupations

(Information derived from the <u>Occupational Outlook Handbook</u>)

Significant Pints: There are seldom minimum educational requirements for entry-level jobs and most workers learn through short-term on-the-job training. Opportunities should be excellent due to significant job turnover, but earnings for laborer jobs are low.

Working Conditions: Many of the jobs…are seasonal, mainly in the spring, summer, and fall when most planting, mowing and trimming, and clean-up are necessary. The work, which is mostly performed outdoors in all kinds of weather, can be physically demanding and repetitive, involving much bending, lifting, and shoveling. Grounds keeping workers may be under pressure to get the job completed, especially when preparing for scheduled events, such as athletic competitions or burials. Those who work with…potentially dangerous equipment and tools such as power lawnmowers…must exercise safety precautions…and take care to protect against hearing damage.

Blades of Grass...

Cutting lawns is an activity. Therefore you can't classify it in the same category as contemplating a fly on the ceiling or watching paint dry. It is nevertheless an excruciatingly tedious occupation. I injected creative effort into my labors, and did all manner of 'things' to make the chore more bearable. Nothing I did seemed to change the fact that these acres of grass possessed the character of the open prairie in the time of Lewis and Clark. It is unforgiving. Leave a few hundred square yards untended, come back the next day, and it's grown knee high and has become as tough as jungle creeper vine. Florida grasses are genetically engineered to be resistant. Resistant to drought, scorching summer heat and the forged steel cutting blades of a riding lawnmower (particularly when wet after a series of afternoon rain showers). Like chalk art on a city sidewalk, your work is transitory. Cut the lawn, and your perfectly trimmed edges and even cut is gone in a matter of days. A hardy mix of matured Bahia and St. Augustine grasses trimmed like a barber's number 4 buzz cut, looks like the greasy dreadlocks of a homeless Rastafarian by the end of the week. The pride I had taken in my compulsive attention to detail was impossible to sustain beyond the first month as a lawn man. I had taken pride in achieving a precisely manicured, former prairie of grass. Now I was spent of any such ambition, and besides the pay sucked. The six-hundred dollars a month amounted to five dollars an hour when I did the math.

There came a glimmer of renewed enthusiasm when Donna offered to help. She was faster than I was. Whereas I took my time in negotiating every turn - using reverse gear more than forward to ensure the most evenly mowed path - Donna drove like a farmer at the wheel of a columbine. The condo lost a few flower beds to her reckless riding, and some thorny bushes got trimmed to ground level. Harvey Saperstein, a septuagenarian resident whose macular degeneration hadn't progressed that far, noticed that where once rows of begonias, bromeliads and jonquils had bloomed had been reduced to patches of scorched earth.

He complained to Marion: "Those beautiful flower beds. You know they cost a pretty penny. Paid for by my maintenance fees...Gone! Apparently mowed down by those careless groundskeepers. That kind of beauty can't be replaced...just like that." I imagined him snapping his fingers inches from Marion's face for emphasis... 'Just like that'...SNAAAP! Marion described his visage as that of a Jewish Golem in lime green Bermuda shorts, wearing canary yellow knee highs and sandals. "Oh, did I mention that he was wearing the tackiest polyester knit shirt. And in this heat no less. I think his wife must be blind as well." Marion was a keen observer of human wildlife.

She told us that she had done her best to assuage the condo complainer's threat to, 'take the matter before the board.' She took the best possible position. She lied. Marion blamed the equipment. A defective lynch pin in the trail-behind mover's coupling...that she swore she had brought up to the condo's former maintenance chief. And which, as she predicted would happen, result in a catastrophe – a *minor* catastrophe, Thank the Lord – because of his neglect. He bought it, and because his memory wasn't that good, would probably forget the whole matter during his elevator ride to his twelfth floor apartment. Marion should be the one in the family to run for election in the next political season. She is better at modifying the truth than I am.

Donna was demoted to push mover driver. She was a pretty sight pushing the fire engine red Toro mower around the property. She could negotiate the tight spots, and trim the edges along the fence line; careful not to lay faro the occasional flowering survivor. Her tanned body, perspiring in the torrid heat was like a carrot

46

before the horse (me). If women are hardwired to
the scent of men's pheromone rich sweat, then men
are attracted to the heady muskiness of a woman in
heat, and I mean just hot and sweaty. Khaki shorts
and a sleeveless blouse that clung to her perky
breasts - nipples erect like plump raisins in the
occasional cooling breeze - helped take my mind
off the servility of my labors and tuned me in to
my baser instincts. I was a man on a mower in
pursuit of quarry. Running through bramble bushes
in pursuit of a mate is far less painful than
running through brambles for your life; say from a
charging leopard. The incentive was a feral
attraction that would last only for so long as it
took for dehydration and heat stroke to take
effect. Surges of testosterone, prostaglandin and
oxcytocin by-pass the survival instinct for water
and rest when running on empty. And so during my
ardent chase after my two legged mate (who now
appeared to have four legs and three heads), I
swooned , not in passion but from heat stroke, and
rolled off the Dixie Chopper while downshifting to
third gear.

I came to lying prostrate and staring into
the sun with a cool towel being pressed to my
forehead. My first thought was: "Is it true that
you'll destroy your retinas if you stare directly
into the sun? If I'm blind would everything still
be bright?" I must have been asking the question
out loud, because the cool towel was placed over
my eyes, whereupon I thought I must be dead. That
would explain the bright light.

"Are you okay? Should I call 911? You seem
alright except you're really red, and your
breathing is…shallow, fast…you look kind 'a
weird." The fact that I could hear every question,
although I couldn't answer Donna (I never could
answer every question she'd ask), reassured me
that I was alive. I tried to rise, but I didn't
have enough strength. I remembered the Alexander
Technique. The system that taught a person how to
use gravity and one's natural momentum to get up

from the floor or to move gracefully through life. Since there was no grace to be had, I used my training to get the hell off the ground. Or should I say, grass. I attempted a roll to the right, hoping the momentum would help bring me to my hands and knees from which I could easily stand. Instead I found myself face down, my slack jaw clamping down on a divot of sod. It was at that moment that an overwhelming anxiety seized me. Like the grip of a strong current pulling me under a sea of grass. I was eye to eye with infinity. Blades of grass in such numbers as to overwhelm the senses. Strange how the mind works, and what goes through your head when experiencing the void. No matter the color- whether the black abyss or an infinitely green one – it really doesn't matter. Donna's advice was, "Just lie still till you get your strength back. You color's better now. Just wait. Okay?" I estimated while awaiting the return of my spirit (both in terms of attitude and spiritus), that there were approximately 320 blades of grass in the square inch of lawn staring me in the face. I'd do the math later, and would learn that one acre of lawn contains roughly, 457,380,000 blades of grass. Times that by the condo's seven acres of lawn and the realization blew my mind. I can now identify with the reaction of the Tax Watchdogs when they estimate the national deficit. This awareness heightened my sense of futility about life. Why make your bed every morning if you're going to sleep in it every night? Why wash the dishes if you're going to eat off them again before the food even dries? Questions we all asked as kids of the parent who demanded that we waste our time on such trivialities when we could be out playing. The existential awakening I had while I lie there, as the backs of my legs were becoming seriously sun burned, was, 'what is the meaning of this job, and what is its relevance to my existence?' Why cut the lawn when it's only going to grow back in a week from now? I was no longer the kid with the borrowed push mower earning fifteen dollars to cut a neighbor's postage stamp sized lawn. I realized I made more then, and had more time for the fun things in life. Some childhood thinking becomes old age wisdom. Contrary to Robert Fulghum's, "All I Really Need to Know I learned in Kindergarten," which instructs the wisdom of humanitarian obedience to good manners and decent habits; I'd rather eat more ice cream, and walk barefoot longer in the summer of my life. Playing nicely with others is good advice, but working for them is another matter altogether. This job sucks. And, I quit.

So I didn't just up and quit. I fantasized quitting that moment; leaving the Dixie Chopper idling, and walking away. I gave the obligatory two-week notice. I told Marion I had a job prospect. In my head I heard myself say, 'I would have one – eventually.' Eventually would, I wished, be soon.

Part III

Guards

(Information derived from the <u>Occupational Outlook Handbook</u>)

Significant Points: Favorable opportunities are expected for lower paying jobs, but stiff competition is likely for higher-paying positions at facilities requiring a high level of security, such as nuclear plants and government installations. Some positions, such as those of armored car guards, are hazardous. Because of limited formal training requirements and flexible hours, this occupation attracts many individuals seeking a second or part-time job.

Working Conditions: Most guards spend considerable time on their feet, either assigned to a specific post or patrolling buildings and grounds. They also may be stationed outside at a guardhouse of the sort found at gated communities…. Guard work is usually routine, but guards must be constantly alert for threats to themselves and the property they are protecting.

Double Dipping…Under the Big Dipper

As for the night security, moon-lighting gig? There's not much to write about. It's hard to have writing material other than what constitutes keeping a dream diary. I was so exhausted from my days in the sun that night rounds at the condominium consisted of finding concealment. That is, finding places to sleep. As luck would have it, it wasn't one of those security guard jobs where you had to turn a key at a dozen clock stations. The biggest challenge was finding a place to catch some zzzs where I would be safe from marauding raccoons, or not be trampled by illegal Haitian's coming ashore. Restful sleep is hard to come by when vigilance is keen for such dangers as I just described. And such dangers did arise.

Raccoons are vicious little bastards when out for a romp at night in search of food. They are also, I discovered, not shy around humans, and a sleeping human to them is something close to a passive food source. Or at least another helpless animal to bully. Raccoons travel in packs, like ravers out for mischief. I write about these pests because they are the main distraction to having a peaceful nap under the stars. I don't indulge in those maudlin, anthropomorphic attributions that naïve animal lovers habitually do. Raccoons are not cuddly, cute, little sugar bears. The buggers are native to North America. They were introduced elsewhere in the world, which proved to be a huge mistake. Of all the names, in the many languages for raccoon, the best fitting is *raton laveur*. *Raton laveur* is French; meaning [hand]*washing rat*. A masked, hand-wringing rat doesn't conjure up a pleasant image. A little black mask doesn't conceal an identity. Like the classic depiction of the bandit, the accessory communicates menace not anonymity. Who did the Lone Ranger and Zorro think they were fooling? A raccoon is still a little rat behind the mask. And the little shits are no fun to wake up to when they've commenced to mug a sleeping security guard. I am not exaggerating this scenario to exploit raccoons for humorous effect. Take for example a recent article from *The Tampa Tribune*. The headline reads: "Raccoons attack woman as she tries to wave them away." The article is presented here *in its entirety*, because people should know the dangers they face from such an unsuspecting foe.

Published: October 4, 2009

> LAKELAND – A 74-year old woman is recovering from injuries she received after being attacked by five *raccoons* at her front door Saturday evening, the Polk County Sheriff's Office said.
>
> Gretchen Whitted of Lakeland was seriously injured in the attack that happened at about 5:30 p.m. at her home…the Sheriff's Office said.
>
> "She was gashed open around her legs," said Sheriff Grady Judd. "We're not talking about a lot of little bites here."
>
> "She was filleted," he said.
>
> "Whitted heard a noise outside her house and saw five raccoons in her back yard. They then migrated to her front yard. She opened the front door of her home to wave the critters away, but when she did, they attacked her, biting and scratching her legs. Whitted fell and the animals continued to attack her.
>
> Later, she told investigators, she wasn't sure whether she fell over her own feet or over the animals, Judd said. She also thought that perhaps the mother in the group was trying to protect her young.
>
> Neighbor Christy Steinmetz said she was

sitting on her couch with her family when she heard something that sounded at first like laughter. She was on her way to check it out when she heard Whitted cry, "Help."

She said she found Whitted on her hands and knees trying to get up and the raccoons coming from the porch area. Steinmetz said she backed up in to the street to get out of the way of the raccoons, which appeared to be on their way to a drain.

"She was in disbelief," Steinmetz said of Whitted's reaction to the incident. "She didn't believe the raccoons attacked her."

Whitted was transported to Lakeland Regional Medical Center where she is in stable condition in the trauma unit. She received dozens of staples and sutures, and will require additional treatment.

Typically raccoons only come out at night. Authorities are concerned as to why the critters took part in what Judd called a "gang attack' during daylight hours.

Deputies enlisted firefighters to flush the drain into which the raccoons disappeared, and traps were being set up throughout the neighborhood. Residents were also being alerted to the attack via automated telephone alerts.

I rest my case. I don't make this shit up. I don't know if Gretchen instigated the attack by smearing cat food over her legs, or she teased them into playfulness by falling on the floor. It may be unfair to say that Gretchen may have asked for it. I'm suspicious that she excused the attackers because the gang leader was a "mother who may have been trying to protect her young." God forbid that motherhood should receive a bad rap. I stick by the theory that she teased them into play; falling to the floor like she did; as if a free-for-all with five raccoons would be a barrel of laughs. To top it off this poor woman "didn't believe the raccoons attacked her." She may have been overly medicated when the incident happened.

I, on the other hand, don't cut the pests any slack. They confronted me as I awoke with a start to find myself surrounded by four raccoons the size of pit bulls. They ran circles around me, the way mobs taunt the object of their hatred. They carried on this mad, frenzied dance as if inviting me to strike first. These demonic creatures actually have a cunning intelligence. They are reputed to be able to remember the solution to a learned task up to three years later. I could easily surmise that this roving gang of raccoons was the same that had attacked Gretchen Whitted. I was after all on the ground. Fortunately, I had no sudden urge to laugh. In spite of all their snorting, hissing and barking I would not engage. I knew enough about my enemy from my college courses and from watching years of Animal Kingdom on The Discovery Channel not to provoke a confrontation. I know that adult raccoons are savage fighters. Few dogs can kill an adult raccoon without suffering some mortal wound inflicted by the critters ripping teeth and razor sharp claws. I truly regretted that I was an unarmed security guard. I felt helpless, and though this feeling had grown familiar, I'd never get used to it. I feigned a submissive posture. Not terribly difficult under the circumstances. I avoided making eye contact with the ring leader, a muscular, bristle-haired, rabid looking animal who resembled Kathy Bates as the homicidal, Annie Wilkes, in *Misery*. I rose timidly; at the same time backing up slowly and exiting the hedges where I'd slept and into the open field beyond.

I unconsciously guarded my privates. If attacked, I'd go down fighting to keep my manhood.

My only guess is that my tormentors grew tired of trying to provoke a fight with an unworthy opponent. I couldn't be sure that they had moved on because the hedges were bathed in the coal black of a moonless night. And given the fact that raccoons have remarkable hearing and possess night vision, I wasn't going to be brave and seek retribution by being mouthy and getting all bowed up. The only satisfaction came with a fusillade of paving bricks I hurled in the direction of the stand-off, cursing the mean little fuckers and threatening to trap and torture them the following night.

Part IV

One if by land, and two if by sea...

From Henry Wadsworth Longfellow's poem, "Paul Revere's Ride"

The Haitian problem is one of Florida's illegal immigration embarrassments. "One if by land, two if by sea," warned of the means of invasion by the British in the War of Independence. By land or by sea warns of the invasion of an illegal immigrant by nationality. Mexicans and Central American's come by land. Haitians come by sea. Cubans don't count because they have a special dispensation when it comes to showing up on Florida shores uninvited. "Wet foot, dry foot," pertains to the rule that if a Cuban has set one foot on dry land, then he's as good as a citizen of the United States. However, a Haitian is unwelcome. Haitian dictatorship isn't as romantic as post-Castro Cuba. And the Haitians aren't as well connected politically in the United States as are the Cubans. So when a Haitian sneaks ashore he is usually as disoriented as a hatchling sea turtle lured back to land by the glare of street lights. Lights which lure him to capture, incarceration and deportation. Haitian smugglers will occasionally pitch their human cargo overboard if the coastal patrols are in pursuit. That's similar to what happened one moonless night during my rounds (so to speak). While dozing on the warm dunes along the condominium's shoreline, I was awakened by two wet feet tripping over me. I saw only what can be described as the shadow of a shadow sprawling head long into a thick bed of detritus deposited by the recent high tide. The whites of eyes as big as saucers peered at me from beneath a mantle of seaweed festooned with shells, discarded plastics and old condoms. I must have been a worse sight then the feared Obeah of the superstitious Santeria. The man, it turned out, was part of a small group of five or six Haitians. They apparently were forced to jump from their wreck of a boat and swim ashore as it foundered – out of gas and at the mercy of an angry shore break. They were lucky not to have plunged into a school of sharks or a pack of raccoons. Yes, raccoons can swim, although they're reluctant to just go for a swim for the hell of it. They are responsible to wiping out sea turtle nests, so it's likely you'll encounter a hungry pack while out for a stroll on the beach. Or sleeping under a sea grape bush like I was when I was assaulted. In the water, they're killers. Raccoons can attack in water – okay, usually when attacked first, say by a dog. But the point is, they're as lethal as Bull sharks. If a dog tries to take out a raccoon in the water, a raccoon will hold the dog's head under water until it drowns. Alright, I digress. Suffice it to say, the Haitians were lucky.

And I was lucky too. Lucky that these were your ordinary immigrants, and not drug smugglers or murderers and cut throats released from Haitian prisons and paroled to American society via illegal entry. They were more frightened of me. Thinking, most likely, that I was Sheriff's Marine Patrol or Customs. They were all carrying on in Creole in what sounded like pleading, or surrender or 'don't fuck with us.' I couldn't make out anything any of them were saying. I simply threw my arms up, and started waving them away. And then I thought of Gretchen again, and how when she waved the raccoons away they attacked. I was fearful that this gesture might trigger violence. If it did in raccoons, why not Haitians? They seemed to have a lot in common with those nocturnal critters all of a sudden. I wasn't one to rat out a band of peaceful people who were seeking asylum from god knows what. Haiti isn't a tropical paradise. In fact, Haiti is worse than third world by economic standards. I would have been willing to grant them citizenship myself if it were in my power – and for a kilo of skunk if they were smuggling any. And so for the second time in a week I backed away from a threatening situation. This job had me exhausted and on the ground in a compromising position like the day job did. My resignation was for both employments at the condominium. Luckily I could use the same excuse for resigning from both.

Chapter 3

Doctor Jack and the Beanstalk

It was an ad in the Palm Beach Post Classifieds that caught my attention that morning. I was still sleepy in the lazy way that you get to feeling all the time when time slows due to unemployment. I have to be honest. I was *sort of* looking for a job. Unemployment can become a terminal condition. It's like the vacation – an indefinite, unpaid vacation in my case – where you finally relax. When you haven't thought about work. When you haven't called the office to check in. Worker's do that because they secretly fear they've been replaced by someone younger, smarter and more ambitious than them. It takes, at the very most, a week to forget your employer and your co-workers. God knows they forget your name a few days after you've gone. A vacationer knows that there is danger in vacations lasting longer than a week. The trance-like hold on a worker weakens after a week away from the hypnotic ticking of the office time clock.

The classified ad I chanced upon was straightforward:

Experienced mental health professional needed to provide individual and group counseling to residents of an in-patient psychiatric facility.

Must have at least two years post graduate experience working in the mental health field.

Prefer licensed, or licensed eligible social worker, mental health counselor or psychologist. Excellent pay, good benefits. Send resume to: SPF, P.O. Box 2245, Port St. Lucie, FL 34952.

I applied. I interviewed. I got the job. The interview was less hostile than the one for the city job. More a consensus of the interview panel in the spirit of, "Let's give him the job, and see if he survives." My resume attested to my resiliency to the abuses of crazy clients and insane working conditions. I had managed, thus far, to remain relatively sane thanks to occasional periods of unemployment. The inertia that unemployment produces is a natural tranquilizer. You shuffle through seemingly endless days, weeks and months. But what will get you eliminated off the bat from an interview is being caught in the headlights; that dumfounded reaction to being caught off guard by that tricky question you didn't anticipate. I'd seen Mel Gibson express it while acting out some agony or when he'd be pissed off in some revenge scene. I managed to contain my emotions. I maintained the composure of a basset hound stretched out on the porch of a Georgia farm house.

I was grateful to be employed. The joy I felt was the joy associated with the honeymoon phase of a new job. I had only the anticipation of work, and receiving the first pay check, without yet having actually earned it. That would come in a week after the customary background check, and the professional vetting that would demonstrate I was more preferably suited for employment as opposed to being a ward of the institution. That I was merely empathic without the debilitating symptoms, and therefore qualified to treat the majority of the population whose bad luck or poor management of everyday life could get them institutionalized.

Here I'd come - full circle; from working as a prison psychologist ten years ago to becoming employed in its commercial off shoot - the private psychiatric hospital. For all intents and purposes it was a locked facility from which the inmates could only be paroled at the pleasure of an examining board. The hospital's 5-star rating compared with prisons' more Spartan accommodations made being 'hospitalized' seem more appealing. Namely, to those making the involuntary commitments. But, then, I would do my time here as well. I'd report to work with the sound of a steel door closing behind me, and the metallic echo of a mortise lock as it found its mark. My charges and I would be hermetically sealed from all the frantic business, and unnerving traffic of the outside world. I would get to leave each evening. They would not.

Vacation over. I prefer to call it that. The months without a job were just a short pause in the breathless panting of a man at work for nearly half a century. What I had recently experienced, and dubiously enjoyed, was a mere hiccup in a forty year history involving countless jobs. I must admit though that there is little consolation in profiting from the misery of others. I am a member of a profession that benefits from hard times and people's misfortune. So in this time of economic recession, a rising divorce rate and absent parents hospital admissions are flourishing. My services are in demand.

A therapist's role is to provide support, heal the hurts and facilitate self empowerment. In brief, act as an agent of positive change in the lives of others. Is therapy effective? Yes. I've seen it work. People want to get better; so with or without a therapist they're likely to improve. Therapy may accelerate the process and medication certainly plays a role. Why tough it out alone when help's available.

If there is a down-side to feeling better, it is when you get well and are facing the pile of ruin you left behind. It's still there waiting for you. The theory is that in order to meet these demands one has to have identified the resources they need, replenished their energy and developed the motivation to work through the problems. So you can see that it's important that a patient continues with a therapist on the outside because that's where their left-behind problems await them. Their hospitalization is like my unemployment: nice to get away from all the hassle but very, very aware that lying low can't go on forever. The obligations of the outside world keep nagging at you; calling you back. First just a whisper from that little voice inside your head. And then that voice gets louder and louder. Sooner or later you have to face the world again. Whether discharged from the hospital or back to work, you pick up where you left off. The travails of life: the fucked up relationships; the mountain of bills; and your outstanding obligations - become instant replay.

I believe that some people are treatment resistant, just like fat people can be weight loss resistant. It doesn't matter that they are doing everything that thin people are doing. Fat becomes a permanent burden, and, yes, a losing battle. Rizzo Malmo (a pseudonym to protect his anonymity) was just such a patient. He was certifiably nuts (e.g., delusional disorder and delusional personality disorder - a double whammy). I met with him my first day on the job. Rizzo, whose last name shall remain anonymous, was an employee at the Saint Lucie Nuclear Power plant. More specifically, Rizzo was involved in the refueling cycle at the nuclear plant.

Part II

Nuclear Engineers

(Information derived from the <u>Occupational Outlook Handbook</u>)

Nature of the Work: Nuclear engineers research and develop the processes, instruments and systems used to derive benefits from nuclear energy and radiation. They design, develop, monitor, and operate nuclear power plants used to generate nuclear power. They may work on the nuclear fuel cycle – the production, handling and use of nuclear fuel and the safe disposal of waste produced by nuclear energy – or on fusion energy. Some specialize in the development of nuclear power sources for spacecraft; others develop industrial and medical uses for radioactive materials, such as equipment to diagnose and treat medical problems.

Job Outlook: Employment of nuclear engineers is expected to grow more slowly than the average for all occupations through 2008. Due to public concerns over the cost and safety of nuclear power, there are no commercial power plants under construction in the United States. Nevertheless, nuclear engineers will be needed to work in the defense related areas, to develop nuclear medical technology, and to improve and enforce waste management and safety standards.

…Consequently, most openings will result from the need to replace nuclear engineers who transfer to other occupations or leave the labor force.

As it were, Rizzo, was involuntarily transferred out of the workforce to undergo a mandatory fitness-for-duty evaluation. According to his supervisor, Rizzo had refused to shed his radiation suit after working a shift in the reactor containment area. His crew was replacing spent fuel rods, and like the others in his team, he was dressed in yellow polyethylene from head to foot. He also wore shoe coverings and a hood with a respirator. He had followed the others to the contamination control point. According to his supervisor, Rizzo had set off a warning indicator when one of the friskers detected a hot particle reading somewhere on Rizzo's person. He had removed his hood and shed his gloves. When he dropped both layers of his coveralls the reading on the frisker's monitor showed the presence of low radiation contamination. Rizzo's reaction was to gather up his coveralls and proceed to zip himself back up. This is a big procedural no-no, and what ensued afterwards is classified. I can only guess that Rizzo caused quite a stir with the decontamination control team. He is a skinny yet wiry fellow, and subduing him, let alone preventing a miniscule radionuclide from jumping onto someone or something else must have been a daunting task.

When I met Rizzo, he looked ill at ease. I'd say he appeared vigilant; on the look-out for some, as yet, unseen danger. He was wearing a yellow jump suit with a biohazard patch sewn over his zippered breast pocket. He also wore a device hanging from a dog tag chain that had lettering that read: microwave oven leak detector. I didn't ask about his choice of wardrobe. He looked like an East Bloc member of the space station team. Just floating about weightlessly and having little control over his orientation. His furtive eye movements took inventory of his surroundings. He was not a happy cosmonaut.

"And who are you? Or, should I say, did *they* send you?"

"Hello Rizzo. My name's Dr. Jack. I'm your therapist. I'll be following your progress while you're here."

"Is that so? Well, Doc. You didn't answer my question: Who sent you?"

"No one sent me. That is other then the ward psychiatrist. She essentially oversees all patient care. So, I guess she did."

"You guess. Then you're not sure who sent you."

"No. I mean yes I'm sure. She sent me. And technically speaking, no one really sent me. I'm here because I'm assigned to this ward. And you are one of the patients that I will see because this is where I'm assigned." Rizzo wasn't making this easy. He is one of those engineer types. All linear logical, and this-is-so-because-here-is-the-proof sort of thinker. My brother Ben grew up to be an engineer. I still can't have a philosophical discussion with him.

"Just making sure you're not one of them. They tell me I'm safe in here, and they can't get to me while I'm locked up. Unless…you're undercover - then I'm fucked."

"I give you my word. I'm a psychologist, and I am here to help. Who are you afraid of…"

"Didn't say I was afraid. Just don't want them doing any more of their experiments on me. Right now they're probably too busy testing their devilish technology on other less fortunate inhabitants of this planet. I'm hoping they've forgotten about me. At least for the time being. Probably thinking I don't know what they did, and so none the wiser."

"Who are "*they?*" And what did they do to you?"

"Didn't you read my dossier? Or maybe you don't have the clearance to access my file."

"I've read your file, but I didn't read anything about experiments. I know that you work at the power plant, and that you freaked - I mean understandably - about some low level contamination you picked up while in the reactor containment area…"

"Well, I see they've sanitized the account of what really happened. The version you're getting is the blacked out copy meant for the civilian population. Most likely trying to contain a potential panic if the real story gets out. Hey Doc, you carrying a cell phone?"

"Yes, why?"

"Because they can track you that way. Don't you know anything? I don't want them finding me if they discover that you are in contact with me. You'll lead them right to me. I can't take any chances. I want a new therapist. One who understands what's going on, or at least one who will follow the proper safety protocols"

"If it's any consolation to you, I leave my phone turned off while I'm here. I don't allow in-coming calls to distract me from my work with the patients. So, lets you and I discuss the safety protocols that are important to you feeling safe. Okay?"

"Look Doc, in-coming calls, outgoing calls, they both can be tracked. Your phone contains a GPS locator chip. That's all they need to locate your exact coordinates. So, if I retain you as my therapist, we need to establish some ground rules concerning my safety. Do you comprende, Doc?" Rizzo was playing hard ball with me; trying to take the upper hand. Sharing control with a patient is ideal, but this guy wants to run the whole show. I challenge his belief system too strongly and he possibly decompensates. I buy into it too convincingly, and I help strengthen Rizzo's delusional system. Although I have to admit he is beginning to sound pretty convincing. Shit, if there are men in black suits out there gunning for the human race I want to know about it.

"How about I start by agreeing to leave my cell phone off - for both out-going and in-coming calls. Secondly, lets you and I talk about these people that you're concerned might find you. Is that good for starters?"

"Well, we'll see. But I reserve the right to seek a change of venue if you compromise my security."

"Okay. Fair enough. So to begin with - no phone service while here…"

"No. Turn off your phone before you leave from home. Better, remove the sim card. Otherwise you're like Hansel leaving crumbs along the trail. They'll follow your trail right to me! Look we've got to be real clear on this from the start - if it's not too late already. Listen, Doc, if you get this right, I might take a chance with you. I'll brief you on the project, but not if you don't follow security procedures. If you don't well all I can say is that it won't matter for either one of us. They'll take us both out. So, you willing to follow my instructions, or do you want out?"

"Yes…"

"'Yes', you want out, or 'yes' you will follow my instructions? Which one is it going to be?"

"Rizzo, please, I hadn't finished the sentence. I'd appreciate the courtesy of a little more patience with the process. Yes, I'll follow…I'll work with you on this problem."

"Yeah, well I'm not too sure about you Doc. But, you already know a lot, and I don't want to have to bring someone new into this. Higher probability for a security breach. So, then, we'll do this on a trial basis. And what's this, 'process,' you mentioned? You are beginning to sound like one of 'them' again."

"The process is our methodology. You know, how we work this through slowly from beginning to end."

"What end? You mean when they find me and erase my memory or put me down?"

"No." 'No, damn it,' I said to myself. "When you're better… being less afraid of…being abducted. Not in any danger, so to speak."

"I never said anything about being abducted. You think I'm one of those alien abduction freaks. Those nut jobs that believe they've been taken by aliens and examined with probes and subjected to whatever other unspeakable violations those sick, little green bastards do to gassed earthlings."

"I wasn't suggesting that, Rizzo. You're jumping to conclusions. I should have said, kidnapped, shanghaied or apprehended. And what about the gas thing. I hadn't heard about aliens using gas?"

"Okay, Doc, don't get your panties in a knot. I don't know anything about aliens using gas on people. I made it up. Although, I'd use gas to immobilize my quarry. Untraceable you understand. Stuff metabolizes quickly. No trace in the blood if it's tested. Forensic examiners miss it all the time. Sure to induce amnesia if the right cocktail of surgical gases - one primarily composed of sevoflurane - is used, although I'd prefer an IV injection of sodium theopental. Impractical though, since the bug-eyed bastards aren't tall enough to stick a human with a hypodermic. Makes more sense that they'd introduce a misted form of sevoflurane…take us down even on the run. I do digress"

"Yes. You do. You appear to know a lot about anesthetics. Have you studied medicine?"

"In my spare time. Never hurts to keep up with the latest in medicine in case all the doctors are wiped out, and you find some wounded individual in desperate need of an operation." I was growing concerned that Rizzo might have taken advantage of women he might have dated. Worse, that he might take it upon himself to operate without permission on some stranger with a ruptured gall bladder. I didn't want to imagine what Rizzo was capable of if released before he was stabilized, and on the right anti-psychotic drug. It was bad enough that I was working with the likes John Nash, Jr., the central figure in "A Beautiful Mind." Rizzo was no Nobel Laureate. However, he did share a paranoid imagination like Nash's, and a fear of them - the men in black.

"Rizzo, let's wrap it here, and get back to work tomorrow, say 2:00 o'clock."

"Okeedokey. Fourteen hundred hours sharp. Don't be late, Doc. And, remember, loose lips sink ships. Keep it OPSEC...You read Doc?"

"Roger that, Rizzo."

The next day...1400 hours - sharp!

"On time Doc, I like that. I hold you to the standards of George Washington in the matter of arriving on time for an appointment."

"Alright, I'll bite. What is the standard you attribute to George Washington?"

"Well, when George's secretary was running late for an appointment he gave the excuse that his watch was too slow. George was on him like the stickler he was about being punctual and said, 'You must get a new watch, or I must get a new secretary.'"

"You're not George Washington, Rizzo?" And I am very conscientious about keeping my appointments on time."

"And you Doc aren't like his secretary. So I'll keep you on."

"The occasion could arise where I may run a little late because of an emergency or some other situation over which I have no control. So, on average, I will stick to our appointment times as best I can. Fair enough?"

"Just give me a call if you're running late. And, oh, be sure to use an untraceable land line."

"Rizzo, I'm not able to promise you I will call. I will respect your time, but since you're not going anywhere for a few days, let's be a little more flexible and relax the standards concerning the time issue."

"Okay...for now. We've spent five minutes talking about the time. Shouldn't we talking about....*Rizzo looks to the right and then to* *the left. He lowers his voice and leans closer...*Them. And how I'm going to disappear from their radar? Do you have connections to the Witness Protection Program?"

"First, you promised that you'd explain the program '*They*' are subjecting you to. Tell me about 'Them."

"They are the ones who sent the fleas. They were hoping that I'd carry them out of the plant and into the general population where they'd spread and infect others. But the friskers are programmed to identify the fleas. That's how they stopped them from leaving the contamination control area. Those idiots at the check point jumped my ass. I was ready to sacrifice myself rather than let the fleas take over. I was trying to keep them contained which is why I re-suited. The plant monitors are pretty naïve. They think that following decon protocol is going to contain those murderous macro-terrorists."

"Fleas? Like dogs and cats carry.

"Are you kidding me? Come on, Doc, that's why I need a nuclear guy on my team. Someone on the elite team who has the clearance, and knows about *Them.*"

"Rizzo, I'm all you've got to work with right now. You promised to clue me in on what you believe happened to you. So, tell me about these…ah, fleas."

"Are you mocking me Doc, because if you are mums the word from me. I don't talk to skeptics."

"No. I really want to know about the fleas. Tell me."

"Well I'll give you the cover story first. But keep in mind there's much more to it that *they* don't want you civilians to know about. The fleas are technically fuel fleas; bits of metal that are made radioactive when they're carried by water into the core of the nuclear reactor. They're tiny little fuckers, but they are mighty lethal. They deliver quite a bite - radiation Doc, not a bug bite - when they land on your skin. *They* want us to believe that their origin is degraded nuclear reactor fuel sloughed off as bits of tiny metal that get swirled around inside the reactor core and are carried out in the water. HAH! Can you believe that anyone would buy that line of shit? I tell you Doc - and keep this quiet because your life depends on your...*Rizzo makes a zip you lips gesture...* those fleas? They don't just slough off the fuel rods. Uh, uh. The fleas, Doc, they're an intelligent life form. I shit you not. How could you doubt the facts. The little fuckers jump on you. I've seen em with my own eyes. Just little tracers of light. You catch em moving out of the corner of your eye. By then? Too damn late. They've zeroed in on you. Impact to target - you - point-two micro-seconds."

"And the contamination monitors picked them up?"

"Yeah, but it ain't like picking tics off a dog. You see, they leave a signature that the friskers read. The fleas, they've already burrowed in...deep. Head right for your brain. Oh yeah, they soap you down and put you through a few rinse cycles at the check point. Just weakens the signature radiation. The devils are already in. Just fool you with the radiation signature. Like a fart, after the beans are eaten."

"So you think the fleas are still inside you…your brain?"

"No, I think I killed the one that got past my suit."

"How'd you kill it?"

"That's a secret Doc. I need to keep that – the 'method'– under wraps for the time being. I don't want someone stealing my invention and patenting it. Besides it's still in the experimental stage."

"How can you be sure you…ah, killed it?"

"Now you're freaking me out Doc. I thought you were a shrink. Are you trying to make me feel worse? Do you know something I don't know about *them*, and you're not telling me. What did the X ray show?"

"We didn't take an X ray. And, no, I'm not trying to freak you out. Just curious about how you did it. It might help others if they knew…ah, how to prevent contamination."

"Not contamination, Doc. That's nothing, just a little radiation. A minor burn. A slight genetic mutation here and there. We're talking, INVASION!"

"And whose behind all of this?"

"Ah ha. I never thought you'd ask. Now that's the sixty-thousand dollar question, ain't it?"

"It's what I've been asking all along…"

"Don't jump the gun, Doc. Would you have believed me if I just started talking about, *them,* before I'd given you the background data? Why, you'd write me off as a genuine nut case."

"Yes, I guess you're right. Now that you given me this background data, tell me more...about them. Please."

"Doc, I'm exhausted. How about we continue this session this after noon. I need lunch and a nap."

"Rizzo, we had an agreement remember. You were going to identify *them*. How can I really help you if I don't have the whole picture?"

"I'm not going back on my word. Do you take me for a welker? The suspense won't kill you. I need my sustenance and a short constitution to gather myself. This ordeal has been...like I said...exhausting."

"Rizzo, nap time is not in the treatment schedule. You have group therapy after lunch."

"Then pull some strings, Doc. I need to re-group myself. I actually have to recharge and adjust my internal balance. So it's later or not at all. And, I want a power nap."

 "Okay, okay. This afternoon. I'll talk to the charge nurse about giving you a half-hour to nap. Then we talk. How's 1:30 sound?"

"You're not such a bad guy after all, Doc. I'll tell you this because I trust you: napping is very important to what I've been working on. It's essential to the 'method' for getting rid of the fleas."

"Is that all you have to do is nap. Is that you're method?"

"Stop fishing, Doc. No it's not just about a nap. Let's say it's an important part of the 'method', and leave it at that - for now. See you at 1:30. Sharp."

I don't know how the hell Rizzo got the upper hand. He's a damn good story-teller if nothing else. His delusion is pretty wild. He must be defending against some painful memories. But for the life of me, I can't imagine what they might be. I read his chart, and I interviewed him. From the start, I considered him to be an unreliable informant and a poor historian concerning his personal life. However, his supervisor and his ex-wife whom Rizzo gave me permission to interview revealed nothing horrible in Rizzo's past. He was just a geek with a life-long fascination with things that glowed in the dark. Information like this bothers me more than anything; more than if Rizzo had some evil done to him. Because it therefore could happen to any one of us…just like that. Like a majestic oak that upon reaching maturity in loose soil falls down. I have danced with many a demon through my years of drug-induced craziness, or plain out hedonistic abandon, but I never took the demon home after the dance was over. Well, maybe I did once and awhile. But at least my she devils left before dawn while I was still unconscious. Poor Rizzo. No telling what in hell Rizzo was napping happily with at this very moment. The psychiatrist was going to have to be heavy-handed on the anti-psychotic scripts to bring this guy down to earth.

Same day: 1:30- sharp - in the afternoon...

No Rizzo. Where was he? I have to admit I was in agonizing suspense to learn who *They* were. The patient, though deluded as a Mad Hatter, intrigued me. I went to the unit desk and asked for Shirley the charge nurse. She came out of the chart room with a quizzical look that made me feel like she was laying eyes on me for the first time.

"Doctor Jack, you look like a kid whose balloon broke. What's the matter?"

"I have an appointment with Rizzo. It's not like him to be late. I checked his room and he's not there."

"Oh, yes. Mr. Malmo. Room 3A. He's been discharged."

"You mean transferred?"

"No. Discharged. Strangest thing though. Didn't go according to hospital procedure. Don't know how JACO's going to look at it when records are audited. But it's not my call. I'm just the lowly charge nurse."

"Damn unusual. It should have gone through you. Didn't you have to release the record with the treatment team's signatures on the discharge plan."

"What treatment plan? They just showed up and spirited him out of here. Our hospital director, Doctor Romeo, came with these three men who kept flashing ID in our face; saying they were federal officers and they had a warrant for Mr. Malmo's immediate release. And...that he was to be released in their custody. Took Mr. Malmo out of here in upper body restraints. Poor man looked like a mouse that'd been cornered by three hungry cats. He not so much as let out a squeak when they escorted him out of here. Like they were in a big hurry."

"They? 'Them!' You're certain they were federal marshals?"

"I don't know if they were marshals. They had official looking IDs with gold badges and a warrant signed by the US Attorney General."

"How were they dressed."

"Black suites. Government issue stereotypes. Dark glasses so you couldn't see their eyes. Spooky kind of; you now when you can't see the person's eyes when they're talking to you. Impossible to have a two-way conversation, although there was no two-way conversation on the matter."

"Shit. Rizzo was right…"

"What did you just say Doctor Jack?"

"Sorry. I didn't mean to say, 'shit'."

"No. About Mr. Malmo being right. Right about what?"

"Rizzo, Mr. Malmo, was afraid *They* were coming for him. He said he was afraid for his life. Looks like he was right."

"Who are *They,* them or whatever."

"I can't say. Rizzo never got to tell me. I don't think either of us really wants to know."

Part III

Six months later...Wal-Mart 2 o'clock in the morning...

Donna hates to shop. She hates Wal-Mart. So here I am at two in the morning getting some shopping done. I couldn't sleep, so why not. The only risk was running into my recently discharged hospital patients, Twilight cultists, night stalkers and other insomniacs. Who else shops at a warehouse department store lit up like Players Field Stadium at two in the morning? I was navigating a cart with one wheel that wobbled and would occasionally lock up causing me to lurch over the handrail and knock the breath out of me. I ended up in the sporting goods department because my auto pilot invariably takes me there. I regularly check up on what's new in gadgets from GPSs to disposable toilet bags containing organic, bio-degradable chemicals. What struck me as I navigated the aisle between racks of weight lifting apparatus and yoga mats was an end-cap display of sporting accessories. The end-cap display was the size of the Eifel Tower and was festooned with sport bracelets and necklaces claiming to boost the average couch potato's energy, strength, and stamina to that of an Olympic triathlon gold medalist. Furthermore, their manufacturers claimed that wearing these gadgets was like taking a dip in Lourdes for those suffering from the nagging aches caused by the earth's gravitational field. Other small print claims included energy balance, and an internal harmonic convergence of the body's energy grid. Yeah right! Another scam brought to us by the makers of homeopathic remedies, crystal chakra balancing, color healing and copper and magnetic bracelets. A sales pitch that would do Edwin Hartley proud. Edwin created Jack in the Beanstalk. These clowns had taken the magic beans to a cosmic level. I'm not easy to fool. However, I admit that I'm intensely curious. So a closer examination of these wondrous do dads couldn't hurt. I have a gift for keen observation. And by adhering to a rational scientific method of investigation, I would debunk the myth. Better yet, I could take the thing apart right here….if it weren't for the security camera pointed down on me. It's much harder to find a sales clerk in a Wal-Mart than a hidden camera. You cannot, I repeat, cannot, imagine my surprise when there written in god's own handwriting (see the stone tablets with the Ten Commandments) was, to again add credibility, god's handiwork. Written in the florid style of upscale commercial advertising (the hand-writing of post modern god) was: *"**Nuclear Flea Repeller, LLD.**"* The active ingredient was soluble, Ti (atomic number 22) – Titanium >/<. Although unwaveringly skeptical, and maintaining my scientific objectivity, I bought half a dozen of each. God Damn, Rizzo, you're out there somewhere.

It still remains a mystery: Who are *"They?"* Was Rizzo working for or against *"Them?"* Whose side are *"They"* on? Who – okay, *"Who,"* is Rizzo *working for now?*

Chapter 2. Post-Script by the author:

Pseudo-scientific scams pitch to the gullible consumer. What is it about the rational person who abandons his reason and buys the "Magic Beans?" I read long ago that it has its origin in the 'magical thinking' associated with children of three - and their interpretation of causality. The time in or lives when thinking makes things happen. If, for example I want something very, very badly, and it happens, then my wanting caused it to happen.

Many adults exhibit this primitive way of thinking. If I pray for rain, it eventually will rain. If I pray for the flood water to recede in the ninth ward, it will eventually recede. The same happens if I don't pray. But somehow, people come to believe that praying makes things happen. This is an example of a superstition - perceiving patterns where none exist. This is faulty reasoning caused by magical thinking.

If I have little motivation and no athletic prowess, and I really want to run a five minute mile or play nine holes of golf like Tiger Woods - and satisfy as many women in a season - I can, with the assistance of God or a titanium bracelet. There really are titanium bracelets, like there are copper and magnet bracelets, and healing crystal pendants, etc. But the difference is, titanium and copper are basic elements and have been studied for decades by scientists. New developments in metallurgy have unlocked the power within them to heal, and to enhance our energies (honest to god they do!). They therefore become legitimate, scientifically endorsed talismans of real power. This is science as religion. Where once more, like children of three, we can experience the miraculous through wow wee chemistry and its sponsor, scientific discovery. And, with a huge leap of faith, because we can leap farther wearing bracelets laced with heavy metals. Abandoning reason has become a bad habit with Western Civilization. We are, as a nation, a bunch of lazy religionists or superstitious physicists of the quantum and 'reverse causality' types. Both abandon reason; disguising religiously motivated moral stupidity, or intellectually absurd notions such as promoting a belief in muons, which like god, have a plan and are indivisible and simultaneously everywhere.

A magic bean that can grow to heaven? Hey, why not? We can reason that this a *space elevator that will take us to a place in the multiverse where people run faster (or fly if you prefer), play a par none game of golf at Club Eden, and I hope to hell, satisfy as many Victoria Secret Angels as Tiger Woods (but for free) for all eternity. Amen!

I did buy a titanium bracelet. Since wearing it I have run faster than a locomotive and leapt a tall building in a single bound. I think titanium may produce a profound mental state not unlike mercury poisoning.

Dr. Jack Mc Kane's Biographer

Chapter 4

Private Practice

Private practice is a bold enterprise. It's not for the meek do-gooder who has no business savvy or doesn't possess certain mercenary ambitions. Selling your services for a fee is a difficult concept to grasp for quite a few private practitioners. Particularly those who received their training in public service agencies like welfare and criminal justice. I was fortunate in the sense that I had numerous internships to include a lengthy employment as a hot shot bureaucrat for the Department of Defense. I had my bleeding heart cauterized a long time ago. I genuinely care for people and am sensitive to the needs of those who can't afford to see a therapist. I will generally work out a reasonable fee or see a percentage of my clients pro bono. Nevertheless, business is business, and you have to earn a living.

I now possessed a license to practice after having spent time in the trenches working with criminals, the hospitalized mentally ill and social welfare clients. These are the populations you can work with without a license while receiving clinical supervision by agency directors who are themselves lifers of a sort. Hospital and private practice work has its correlates in oppressive institutions such as the prisons and probation agencies. There is even an overlap, since prisons, psychiatric hospitals and private practice clinics often share the same populations. Of course there are those people from the general population who aren't taking powerful, psycho-active medications and don't have a prison record. You have to ask them, "What brings you here? How can I be of help to you?" By asking such a non-threatening question you discover that they haven't tortured and killed anyone and appear to be relatively law abiding and well adjusted. Often they'll confide something terrible like, "I don't have any friends," or, "My wife left me, and my dog died. I really miss my dog." Oh, sure, there are those who have suffered horrible insults and injuries, but they have muddled through life surprisingly well in spite of it all. Most of my peers prefer working with the "worried well" population. Preferring those who have good private insurance coverage, or who can afford to pay out-of-pocket. Although every human being has a unique story to tell, I have a proclivity to seek out those whose stories might have been written by Stan Peckinpah, Stanley Kubrick, Roman Polanski or Steven King.

Clients are referred by a variety of sources in a well managed private practice. The Tri-County Therapy Center, my practice, had numerous contracts representing the private, state and federal sectors. It seemed a shame to ignore the real challenges to the profession and only see depressed and anxious clients who tried to infect you with their relentless pessimism. It livened things up when a manic client would show up and present his or her plan for world peace or domination. On the other hand, a borderline client was anathema to therapists who would burn sage and try to pass the client off to someone else rather than spend five minutes with one. I believe that borderline clients get a bad rap. Yes, they are typically ornery types who initially tell you you're great and that you're the best therapist they've ever had, or for that matter the best therapist in the universe. Only to ultimately condemn you for not being available during their ninth crisis in a week because you had taken the week-end off. Their often hedonistic appetites are 'tsk'd tsk'd' by therapists who try to encourage them to have stable monogamous relationships and to abstain from recreational drug use. The theorists maintain that borderlines have an attachment disorder. That once upon a time their mother - or some significant other - failed to bond with them, and consequently they are always expecting someone to abandon them thereby confirming that they are unworthy of both love and belonging. So, it goes that these poor unfortunates will idolize some authority figure or strong person to whom they are attracted, and set things up so that they are ultimately rejected. Going so far as to unwittingly plan for rejection by setting their expectations so high that the people they idolize can never meet them. They end up being "fired from therapy," thus proving to themselves that you can't trust anyone to be there when you need them.

In my opinion therapists created borderlines to excuse their failures with clients who never wanted to join the club in the first place. Borderlines are habitual social contract violators. Who reading this right now hasn't ended up hating someone they loved; who meant the world to them, and who let them down only to end the whole thing acrimoniously. And who upon leaving, drank and screwed indiscriminately because you needed desperately to be validated as desirable and loveable by someone else - usually another early rebounder or woman you paid to like you for an hour. If anything, borderlines accelerate a process that takes the normal, serial monogamist (repeatedly married American) five years to accomplish. Women represent the majority of borderlines according to therapists. But then again, the marriage contract isn't exactly fair to women whose matrimonial relationship to her spouse hasn't changed much since King Henry the VIIIth. There are plenty of male borderlines. But it's hard to tell them apart from non-borderline males. The appropriate diagnosis for them should be: "Those men who just don't get it." I had the champion of male borderlines; who, had he lived two-hundred years earlier, would have been indispensible to helping settle the American frontier. These are the mono-self-sufficient guys who can go it alone for weeks or months at a time, and not be lonely for human company. A ride to the nearest settlement a hundred and fifty miles away for some quick nookie and a bottle of hooch, and he's ready to ride west once more. His horse was his closest companion. You don't want to imagine how close.

Gary wasn't born that long ago. He should have been. When he came to see me, he had gotten into trouble with the police for accosting some bicyclists. Gary wasn't a big guy. He was maybe 5', 8" and weighed about 175 pounds. He was barrel-chested with a substantial gut. All of this was unevenly stacked on top of spindly legs that gave the impression that Gary might just come unhinged at the hips and topple over at any minute. His physical appearance, unusual for its disproportion, was less dramatic than his lumps and bruises. There were too many to count. He appeared to have been beaten with a Louisville Slugger and used as a backstop for batting practice. He walked with a painful hitch to his step and sat down in a grunt of discomfort. He stated the need to clear his good name so as not to be fired from his company. He knew they'd eventually find out because they reviewed the police blotters because of the sensitive security requirements they had to maintain as defense contractors. I couldn't imagine that a bicyclist attacker was a security risk to a company that employed aircraft mechanics. Nevertheless, Gary wanted to initiate an evaluation. He anticipated that his employer would require one once they found out about his peccadillo. He intended, he told me, "to set the record straight that I'm a descent guy, and that I'm not violent. I wanted to start this on my own. I think it will look good that I volunteered for a psych eval." Gary understood the value of CYA in employment politics.

"It's a good idea to initiate an evaluation. However, you need to be sure they'll accept my summary and recommendations."

"You're on our EAP provider list, aren't you?"

"Yes, but it's possible that they may request an independent evaluator outside the EAP, or have someone they use internal to the company; say through the company's home office."

"No, they'll use you. Before you were contracted as Gunmann Air Industries' EAP, I saw the old EAP shrink for an evaluation."

"So, you've had as assessment done before. What was the reason?"

"Oh, nothing big. My girlfriend and me sort 'a got into it. She was a drunk, and used to go nuts on me when she'd had a few snorts. So, one of the times that she was kick'n the shit out 'a me I had to you know, restrain her."

"And how did it come about that the company required an evaluation. I mean, the company did require one. Is that right?"

"Yeah. Because of the arrest blotter again. But I was cleared to go back to work."

"Gary, what exactly did you do that caused the police to get involved?"

"Noth'n. Like I said I was just protecting my balls. She was screaming like a banshee, calling me a cocksucker, a queer - all kinds of names. The neighbor called the cops. I suppose it sounded like someone was being killed."

"And you were cleared of the charges?"

"Hell, yeah. She a fuck'n looney. I was doing my best to calm the situation down. She's gone off on me before that, but that time was a doozy."

"What happened to her? Where is she now."

"Oh, she's at home. She wanted to come with me and speak for my character, but I told her I had to feel things out first."

"Aren't you concerned about her behavior? I mean you describe her as unstable…an aggressive alcoholic you said."

"Yeah, but I love her to death. When she's sober, she's the warmest, lovingest person you'd ever want to meet. And besides she's cut down on the booze since going ballistic on me. Says, she's do'n it for me. Now ain't that a hell of a thing? Gotta love her for try'n. Ain't easy to back off the booze the way she drinks. I know from personal experience."

"Do you drink a lot?"

"No, got the demon off my back two years ago. Go to AA once in a while. Do a little weed now and then, but don't have a problem with it. Calms me down. Helps me cope with Claire when she gets radical like when she's on her period. Hey, you're not going to write that down; about hit'n the pipe once in a while are you?"

"Well, no. Not if it isn't a problem insofar as interfering with your work. Besides I need to have you sign a release of confidential information before any report leaves my office. And…Don't they drug test you at work?"

"Only if there's a work-related accident. Or if there's a police report or an arrest."

"So then you have to submit to a urinalysis…"

"Did already. Came back clean."

"I'm surprised that you did, considering that you use…what? 'Every so often'."

"It helped that I drank about a gallon of cleanser. Detox was a bitch. Pissed till my kidneys just about collapsed."

"Oh, I see." I wasn't sure how to phrase my question about his injuries. I was thinking: maybe this guy has a rare blood disorder and a colony of fatty cysts. So I erred on the side of automobile accident or spouse beating. "And the bruises and bumps; did your girlfriend do that?"

"No. It's embarrassing to admit it. A bunch of cyclists beat the shit out of me."

"You got into it with the Outlaw bikers."

"Now, you know how to hurt a guy, don't you? No, a bunch of pansy bicyclists. Except'n they weren't the pansies I thought they were. Dressed like a trail of neon ants on bicycles."

"I'll tell you like it was. You see, I was in a pissy mood after my old lady gave me hell that morning. I was driving to work when these bicycle riders were take'n up the whole single lane. Cars com'n in the opposite direction, and no room to pass. Y'see, I'm run'n late for work, so I sort'a nudged one of them who was rid'n too close. So this creep, he kicks my door, and picks up speed, passes two or three riders ahead of him, and to top it off, he flips me the bird."

"I was rip'n mad. I was so mad I couldn't see straight. I took off after the bastard, and pulled in front of him. I knew I was wrong, but my Irish got the best of me. Before I knew it, the whole pack of them pulled up, got off their bikes and surrounded me. I don't remember who hit who first, but I went into Corps mode, Semper Fi, and went down swing'n!" Kicked the liv'n daylights out of me. I'm get'n too old to take a beating. Takes me longer to heal."

Gary should have known better then to pick on a column of cyclists. Never let the spandex fool you. All those tights and knickers that show every nook and cranny of the human anatomy are battle uniforms. Their helmet graphics with their iridescent swashes denote rank and combat MOS. These guys dress like ants, and emulate their habits and battle strategies. They are generally smarter, better organized and more dangerous than the Sons of Anarchy. I kid you not; these cycling enthusiasts are Formicidae incarnate. In other words, ants. I told you before I'm not one to anthropomorphize nasty animals with human traits – like friendly, sentient and cuddly guard dogs. However, the reverse is more likely: humans will mimic insects and animals. Just look at how we design and engineer our machinery. A car is a horse on four wheels. Cyclists are ants leaving a pheromone trail for others to follow single file. A riding helmet is a serious imitation of an ant head made of man's improvement over keratinized epithelial cells – ant armor. Riders' shorts and bibs leave a lot to be desired in terms of armoring. However, the helmet rivals a soldier's Kevlar pot. I've examined these marvels of head protection: Fusion-mold micro-shell with channel ventilation, cam lock levers, massive air vents and blade visors with a GPS fit system. Jeez…zuss Christ! Add wrap around Oakleys and what have you got; a fucking two-legged ant with a head that can deflect a sledge hammer blow. I wondered if Gary realized the risk he had taken…

"Gary, did you under-estimate these guys? I mean did they strike you as menacing in any way?"

"You're creep'n me out Doc. Yeah, now you mention it. They were kind'a grade B horror movie look'n."

"What do you mean by that?" I know I'm not supposed to reinforce bazaar associations in my clients, but I couldn't help leading Gary in this direction. Maybe it would put the primeval fear in him that keeps most civilized people from cavorting with wild beasts or wrestling Russian bears.

"Did you ever see the flick, I don't remember the name of it, where these spiders that got irradiated from an atomic bomb test and grew as big as a house and started killing off people left and right?"

"Yes, vaguely. Are you saying these cyclists were like those mutated insects?"

"No. I was just thinking about the old movies, and how cheesy the special effects were. Hey, you okay, Doc. You sure ask weird questions."

This guy had no imagination, and the lack of a little imagination can get you into serious trouble. It is from our ancient tenebrous instincts that we fear the dark and react with alarm when discovering a rat in the toilet. These reactions are hard wired into our brains. It represents our survival instinct. Our future as a species depends on t. I don't know how Gary made it this far. I suspected his future progeny were bound for extinction by the next generation.

"Yes, I'm fine. I'm just concerned about your risk taking, and being so angry."

"Yo. I'm pretty laid back compared to how I used to be. I was a real hell raiser in my youth. It's just recent with all the guff the ole lady's been giv'n me. And those creeps…the bikers. It was…well, the combination of things all gone to shit. What would you do if you was in my place, Doc?"

"I'm here to complete your evaluation. So, it's what you do that's important. Do you want to continue with the evaluation, now that you've told me the background information to the incident?"

"What are you going to write in your report?"

"Some of the things you've already told me and more information based a complete social history. I write a summary of my assessment and include recommendations to you and to your employer."

"You mean you're going to mention that I smoked pot? And about taking an ass kicking from the bike freaks?"

"Well, yes, in so many words. I'll allude to your experimental or social use of alcohol and other recreational drugs. And about the attack; isn't that why you're here?"

"Yeah. So tell them about the *incident,* and my side of the story – except about going ape shit. That's not really me. But don't mention the pot, man. They'll make a big deal out of it. And what's it got to do with a mental health evaluation?"

"It's medical, so it's part of the history. Only if it's causing problems in your life is it noteworthy beyond merely mentioning it. I know that you work in a Drug-Free Workplace, so yes it could raise a red flag and invite closer scrutiny. But I'll cover that in my assessment." And about losing your temper, well that happens. If you have some impulse control problem then your treatment may include remediation."

"What's all the mumbo-jumbo: closer scrutiny and impulse control and re-medication."

"Remediation, not re-medication. It means possibly having to enroll in an Anger Management group. In fact, because of the incident it would be the minimum requirement stipulated in your back-to-work agreement. I don't have all the information I need yet to make a solid recommendation."

"You're being a jerk, Doc. I don't like the sound of where this is going. I just want you to tell them it was a one-time deal – the cyclists' thing – so when they see the blotter they'll understand it's no big deal."

"Gary, there's no need to be offensive. You came to me to have me do my job, and complete an honest evaluation. You're being a bit premature in assuming the worst outcome."

"I came here Doc because I heard you're the best, and now you're trying to screw me over." Gary was getting pretty worked up, if balling his fists and dropping his weight to his knees in preparation for a lunge was any indication. I hadn't seen a face get that red in a long time. I didn't wish him ill, although if he had a stroke I'd feel safer at the moment.

"Gary, I can see that you're upset (astute therapeutic observation). You don't have to have the evaluation done here. If you don't like where this is going, as you say, then I can give you a recommendation to see another psychologist."

"What the fuck. And start all over again. Do I get my money back?"

"It may be worth it to you to see another evaluator. And, no, I won't return the entire fee. I'll refund you the portion that covers the written report."

"I want a full refund. And you are a jerk!"

"I thought you had mellowed since your scrapping days. Let's settle this amicably. I'll refund the majority of your fee. You've taken my time, so that's only fair."

"Yeah, I've mellowed…but I could make an exception in your case…"

"If that's a threat Gary, I may have to call 911…"

"Fuck you, Doc. I'm leav'n. Don't need no more trouble. Some help you are, and you call yourself a psychologist…Dick head!" With that Gary left, restraining himself with great effort not deck me or slam the door on his way out. I'm sure Gary has an impulse control or intermittent explosive disorder, which simply stated means Gary is a walking time bomb and one mean son-of-a-bitch. Something tells me - call it a hunch - that Gary will be back. Hopefully with a change in attitude.

Doctor Jack reminded himself that it isn't good practice to encourage bazaar associations with a client. Particularly a client, who from the beginning of the session, presents as unstable. His instincts should have told him to stop right there. But then Doctor Jack is known to provoke a situation where restraint would be the prudent course of action. I know him, and he has this thing for drawing comparisons between human and animal behavior. He told me it's a major theoretical underpinning to his work. The theory is called Ethology. Ethology studies animal behavior across all species; looking for one behavior that is shared by all of them. Like aggression in a number of unrelated animals. One branch of ethology delves even deeper; trying to quantify animal emotions, culture and learning. In response to scholarly works written about this specialized branch, Doctor Jack replies, "Bull shit!" He is adamant about keeping his animals objective sources of meat on the table. He will not name an animal – like his backyard chickens – that he's going to be-head and cook for a Sunday dinner. Jack rather emphasizes the commonalities across species to include Homo sapiens (us). And it is on this point that Jack radically departs from the professional norm. Like with the 'ants.' Jack sees a column of bicyclists as an ant procession. I believe he was genuinely concerned for Gary's well being when he pursued this avenue of inquiry. He would have liked to have come right out and warned Gary not to mess with an angry colony of ants [slash] cyclists at the risk of being dismembered and eaten. To Jack this is no prosaic metaphor. Jack perceives such an encounter as a real danger.

Doctor Jack is not a whacko concerning animalistic attributions to human behavior. He is not strange for having a fascination with the ant as a case study. One of my favorite author's, the Transcendentalist, Henry David Thoreau, included a section in his famous Walden Pond that discusses his fascination invoked by the complexities of the ant world.

Bear with me here...I don't always agree with Doctor Jack McKane's theoretical applications. However, in this regard he may have a valid point. I give you the following decision rules that apply to this theory because it may enlighten you. It did me. They come from one of ethnology's revered theorists, Niko Tinbergen. Niko was a contemporary of Konrad Lorenz – the Learning Theory guy who had newly hatched geese and chickens following him around thinking he was their mother. I don't know what Konrad was dressed in that caused that to happen. It has something to do with imprinting, and less to do with dressing up like Big Bird. Anyway, to the point.

Tinbergen insisted that ethology always needed four kinds of explanation in order to categorize a certain behavior:

> **Function** *– How does the behavior affect the animal's chances of survival and reproduction?*

> **Causation** *– What are the stimuli that elicit the response, and how's it been modified by what was recently learned?*

> **Development** *– How does the behavior change with age, and what early experiences are necessary for the behavior to be displayed?*

Evolutionary history – *How does the behavior compare with similar behavior in related species?*

Related species? Doctor Jack would insert, 'humans.' Our early ancestors functioned primarily with the brain of a reptile. Early social behavior was governed by the instincts and behaviors answering Niko's four questions. I mentioned earlier that one type of behavior studied by ethologists is aggression. Not all behaviors in animal groups are altruistic (directed toward survival of the group and reproduction). Take revenge for example. Revengeful behavior was previously thought to be a nasty trait observed exclusively in Homo sapiens. It's since been observed that other species have been reported to be vengeful, including reports of vengeful camels and vengeful chimpanzees. And you didn't already know this! I saw the reality TV episode, "When Animals Attack People." I was convinced of animals' hatred toward us way before it aired.

Doctor Jack told me that the ultimate perversion of animal behavior is when people start dressing like animals and run amok. Or people seeing other people dressed as animals and exhibit wolf pack hunger and attack. I'm thinking of women wearing mink coats being attacked by naked women throwing paint balloons. I like the imagery.

Back to 'ants,' and cyclists. *This is where all this beyond-your interest theorizing comes together. Bicyclists look like and behave like ants. Period. Doctor Jack convinced me that the two species have merged into a distinctly separate organism. Here is a table of comparisons that will prove unequivocally that I am right (and therefore so is Doctor Jack):*

Ants

Ant busses- Ants utilize a public transportation system. I kid you not. Because of the size difference in some worker ants, the small ants ride on the backs of the larger ones (called, "bus ants"). The little piss ants do all the toting, while the larger ones convey them to and from the work site.

Cyclists

Bicycles- Two-wheel and some three-wheel riding systems transport cyclist to and from their destinations. The cyclists are seen carrying back backs, water and power gel while riding atop their bicycles.

Ants

Ant Trails – Why do ants always travel along the same trail? They do this because they smell their way along rather than seeing. They use pheromones to mark their trail the way trekkers use way points when geo-coaching. They find their way back by this method. When they've completed their foraging and return to the mound, the trail gradually disappears as the pheromone wears off. Humans produce pheromones to attract the opposite sex. Human pheromone is a cocktail of sex hormones and rancid sweat.

Cyclists – Ditto. All the male cyclists will follow a female cyclist to the end of the earth, focused upon her voluptuous rear and drafting in the waft of girl dew.

Ants are vicious defenders of their own kind. Ever crush an ant – I admit I have – and watch the other ants start running around all crazy. I read once that crushing an ant releases a pheromone that alerts the other ants of imminent peril. The alarm brings in reinforcements of other ants. If the queen is attacked by enemy ants or some other insect species the workers and soldier ants rush to her defense and tear the aggressor to pieces.

This is what happened to Gary. He dared attack the queen of cyclists. Its workers descended on Gary and commenced to tear him to pieces. Had he studied ethology or understood the behavior of ants, he would not have been in the predicament for which he was required to see a therapist. Gary undoubtedly was once a kid who pulled the wings off flies, burned caterpillars alive and crushed ants underfoot for the fun of it. He deserved the revenge of ants or their evolved successors – cyclists dressed like ants.

Why the long treatise on ethology and ants? Because it so influenced Doctor Jack's good intentions toward Gary, even though his efforts went terribly wrong. Or could have if Gary hadn't mellowed since his days as a bully of creatures both large and small.

In conclusion (of my fixation on ants), ants are alleged to be the smartest insects. With a whopping 250,000 brain cells they have more brain power than a former US president. With over 12,000 identified types of ants in the world, they are more numerous than any other species. If you took all the people in the world and placed them on a balancing scale opposite all the ants in the world, the ants would weigh more. In the end, the ants will out-live everything. They will survive the extinction of all other life on the planet. They, not the cockroach, will thrive after the coming global ice age or the endless nuclear winter. When the automobile becomes extinct and our fossil fuels are depleted, the cyclists will ride the earth annihilating everyone and everything left alive in their path....

Maybe I exaggerate.

Dr. Jack Mc Kane's Biographer

Chapter 5

Gary's Return

In private practice you, you expect clients to return to therapy. Not for the same issue for which they first came, rather because life presents new challenges throughout the life cycle. It is a statement of their trust and confidence in you that they come back. It is reasonable for them to expect that your will support them through the new challenges that life has thrown at them. And that they will again successfully overcome the present obstacle and move forward. There are some former clients that you dread seeing for a second time. Gary is one of those clients. I saw his name on my schedule and thought, or rather hoped that it was a scheduling error. Some glitch in the 'Therapist Helper' automated booking software. However, my base instincts told me that Gary *was* back, and that I was in for another round with the classic therapist bully. I secretly held that Gary had seen the error of his ways and was ready to accept the consequences of his poor choices. Gary's entrance made me pause and reassess his motives. He looked the picture of innocence, pious in demeanor and not guilty of said charges. I might say, deferential and humble, if I hadn't already tangled with him.

"Hi again, Doc. Take it easy I ain't pissed at you no more. In fact, I want to apologize for being such a dick…I mean block head. It's genetic, I think. You believe in bad genes Doc.? Well, I still got that fight hang'n over me, and the EAP says I got'a get it done with you. I quit pot, so it ain't a problem no more. And the ole lady and me; everything's copasetic. No major blow ups. She loves me like a rock…"

"Okay, okay Gary. But let's have an understanding. No blow-ups with me either over how I do my job. I will represent you, and I'll advocate for what's in your best interest. Agreed?"

"So, you won't mention the pot, since I just told you I don't use no more?"

"Let's just move on from there. It's where things got…ah, difficult the last time."

"Alright. But first, one question…"

"Yes, what is it?, and not about the drugs again."

"Are you a cyclist?"

"No. Why is that important?"

"Cause those guys are still creep'n me out. I think they're follow'n me. I'll check my rear view mirror; first I don't see 'em, and then I look again a few minutes later and there they are. Bastards ride like bats out of hell. Fast for peddle push'n twerps."

"Are you sure they're the same ones you confronted?"

"Hard to tell. They all look alike. But they got'a be the same dudes. They looked right through me as they rode by me when I pulled over to let them pass - really pulled over to check em out. They got these wrap around dark glasses on that make their eyes look like…well, weird, like them mirrored balls at the disco clubs."

Gary had me wondering if there was a disco club that survived the eighties. I seriously hoped not. But it is Gary's reference to people with multi-faceted lenses, bug eyes, that really grabbed my attention. Had he looked into the eyes of a trail of cyclists and glimpsed their inner lives? As ants on the march, or ride, to world supremacy. "Are you saying that their eyes appeared insect-like?"

"No, but far out looking shades. I wouldn't mind buying a pair for me and the ole lady. Wonder where you can get em?"

"I thought you were saying you felt threatened by the bikers?"

"Yeah. I sure as hell been think'n their follow'n me. I think maybe they want another go at me. I wouldn't say, 'no' to a re-match if it was only one or two of 'em at a time."

Evidently, Gary is not the kind of person who learns from experience. I feel compelled to set Gary straight. I can't imagine how he's kept his job this long or how he's managed to survive at all. He reminds me of, Brock Lesnar, the mixed martial arts fighter whose opponents exhaust themselves landing punches on his face. Brock ultimately shakes off the earthquakes in his head and KOs his opponent. He does this fight after fight.

"Gary, are you looking for trouble?"

"Nooo...'course not. I said they're gun'n for me."

"You said you thought they were following you. It may be just a coincidence that they happened to be riding on the same road that you drive to work every day. That's not the same thing as stalking you for revenge."

"I hadn't thought about them stalking me because they want revenge. That sounds pretty serious when you put it that way."

"No. I'm not saying that they are. You said....never mind what you said. Let's move on with the assessment. Okay?"

"I think that's a damn good idea, Doc. One last question though…"

Yes. What is it?"

"How'd you get here today?"

"I drove my car. What's that got to do with anything?"

"Don't know. I saw a bike chained to the post out front. Wonder'n if it was yours. Do you own a bike?"

"No, that's not my bike. I sold my bike last year. I own a motor scooter. It's the only two-wheeled thing I ride."

"Fuck'n A, a scooter, like the sissy-ass rice burners them little Chinks tool around on? Jeez…zus, Doc. Are you kid'n me?"

I can honestly say, I have never felt hatred toward a client in all my years of practice. I can't say that anymore. I really hate Gary. I'm not ashamed to admit it. I hope the "Soldier" cyclists catch up to Gary at the next stop light, and tear him to shreds.

Postscript:

Gary's Mental Health Evaluation was eventually completed. A cool professional air was assumed by Doctor Jack. He had to in order to detach and remain "clinical." He didn't want to emotionally react and discharge Gary for non-compliance because of his continual provocations and distractions from the task at hand. The recommendations to Gary's employer included his participation in Anger Management group and some psycho-education classes addressing Substance Abuse. He wasn't happy about the Substance Abuse classes, but he capitulated without going, "Corps All-the-Way" with Doctor Jack. Gary valued his job, so he was willing - with reservations - to do what was necessary to keep it, and his regular pay check.

Gary's lingering obsession with the cyclists was to be addressed through occasional one-to-one sessions, which Doctor Jack dreaded. Nevertheless, he'd try. Maybe Gary would have a sustained rational period where he'd re-direct his suspicions and hyper-vigilance to some conspiracy theory or other. Doctor Jack suggested that he write to Jesse Ventura, the ex-governor of Minnesota, who had turned his attentions to investigating government conspiracies. Gary had watched season one of his television show, and was suitably impressed with Jesse's reasoning. He proposed passing his Cyclist Hit Squad theory on to Jesse for a future episode. In this regard, Doctor Jack believed that Gary was making progress. If you're going to act crazy, it made sense to exploit it for capital. I understand now how therapeutic success can transform something twisted into a creative outcome. Doctor Jack subscribes to the belief that there are Successful Psychotics living among us. They are the crazy folks who are happily adjusted to their conditions; often profit from it; and attract eager followers. Look at the key figures representing the Republican Party. Now look at a group of Tea Party members at a posh neighborhood rally. Now, stop looking or you'll start seeing them everywhere.

Chapter 6

Returning to Government Service

Karma

*Karma - the concept of Karma - is ubiquitous
throughout world cultures. Theological
interpretations notwithstanding, Karma's about
everything. It's become a sectarian term which
stands for everything we as humans act upon
consciously and subconsciously- acts that are also
influenced by everything within our immediate
field of experience. If you will accept that
immediate experience is the entire collection of
past actions concentrated on the head of a pin
being pushed through the fabric of time. Call the
fabric of time, "NOW." The needle, "I." As I am
pushed through time for the length of my life. And
there you have it. That's all there is to it. As
for the future; well, it's a useful Grammatik
invention. Writers find it particularly useful in
their plot constructions. To plan how things will
turn out for the protagonist. They give their
omniscient readers what they want: a happy ending.
We are hopelessly optimistic; endlessly plotting
out our future, unrealized lives to ensure the
same outcome.*

*The future, if you insist on believing in it, is a
wishful consequence of an action not yet
completed. It's a pause that's immediately filled
with unsubstantial things unbidden. The way air
rushes into a broken vacuum jar. We screen our
fantasies we call future in the private theater of
our minds. We cut and edit to produce a picture of
our future that, at first, looks like a collage
assembled from the fragments of dreams, and
jumbled allegories, and acted out by the bazaar
and implausible characters of a Fellini film.
After the final cut it looks pretty much the same.
For most of us the void of our imagined futures is
filled, paradoxically, with nothing more than the
cacophony of a noisy universe inside our heads.
Noise made by the instruments of constant
judgments, relentless internal dialogue and self
talk that is orchestrated by the omniscient Grand
Illusionist. And we rely upon this constant busy
signal to label the illusions which pass for our*

vision of the future. The best way to predict the future, I say, is to stock up on fortune cookies, or read your daily horoscope. In other words go easy on yourself and leave prophesying to the fortune tellers. Enjoy the negligible risk of seizing the day (the most common advice) with the stubbornness, the recklessness or the finesse our zodiac personalities would have us do.

The best future to have is the one that is happening right now. In fact it's the only way I can grasp it. So, carpe diem and amen.

Now I know how Jack's clients must feel after he's explained things to them.

Dr. Jack Mc Kane's Biographer

And this is the convoluted gibberish that Jack prattles on about. I have to admit, in plain talk, he makes sense. Doctor Jack believes that his returning to government service is some kind of unfinished business. Not unfinished so much from where he left off twenty years ago. Not literally. Rather some little handful of unfinished business from a lifetime or more ago. To me one lifetime presents enough work. I've left many projects unfinished; hundreds of calls unanswered and a few promises broken. I've never had enough time to complete everything on my honey-do lists. I don't wish to come back to them in this life or the next only to get further behind. To Jack, however, nothing's ever so simple. The accumulated Karma, according to Doctor Jack and the Hindus, is called *Sanchita*. And it can constitute an enormous amount of screw ups and disproportionately fewer at-a-boys. Of course it's always the screw-ups that anybody notices. And of course leave it to the religionists to put the gods in the picture so that nothing gets missed because of their all-knowing and all-seeing minds. And it's these major blunders and small larcenies that require pay back. But, the gods are merciful and dole out a only little pile of the past's peccadilloes for a human being to work on in his most recent incarnation. These thorny Karma blossoms are referred to as *Prarabdha.* Our job is to cultivate these blossoms minus the thorns. In other words get it right this time around. If you are inclined toward horticulture study, taking a course in the hybrid engineering of flowering plants might help.

Jack's Prarabdha is some retribution for his past sins. Then, Jack is Irish and sin is a psychical constant for which he and his Catholic Irish kin must atone before they shuck their earthly coils. Now Jack, being a devout atheist, refuted my insinuation that it was the influence of his Irish Catholic up-bringing, not Hinduism that formed the basis of his belief. He rejected my assumption as being Abrahamic original sin nonsense. "Karma," Jack says, isn't about punishment or retribution, but simply an extension or a consequence of our natural acts." He added, catching himself about to step into a trap of his own devising, "These consequences aren't immutable. It's not like it all pans out in some predetermined outcome. We can change it along the way," he argues. "We can mitigate our experiences hence redirecting their course and outcomes." Of course this is where *therapy* plays a role. Jack subscribes to the Jungian view that Karma is an emotional condition resulting from exposure to cultural biases and off-setting personal beliefs. These human fallacies don't mix well with a person's ideal self or the Ten Commandments. The one that jives with: "Do unto your neighbor, etc." The immediate unconscious thought that should occur when encountering a stranger on the road – if you hadn't already pegged him as a welfare bum and a worthless piece of shit. Jack and the Jungians are all for people developing better emotional hygiene – even before ridding them of bad breath and body odor. Psychoanalysis aims to enhance emotional self-awareness, reduce cognitive dissonance and…get the stains out…thus, avoiding negative Karma…Amen. Well there it is: for the few sessions approved by managed care, you can achieve better emotional hygiene and reduce Karma's impact. Religiously translated: you can fly direct to heaven without a lay-over in purgatory. Scientifically translated: Permanent neuronal changes within the amygdala and left prefrontal cortex of the human brain attributed to long-term meditation and metacognition techniques………have been scientifically proven. This all sets about to accelerate our emotional maturity. To have peak experiences, and achieve the lofty goals of Individuation and self-actualization. Which if I understand it right, is to be damn near perfect. Sign me up. On the other hand, I think emotional immaturity has gotten a bad rap. A great many people comfortable with the seminal works of Jeff Foxworthy and their cable sports subscriptions might become unnecessarily upset by all this.

[Yada…Yada…Yada]

Insofar as his actual past venialities are concerned, he is mute on the subject. He will slip up every now and then - usually when flirting with some exotic therapy like past life regression - and he'll begin speculating on the many former lives he might have lived. He is always more eloquent when he's been drinking or having a flashback and recalling a particularly mind-blowing acid trip. By the next day he will invariably recant these, "lunatic ravings of a man clinging to his ego." He'll say something like this to suggest that believing in surviving death in some form of intelligible after-life is mere wishful thinking. "Fear of death", he says, "will empower the ego to instruct the dying to end the fairytale of their lives in the predicable, 'happily ever [here] after.' Dead is just gone," he insists. His reverie about the past lives he may have lived is, "merely symbolic of our human collective conscious," he explains. "Just a lot of undeleted, obsolete brain software stored in the genetic strands of our DNA. No less grist for therapy than recurring dreams."

What a cynic. As if Jack's own fertile imagination might not intimate that maybe, just maybe, there is something more - out there. Didn't he watch just one episode of the X-Files? For Jack, Karma will have to do. He and his consortium of brainiacs can use it to rationalize everything from new age psychology to quantum physics. He has, like his academic colleagues, propounded more theories then there are…well…ants in the world. In Jack's *Return to Government Service,* his Karma-as-universal-solvent-for-explaining-just-about-everything stands out as his most overstated theory. Karma may turn out to be the absolute *Theory of Everything (TOE).* Doctor Jack is no mathematician, but he may be mathematicians' fool or hero - depending upon the prevailing consensus - in having answered that scientific conundrum. Jack's intuition has steered him away from Myteria Mathematica. Instead he's sat and meditated; possibly having channeled a passing astral Bodhisattva who revealed a divine *and* quantifiable mystery to him. TOE is not 11-dimensional M-theory, the elegant and intricate shape known to mathematics as E-8, or a coherent model for all the fundamental interactions of nature. It is simply, "KARMA." Like gravity and the other fundamental forces of nature, karma is so basic, so ubiquitous we often don't even notice it. Leave it to Jack to have figured out what greater minds than his have pondered for centuries. And Jack didn't waste any scrap paper trying to solve it. The shape E-8 - which is literally an 8 dimensional mathematical pattern with 248 points onto which all the forces which bind the universe can be neatly arranged and held in check (think of angels dancing on the head of a pin and now you're thinking like Jack) - was first found in 1887. However, scientists, only a few years ago, worked out the calculations, which if written in print this size would cover an area the size of Manhattan. Jack knows that simply by tapping into the collective unconscious everything can be understood. This is why Jack, as a first year calculus student, failed the class. He would arrive at the right answer and skip all the theorems, proofs and corollaries required to support those complex mathematical problems. However, all these proofs constituted eighty percent of the grade.

If the Human Potential and New Age Movements bore off-spring, they would name their first child, "Karma." What now passes for theoretical research in the fields of psychology and astral physics is what I refer to as "Karma's" dirty diapers. Jack thinks I'm beyond salvation. Not in the religious sense mind you, rather ignorantly bound to my own brand of cynicism. I think Jack was avoiding using the word, "stupid." Not wanting to outright piss me off. He should exercise the same restraint and sensitivity with his patients.

Part II

*"Maybe this is the place to begin, the reviled
Hemingway hero, the figure who faces the collapse
of democracy and civility during the First World
War and retreats into a self where a man takes his
own measure by an internal code of conduct—
silence, slaughter of large animals, risk, strong
drink, but never, never belief. No, never believe
again because belief leads to betrayal."*

Blood Orchid - An Unnatural History of America

by, Charles Bowden, published in 1995

A *Karmic Episode*....

Jack stared blankly at the stack of mail separated from the junk mail and placed in his inbox by his secretary. It was the usual stuff: insurance reimbursements; managed care newsletters; discharged clients' sworn affidavits of bankruptcy forwarded by their attorneys; returned bills stamped "Unable to deliver." On this particular morning Doctor Jack picked up the letter screened by his secretary on which she had scribbled the message: "Thought you might be specially interested in this one....didn't you do this kind of work before?" Renee had been my unofficial bloodhound on the scent for a potential job opportunity. She knew I was antsy for a change. I had sold my private practice six months ago, and was hanging on through an indefinite transition while the new owners got their feet wet. I had done my time; Spiritism's version of Karma. Accordingly, my spirit had chosen how and when I was to suffer retribution for the wrong I'd done in my previous life. A prisoner in a small office listening to the miseries of the emotionally sapped and the socially disenfranchised was it. Fortunately I hadn't been born with a disability for having made fun of the town leper or for tormenting a fat woman with rotten teeth who'd had the hots for me when I'd lived my former life in medieval Saxony. I hadn't been born as a female in 1949 to grow up to become a fat, lonely, toothless woman with psoriasis. I wasn't that bad off as bad karma goes. Actually I had had it good. Ministering to those I'd wronged in the past is just I suppose. This letter, though? It called to me from some far away time and place; somewhere deep inside. It wasn't all that unusual a letter given the daily correspondence I normally received. It was another Managed Care Company inviting providers to join its network. This one, Military Consultants International (MCI), actually wanted psychologists who'd be willing to travel to see clients. Soldiers and other members of the armed services on whom the war years had taken a heavy toll. The multiple deployments that soldiers had been recycled through had worn them down. And the war machine still needed them to keep the bullets flying and the strikers moving. America still relied on foreign oil, and it needed the military to spread Democracy throughout the oil rich countries of the Middle East. It was the great American conscience realizing an opportunity to look good. Like the establishment was doing the right thing. The right thing the government hadn't done for Viet Nam veterans. Soldiers of that war were spent and discharged; used up like so many old soldiers of foreign wars who were expected to pick up where they'd left off before the Great War or *those* Asian wars. Left on their own to deal with the private nightmares and fucked up marriages like all the old soldiers before them. They had their purple hearts, their broken hearts, and the VFW. There were the sad visages of lost youth, disillusionment, forgotten memories – thank god for those – and lingering fears. There are stories the real combatants will never talk about – it's was just too long ago. Bitter memories that old aren't worth sharing. It's better to bury it all and listen to Country Western music. It's remarkable that any effort whatsoever was being made to help soldiers and their families. It generally requires a century of guilty conscience to move our government to disingenuous tears. To say a Mea Culpa for past atrocities, like those done to Indians…, I meant to say Native Americans, and Negro slaves…though I should say, Blacks, or is it African Americans?

Doctor Jack believes it's in the best interest of Americans to say, "I'm sorry for what my great, great, great grandfather did to your great, great, great grandfather. A history of ethnic cleansing and genocide compels a national act of contrition. These acts of *Sanchita karma* cost *the* American tax payers millions of dollars.

Penance is an expensive proposition. The drive behind these acts of contrition? Not guilt, so much as fear. Fear, like Karma, is everywhere. It waits patiently to collect your back taxes. Jack tells me that the New Age politicians are as crazy as the Right Wingers of the Republican Party. He believes that the former Neo-pagans are making reparations to the generation descended from our pre-colonial squatters and our pre-civil war affordable labor force. Why? Out of fear of retribution. The *Law of Return* is pulling on the American sub-conscious like a mean aunt tugging on the tender ear lobe of an obstreperous nephew. The *Law* (doubtfully an immutable law) is based on the superstitious idea that the harmful effects one has on the world, will return to oneself. Colloquially speaking, "what goes around comes around." Jack knows that as an endangered American species, the WASPs (he and I) are potential muscle (albeit atrophied) for the slave market or a well deserved scalping. Better now to buy our "Free Man" papers and be seen spending our money at the Seminole casino.

Jack sees an opportunity when one presents itself. For a draft dodger he certainly has a soft heart for the war mongered. His "Make Love not War" credo would have sustained him in Viet Nam had he been drafted. His good friend, John Barlog, wasn't as lucky. He was drafted in '65. John never killed anyone. His most hazardous mission was setting out every pay day for a little island inhabited by Vietnamese/Cong prostitutes – which his friend had said was dangerous but worth it. Guided by a clouded half-moon and a swift river current, John made love, not war. There are equal dangers in both. John told Doctor Jack, they would have made good war buddies. It was compliments like this that swelled Jack's spirit with patriotism. Now, here was another chance to make a difference. Make no mistake about it, Jack is not motivated by a naïve obligation to duty, god and country. Jack saw the opportunity to travel and to earn a good income. He would seize the opportunity. He was a mental health mercenary. He'd help the war weary understand that love and war are not incompatible.

"An Ill Wind Blows Nobody Good...."

"The war - the real war, the one that had been going on for a thousand years and would go on for a thousand thousand more - the war between Us and Them, between the Haves and Have-Nots, between my gods and your gods, whoever you are - would be fought by men like Richards: men with faces you didn't notice or couldn't remember, dressed as busboys or cab drivers or mailmen, with silencers tucked up their sleeves. It would be fought by young mothers pushing ten pounds of C-4 in baby strollers and school girls boarding subways with vials of sarin hidden in their Hello Kitty backpacks. It would be fought out of the beds of pickup trucks and blandly anonymous hotel rooms near airports and mountain caves near nothing at all; it would be waged on train platforms and cruise ships, in malls and movie theaters and mosques, in country and in city, in darkness and by day. It would be fought in the name of Allah or Kurdish nationalism or Jews for Jesus or the New York Yankees - the subjects hadn't changed, they never would, all coming down, after you'd boiled away the bullshit, to somebody's quarterly earnings report and who got to sit where - but now the war was everywhere, metastasizing like a million maniac cells run amok across the planet, and everyone was in it."

Excerpt from, "The Passage," by Justin Cronin

Oh, yes. War is profitable. The cost is some cannon fodder. It's a loss accounted for in the collateral damages column of the corporate actuarial sheet. Halliburton, Black Water, KBR and Fluor, to name a few big players, jokey for a piece of the action. Ex-presidents, vice-presidents and politicians backed by PACs and corporate constituents are shareholders. The taxpayers foot the expenses. Jack wasn't born yesterday. In fact he was born into a generation that prepared its young men for military service at an early age. There was Cub Scouts, Boy Scouts, Sea Scouts, Civil Air Patrol, and a steady diet of World War Two films, both serious and sitcom, on TV and at the movies. The draft evaders and conscientious objectors invariably felt gyped out of an opportunity to act out their early war fantasies. Men like Jack sought it through mock service; men for hire in peace time and war who would go to work for some quasi-military agency or government bureau. There are contemporaries of Jack Mc Kane who work as summer hires for the Department of Interior. They wear the uniform of the National Park Ranger and patrol the forests and National Seashores keeping nature lovers and bathers safe from brown bears and beach litter. Some keep low on the establishment radar and work for the Probation Department or local police agencies as advisors and consultants. Others, like himself, cut to the chase and work for NATO, the NSA, the CIA, the FBI, the State Department or the DOD. Jack did his time with a few of these agencies. He left government service twenty years ago with an itch that didn't go away. So here he is, ready to relieve an old itch. Eager to bare his skin to the sharp talons of the government hawks.

In America there are factions,
but no conspiracies.

-Alexis De Tocqueville -
Democracy in America (1835)

In America there are weak factions, a dominant
single party and big business in control of
American lives. This eliminates the need for any
other brand of conspiracy.

the second book of job(s) (2010)

Jack's Interview with MCI...

The office of MCI was a vacated store-front located in the city's combat zone. How apropos. You didn't wander into this part of town after sundown unless you were with the SWAT team and armed to the teeth. My interview is in fifteen minutes. I'm circling the block looking for a safe place to park. If I escape a mugging, I want my tires to be on the car when I'm ready to leave. I finally double park next to a car with an MCI magnetic sign fixed to its driver-side door. I give brief consideration to swiping it for a souvenir, but decide to wait and see how the interview goes first. If it's still there when I return, I might relieve the vehicle of its special identity. Besides I like the logo. Real eye-catching: Planet earth encircled by orbiting energy belts. "MCI" written across the Atlantic Ocean. It had the look and feel of power. Nuclear power along with world domination. I wanted to work for a company with that kind of imagination.

The frontage wasn't exactly inviting, but then they weren't selling furniture or home fashion accessories like the faded sign above the door read. I didn't detect the presence of any life forms. Cigarette butts and an assortment of old food wrappers that littered the sidewalk hadn't been disturbed by human traffic for some time. Pretty deserted. I'd have turned around and left if I hadn't seen the marked car on the block. Oh, hell, what did I have to lose?

The glass door was opaque; reinforced with imbedded chicken pen wire. I could barely make out the hexagonal lattice work through the smoky glass. It was gray like weathered plastic and had cracks spreading out like spider webs from a deep indentation where a rock had hit its target. I knocked, and instead of a welcome greeting, the door groaned open on its rusted hinges. From the deep shadows at the back of the vacant show room, a voice bellowed, "COME ON IN…UNLESS YOU'RE LOST…IF YER HERE FOR AN INTERVIEW, COME ON IN AND…AH…FIND A SEAT…BE WITH YA IN TWO SHAKES OF A LAMB'S TAIL!

My eyes were beginning to adjust to the dim light that seeped in between the irregular seams of boarded up display windows. A competing dusky light strained through soot stained dormers. Particles of dust danced in the unfiltered light as if in the gentle embrace of a mysterious draft that stank of mildew, and mice urine. Dust covered everything. It covered the floor like a thin carpet; and revealed the fresh footprints   of a recent intruder. The atmosphere was eerie. I had seen all the SAW movies, and hoped I hadn't been selected to solve the riddle. I'm thinking: 'This is a stage set for urban combat training.' I should have come armed or at least brought my grand-son's paint ball weapon. "I don't like the feel of this,' I told myself, and was beginning to withdraw slowly with my back to the door, and a trained eye on the distant shadows. Shadows that began to move the way smoke behaves as it fills up a room from a smoldering fire. I felt like I was moving in slow motion. My amygdala was processing danger, and I was in hyper-alert mode. Was I expected to be proficient in hand-to-hand combat for this job? Was a shadowy figure with ninja stealth creeping up on me? My eyes were keen to the slightest hint of movement. My visual senses scanned left then right with autonomic precision. I remembered seeing, "Crouching Tiger, Sleeping Dragon," thus reminding myself to check the ceiling for intruders who moved like spiders and defied gravity. My enemies suspended above me; waiting for the precise moment to drop like a falling piano and crush me. I was a little disappointed that what stepped out of the shadows was the body-double for Lil Wayne wearing a black suit. He wore wire-rimmed glasses with transition lenses that darkened as he approached. Changing from clear to dark to protect his pink rodent eyes from stray photon fragments - in the fucking dimly lit, nearly-too-dark-to-see-anything-clearly-anyway...room. Except this is a spray-tanned white guy sporting dreadlocks inspired by the Nappylocs handbook. They were thin like licorice Twizzlers and looked like the rattails worn by the Alien Predator. His choice of wardrobe was more impressive. He was wearing an expensive custom tailored Armani suit that was worth more than my car. Life was still a movie casted with characters from someone's warped imagination. Either God's or Hollywood's. It was the same.

"Hello. You must be Mc Kane. Here on time. I like that. Something innately trustworthy about a man who shows up on time for an appointment."

"You're reading a lot into punctuality, aren't you? I mean, this place isn't the easiest to find. As for myself...I was ready to do an about face and leave. This address is sort of...ah...hidden...off the beaten path you might say."

"Yeah. You are right as rain 'bout that. Really disappointed with the digs myself. Our sandals-on-the-ground guy told us this was a bustl'n business area. Guess his intelligence is a few years off. Places like this go to seed so fast, you'd think you were run'n with a fist full of them white, delicate dandelions instead of whole city blocks. If it don't beat all. Hard to make a good impression on our applicants with the likes of this place. If it's any consolation, our corporate headquarters in Houston is ultra-modern. Takes up a city block, and not one that looks like this one. So, shall we try to ignore the less than satisfactory accommodations, and get on with business, Mc Kane?"

"Name's Doctor Jack Mc Kane." I usually don't resort to titles, and get formal in a way that sounds arrogant to most people. But this guy was too cocky. His chumminess and Texas manners were rubbing me wrong. I didn't trust the guy. He acted like a spook sent to dispatch me to the dumpster behind the building.

"Well, one thing we need to get clear on from the start, is none of us with MCI use our monikers. Get used to first name intros. That is if you end up working for us. Our decision… and yours of course. Take me, for example, I have a doctorate in behavioral science, and a masters in molecular biology. Don't practice anymore. Prefer to head hunt for the corporation."

"So mister…Doe, or whatever your name is… what by the way?"

"Black….Tyler Black. Call me Ty if you like. My colleagues do."

"Mr. Black…alright, Ty, what's the job entail? And I hope it doesn't require that I keep office hours here."

"The job. I'll think you'll like the work. See here [*as he riffles through a stack of application forms*] you've got prior military experience. Worked for the State Department as an attaché to NATO, Ran around with the 3/11 AC on the German Border, and did a gig with the DOD in Europe. Like to travel, Jack?"

"Yes, Ty, I like to travel. But as you can see from my application, I was working long hours and didn't have many days off to see much other than the local scenery. Some of it pretty bleak." I and the East Germans weren't exactly comrades on holiday."

"No surely not. I read your dossier, and from what I can tell – reading between the lines – that they didn't like you much. Took a shot or two at you on one of your unofficial sightseeing tours. Stepped a little over the line; the one they used to call *The Border*."

"Well, that was then, and this is now. Besides you're making me feel old. Since *The*

Border is ancient history. And the East Germans? They never could take a joke. No sense of humor. Always serious. Looking at us through high powered scopes as if we were geese and they were hunting us from a duck blind. No sporting blood at all." Is this about Germany? If it is you're making me homesick."

"No it's about a whole different kind of work. Maybe a bit too tame to your liking. It's a whole new world out there…"

"Okay, cut it out. I haven't been living under a rock since I left federal service. So what's the job?"

"I'll sum it up in a few words. You travel to military installations; you provide brief counseling sessions to the uniforms and their families. You don't keep notes or document your consults, and that's that. There, you have it."

"And the purpose of these sessions is…what?"

"You give them an outlet for their stress. They need to have someone they can vent to. Somebody to help them normalize what they're experiencing. Lot 'a normal adjustment difficulties making the transition from battlefront to home front. Soldier and his family have a hard time learn'n how to handle it."

"You mean little adjustment problems like post traumatic stress disorder, and going bonkers on the wife when the wake up alarm goes off next to the bed? Or normal things like not remembering where you parked the car when you came home at four in the morning?"

"It's not all about the heavy stuff. Mostly it's about get'n on with the day to day things: communicating with the wife, spending time with her instead of spending all day with his buddies."

"And you need people with my credentials to do that?"

"We have high standards for our teams. All are licensed, credentialed, mental health professionals. It's what our customer requires."

"Who's your customer?"

"You're old bosses. The DOD. Want the highest caliber of professionals we can recruit."

"Are we talking about ordinance or therapists?"

"Very funny, Jack. Won't hurt to keep your sense of humor. Just don't get funny with the top brass. They aren't the best audience at the Comedy Club."

"I don't know. I'll have to think about it. It sounds like you need less experienced therapists for the job." *Of course I'm thinking, 'I have my standards and self-respect to consider as well.'* "Like I said, Let me think about it."

"The work pays well. Work a month to three months on a job. Get to travel. MCI pays your expenses…"

"What's the pay?" Mr. Black…Ty (no pun intended) writes down a dollar figure on my file folder based on a nine month work year. He shows it to me like he's cupping an insect under his hand so it won't fly away.

Jeezus…who do I have to kill?"

"Oh, we'll send you the list when you get there."

"WHAT?"

"Just kidding, Jack. What's your decision?"

"I'll take it. When do I start?"

Two weeks later...Telephone call 2100 hours...

"Jack, telephone call for you...."

"Who is it? Jeeze, it's nine o'clock. Is it the answering service?" Donna had adopted the habit of remaining incurious about late night calls for me. They were usually from the answering service for the practice telling me that a client had called and it was absolutely urgent that I contact him or her. The screener at the service had a short list of questions to ask so they could screen out the ones who's 'emergencies' could wait till the next day. On more than a few occasions the caller was hanging over the dark precipice with cell phone in hand as if it were a safety harness. I wasn't on the call list since I sold the practice six months ago.

"I don't know. Some woman says she wants to talk to you." Only a wife of incurious habit could be nonchalant about a woman calling for her husband late at night. "Just answer it."

"Hello, Doctor Mc Kane. How can I help you?"

"Doctor, this is Melanie with MCI. You interviewed for a job with us, and I'm prepared to offer you an assignment. Are you still interested?"

"Yes...I might be interested. Tell me more about it."

"We need someone who's willing to commit to a sixty-day assignment in Korea. Do you think you can handle the travel conditions? You've got to be fit, because there is no rental car authorized for this location, and you'll be required to do a lot of walking."

"Yes, I'm fit. I run four miles and work out at least a few times a week." Donna was eyeing me suspiciously; probably wondering if I was being solicited by a sperm bank, or a senior male, escort service.

"Good. But are you interested in accepting this offer? I need to have your answer now; otherwise I'll have to call the next consultant on my list."

"I'm sure it's okay. Let me confer with my wife. Can you hold for a minute?"

"Yes, I'll wait…"

Holding my hand over the mouthpiece of the phone… "Donna they want me to go to Korea…to work with the army garrison….it's a couple of months work…you okay with me taking it?"

"Do what you want. Besides, we need the income."

"Is that a yes or a no?"

"If you decide to take it, it's yes. If you don't want to do it, its no." I wasn't up for solving riddles this late at night. I was tired and my thinking was fuzzy. Donna could be real difficult in a tight spot, like when something had to be decided, 'right now,' or if anything came up unexpectedly. I went for the tie breaker…

"So it's okay by you if I accept it?"

"Just give her your answer."

So I did… "Yes, I accept the offer. What's next?"

"I'll be sending your travel orders within twenty-four hours. Let me make sure I have your correct email address…its doctorjack@globalnet.com. Is that correct?"

"Yes, that's correct. And you'll be sending the itinerary along with it regarding the flight, lodging and expenses?"

"That's right, Jack. All the details are worked out at this end. Check your email, and confirm receipt when it arrives. And, thank you for accepting the assignment. I believe that you will enjoy it." How quickly I became just...Jack again with saying, 'yes,' to the job offer. I was now a *humble* member of the elite corps of military consultants.

"So, you told them you'd go?"

"Yes. You agreed didn't you? I included you in the decision."

"Some choice I have. When do I ever have a say in what you want to do?"

"Well, just now. You just did. I asked you, and I only accepted it after you said it was okay." Years of experience as a therapist wasn't nearly enough time to even begin to understand the mind of this woman...any woman. I had to assume that Donna was struggling with some underlying feelings that she wasn't willing to reveal. Probably too painful. Possibly loath to admit the loneliness she'd experience during my long absence. "Look if you don't want me to go, just say so. I'll call them back and decline the offer."

"Why would you do that? You just accepted the job. Don't you want to go? It's the kind of work you've wanted to do since we left Germany."

"We haven't been apart for as long as this assignment lasts. I mean ever...you'll be here by yourself...unless you come for a visit."

"No. It might be good for us to have some time apart. And I don't want to go to Korea. Besides, I can't take the time off from work."

"That's a lot of answers to a simple question…"

"It's complicated…"

"What's so complicated about visiting me in Korea? You're always talking about wanting to go to China."

"Look at a map, Jack. Korea isn't in China. They don't even speak Chinese. I'll visit when you go someplace interesting."

"Where would that be?"

"I don't know. Maybe Japan. And you know I have to work. I pay for our health insurance. And I told our daughter that I'd help her with our grandson while she's in school." I could see the walls going up. A lot like the old German border. Three generations of construction; each one a better attempt over the other to keep the people in, and prevent outsiders from getting very close. It was a freaking metaphor: here I was, again, going to a country with a hostile border comprised of layers; each one equipped to pin down and hurt any would-be transgressor. I was preparing myself for what I had anticipated for so long. Our timid divorce. That's what I would call a client's marital separation. A way for a husband or wife to back out of the marriage. To take a sabbatical from being married with the intention of making it permanent. Living apart gives the one with the divorce agenda time to decide which one of Paul Simon's twenty-seven ways to leave your [ex]lover will work for them.

Sometimes you want your alienated partner to miss you a little. Even before you've left. You know, missing the idea of you being gone. It just goes to show that you can be married long enough for a separation to have happened before you both realize it. For me it was a familiar wake-up call. A call I had heard and answered thirty years before. A call I was answering again. The call to join the American Foreign Legion. The American Foreign Legion is no Shangri-La. It is some far-away place where local troubles vanish in the prestidigitation of distance and time. A far-away place where the unfamiliar state that your life has become is normalized in the foreignness of a language, a culture and customs in which you willingly lose yourself. There are many such fugitives living abroad. I was going to be one of them.

I shouldn't act all hurt that Donna used this opportunity to initiate our timid divorce. After all, our relationship barely sustained the attributes of a friendship. There had been mutual threats of divorce in the heat of many of our, paradoxically, fewer serious arguments. It takes balls to divorce a mate of thirty years. Surprisingly hard. You'd think it would be easy. All those skirmishes which destroy the intimacy, and the less frequent bids for affection. Avoiding the real issues for fear that another argument will only cause bad feelings because nothing ever gets solved. Because somebody's always feeling threatened or implicitly blamed. Oh, and the community property we shared, and the investments we put away for our retirement, and the idea of being alone in old age without an accomplice to pull the plug when the time comes. On, and on, and on. Pity, pity, pity… Little wonder then that it's so hard. It's very, very hard.

"Jack, what are you so glum about?"

"Nothing. I'm not glum. I'm just letting the idea settle in. Korea…sounds interesting."

It is amazing what Jack can do with something as potentially innocuous as Donna thinking that some time apart might be actually good for their relationship. And what does Jack do? He goes off on a cerebral divorce trip. I asked him if this is what he wants. A divorce that is. He would only admit to the possibility of some minor projection on his part. He said he'd bring the question up with his therapist – who not coincidentally is going through a divorce of his own. Jack cops out once again; deferring an answer to a straightforward question by subjecting himself to analysis with a therapist who probably isn't the best counsel for him at this time. Jack is not to be trusted with his own counsel because of his inability to be honest with himself. I don't dare say this to him. He left me with the doubtful assurance that his therapist was a professional of the highest regard, who would remain steadfast and objective with him in this matter. Sure.

Part III

Charlotte North Carolina to Inchon, South Korea...

The FBI investigates terrorism-related matters
without regard to race, religion, national origin,
or gender.

- Terrorism in the United States
FBI Publications, 1997

The TSA treats every American Airline Traveler
as a potential terrorist without regard to race,
religion, national origin, age, or gender.

- Terrorism Against Americans
the second book of job(S), 2010

I hate packing for a trip. I don't have to remind myself why, as I haul two suitcases and shoulder a forty-pound back pack through the Charlotte Airport. Air travel sucks. Flying like a packed sardine for fifteen hours in route to Korea doesn't thrill me with anticipation. Think positively. Think happy thoughts I tell myself, as I'm nearly run down by a tram carrying overweight Americans who are busy funneling Starbucks Frappuccinos and scarping down Cinnabuns. Their glazed over concentration is briefly interrupted as their tram clips my suitcases and nearly sends me headlong into a shoe shine stand. I wobble uncertainly like a pack mule at the edge of a trail overlooking the bottom of the Grand Canyon. I have the urge to shout an obscenity at the tram operator, but catch myself. Aware that I'd make Homeland Security's day by giving them someone to Tazer and send to the Charlotte Airport underground complex for 'questioning.'

It's my fault for traveling so heavy. It turns out that I'm carrying more 'things,' than clothes. Important things, like my computer, a printer, a scanner, two GPS navigation systems, hiking boots, running shoes, canteen, camel pack, Leatherman tool, two hunting knives, trekking poles…to name some. Donna encouraged me to bring more clothes, "You'll be there two months. You should pack enough changes of clothes to last you a couple of weeks. You may not have laundry facilities available." I didn't argue with her. I tossed in another shirt or two; and a pair of combat BDUs just in case I encountered hostiles. Donna seemed satisfied that I had packed enough to wear for my long trip. I was confident that I had packed enough supplies for an African safari. I wished I had an elephant gun at the ready as the tram passed. I again need to bring my attitude in check. There would be karma to pay for such thoughts. I should have left my Garmin Trek out because I needed it to navigate through a mile of concourses to reach my departure gate. I was tempted to sit awhile in one of the white picket style rocking chairs lined along the main concourse. The thought of sitting in one conjured up thoughts of retirement. I wondered if people without south facing porches who had retired in Charlotte came here to rock to-and-fro while harried passengers scurried by. Thinking: 'These damn fools…all of 'em skitter'n along in a hurry to git somewhere fer away when they could jes a well be tak'n a load off their feet and lay down their satchels and sit a spell.' I'd have enough time to sit – longer than a spell – while streaking through the stratosphere at four hundred miles an hour for fifteen endless hours.

Check-in is the second ring of hell at the airport. I arrived early enough so as not to have a long wait in line. I was the only passenger in line. Well, actually there wasn't a line because I was it. My panic began to rise, but quickly subsided, when I realized that check-in wasn't open. I was assured by a passing Red Cap that it would open in an hour. I took advantage of the wait by seeking out a lavatory to lighten my flying weight by a pound or two. It was a luxury to sit even if it was on a toilet seat that god knows whose hairy asses had sat on. I felt relieved to have obeyed nature's call, because if you don't you throw off your body's entire constitution. Jetting through several time zones doesn't respect the body's delicate timing of its important functions.

I returned to check-in to find a line thirty travelers long. It looked easily a block long counting the suit cases and oddly shaped hard sided cases containing everything from golf clubs to tubas, and one container that looked like it might contain an RPG 29 tank killer. There is no point in being impatient. I'd wait and slowly walk the trail of tears to my next internment station, the gate check.

Check-in is better than a standard IQ test. If you can pass the automated check-in kiosk, you will be called to a ticketing agent and baggage checker while others who were well ahead of you in line are still challenged by the codes and incantations you have to recite to receive your e-ticket and baggage confirmation. I was called to the desk by a haggard looking guy whose eyes had bags under them as big as carry-ons barely able to fit in an overhead compartment. I hoisted my first bag on to the scale to weigh it as if it were qualifying for a weight class in an MMA bout. I knew the bag would make weight. It was relatively light. Forty-seven pounds. Three pounds under the limit. The agent smiled wanly; in tacit approval of my adherence to airline regulations. I knew as soon as I strained against the weight of my second bag that I might be in trouble. Trouble meant having to pay practically the price of another airline ticket for excess weight. I made an effort not to contort my facial muscles or grab my low back as it spasmed against my will. I tried to make the lift in one clean jerk. I stuck the toe of my shoe under the bag and leveraged it to bear some of the weight on my foot. Problem was that the scale read like an EEG during an epileptic fit. Going from fifty-six pounds to forty, plus, minus, plus pounds while my foot trembled against its massive force. The agent had me in his cross hairs, and commanded me to, "sss…dep avay fom de bag, zir." I knew his hand was inches from the buzzer that would call in armed security if I refused his order.

"Zir yu arrh ober de veight limit. Holt on vile I zeck de vrate fur yer ov..rage. zunless, you vant do zransfer som of yer arrh..ticles indo de otter bag. Or if yer have vroom in yer garry-on?"

"I'm traveling on military travel orders. Can't you make an exception?" It wasn't beneath me to solicit patriotic spirit in the name of those courageous men and women who were making the supreme sacrifice for their county. And his. Possibly not his, because he spoke with a thick Romanian accent." I couldn't remember the last despot I could summon to the same purpose. The only political celebrity that came to mind was Vlad the Impaler, and I didn't think this was appropriate given the agent's power over my situation.

"I'm zorry bot de airline company ist very zstrict a…bout deez require…ments. Sponzor fer dis flight ist U…nited, and I vill haf to loke upt der vrates." He confers with an accomplice in the Romanian black market and tells me, without blinking an eye, that I'll be charged an extra fifty-five dollars…"Do yer vont de charge put on yer plas..teek gard?"

"You mean my credit card? No. I'll repack a few things. Although I hate backing up the line to do it."

"Ist no prob…lem. Deeze people ken vait. Zo tak yer time." As he was telling me this I began pulling things out of one suitcase while trying to compress the jetsam into the other one. I was aware of the pity showing on the faces and slumped shoulders of the passengers behind me. I was surprised they weren't mumbling and pissed off in the customary American way. I realized that travelers were like refugees. They knew that soon enough they would be subjected to the same humiliation and extortion by the powers in control. We were a disenfranchised brother and sisterhood. We would suffer our fates in the mutual huddle of the trodden masses.

Somehow, during the transfer of things from one bag to the other, an equalization of shared weight not exceeding fifty-pounds apiece resulted. There are wormholes into which matter gets swallowed and lost beyond the event horizon of travel to far-away places. If my math were correct, there should have been three pounds over no matter how I distributed things. I was never very good at math.

Although my personal belongings were bared naked before the airport voyeurs, I was not ashamed. We were all god's children in the eyes of one another. My underwear, although kind of brief with prominent Playboy logos stitched across the groin, raised only the eyebrow of an Episcopal minister. My essential travel tools may have caused suspicion among the ticket agents had I not discretely buried them deep within the side-pockets and bottom recesses of my suitcase. The knives, if seem by the passengers, might inspire hope that I would be their revolutionary martyr if I were to become agitated and moved to rage against the ticket agents. I was now thoroughly exhausted according to the plan of airport personnel, and ready to slouch toward gate check-in.

By the time I got to the gate, I and the other passengers were as sluggish as a herd of bovines being prodded through the chutes of the Chicago stock yards. Worse, it was reminiscent of what I had seen in the old newsreels where concentration camp prisoners are seen taking off their shoes, stacking them in piles, after which they are stripped naked and led to the showers for some permanent hygiene. I wouldn't doubt it if Jesse Ventura told me that these old newsreels are used for training TSA security staff. Getting practically undressed to walk through a scanner is tedious. It demands a lot of coordination, and a good memory for what you dropped in the bin on the way through the gauntlet. You invariably hear the intercom announcer summoning some passenger back to the security check point to retrieve some lost item. Things as big as laptops and as small as retainers get left behind by flummoxed passengers. The suspicious contents of a bag drifting past the fluoroscope machine gets emptied, rifled through and examined by a machine equipped with tiny succodes that sniff the air. Checking you and your bags for the faint residue of chemical explosives. If drugs are indicated, a dope dog, held in semi-attacked mode, probes you and your belongings with a nose that is determined to locate a pot seed buried in your navel since '65. I've traveled enough to have had the privilege of being molested by every security protocol invented. In muted protest, I tolerate the inconveniences of flying in post-911 times. I am convincing myself that it is all worth it. Worth it because of the opportunities awaiting me at my destination - the exotic Far East. Those of us who have flown during the 60s have been spoiled. Plane travel was a luxury then. Coach travel was relatively comfortable. And there were stewardesses. Real stewardesses, not flight attendants, who were all females and resembled cute little Humboldt penguins with hips narrow enough to clear the aisles with room to spare. I won't get nostalgic and list all the amenities of air travel that made flying a treat. Now? Well if you've flown even one time in the last eight years, you know what a Mexican Bus Ride is like even if you've never been to Mexico, or ridden the bus, or for that matter a bus with wings, from Juarez to Acapulco. Its kind and socially correct to hire flight attendants regardless of gender, sexual preference, age and girth, but I hate trying to sleep in an aisle seat and getting sideswiped by the huge ass of a chubby flight attendant or the cart he/she is pushing haphazardly down the aisle. No apologies are ever offered. It's plain out hit and run. Taking advantage of the passenger's momentary disorientation from being rousted from fitful slumber; as if you didn't know that you'd just been grazed by a moose or the metal runners of a beverage cart. As if being a fatty and a bad cart operator is my fault for exceeding my seat and leg room allowance because I'm 6',1" and much bigger than a dwarf. If they bring back transatlantic steamship travel I might consider it. For now, I'll stop bitching. I'll take my beating like every other docile traveler.

I'm running this all through my mind before I've even boarded. So, I go to the ticket desk at my gate, and ask if there's a window seat available. To hell with having to pee four times. The middle and aisle passengers are in it the same as I am. I'd do my best, nonetheless to hold my water, and retain the alcohol content of my in-flight beverages. I am lucky. Probably having made some sucker happy who last flew somewhere back in '65; thinking he was in for a comfy aisle seat with a fast-track to the lavatory and a quick exit to the emergency hatch in the event of a nose dive into the Sea of Japan.

The Charlotte Airport is a marathon course for travelers racing to their departure gates. I had settled into a cramped seat facing the windows overlooking the off ramps. Our plane hadn't yet arrived, so I got to stare out at idling baggage transporters trailing caravans of overflowing luggage. Their drivers were lounging expectantly while cat napping on the clock at thirty-eight dollars an hour. I guessed that they were saving their strength, anticipating another training day for the Scandinavian winter games of boulder tossing and pole pitching - only with my luggage. I couldn't bear to watch when the time came to 'place' the bags in the cargo hold.

The sun had begun to set when our plane arrived. A fairly wide-bodied Boeing 777. Still a tightly confined space when crammed with three-hundred-plus passengers. A miracle of aerodynamic engineering that is still basically a cigar tube propelled by rocket engines. Lifting off into the setting sun strikes me as symbolic all of the

sudden. I am mulled in the lambent glow of a
Carolina sunset. Soon our plane will follow the
sun's slow path over the western horizon. Tracking
the sun's Mercator to a run-way seven thousand
miles away. I already feel like I'm a million
miles from home.

I am seated in the forward cabin behind first
class. I get to board soon after the first class
passengers have been seated. This way I get to
watch the circus as people juggle their carry-on
luggage, balancing bags in mid air while timing
their aim and angle of entry into the overhead
compartments. Either the bins have gotten smaller
or the carry-on has expanded while in storage
between flights. You can see the puzzled looks,
followed by broken blood vessels and sweaty faces.
It amazes me how an item the size of a hay bale
can be reduced to something resembling a dry bath
sponge. Only Barbie and Ken can travel light and
comfortably by today's airline standards.

The senior flight attendant has already made
two announcements encouraging passengers to finish
stowing their bags and to take their seats, "so
our flight can leave on time. If your bag won't
fit into the overhead compartment, please notify a
flight attendant and we will check your bag for
pick-up when you arrive at your destination." In
other words, *we will teach you a lesson and send
it to a foreign military compound in a war zone.
You may pick it up after we drop you from an
emergency exit at thirty-thousand feet.* It is
amazing what passes for a carry-on with some
travelers. There is no fucking way you should
expect an object that looks like a shrink wrapped
shipping pallet on wheels to fit into a space the
size of a microwave oven. I don't know how they
make it this far without being steered to the
cargo hanger. But every so often in spite of all
the cautions along with those little dummy
contraptions at each gate into which you can place
your carry on to see if it fits, some muscle head
gets one by. I understand their reasoning. They

want to arrive during the same month as their luggage. Even if it means stuffing a walk-in wardrobe into a single, small suitcase that has the stretch and flexibility of a pregnant woman carrying sextuplets.

I deplore the abuse of prescription drugs! However, Xanax is a wonderful travel companion. Don't misconstrue what I'm saying as an endorsement for Pfizer Pharmaceuticals who had the original patent (which has expired). I'm not endorsing any manufacturer or distributor of this drug. I'm just happy someone's making it. My patients will particularly misquote me here, because I have come down hard on long-term users of drugs in this class because they are powerfully addictive. It will under normal use quickly reduce anxiety, and powerfully distort your perceptions of who you are, where you are and what century you're living in. It's because of these latter side effects that it is great for taking just before take-off in preparation for a long flight. A good time to take it is while you still have some liquid to wash it down. This is a bit of a problem because they confiscated my four-dollar bottle of fancy tap water at the main boarding gate. So between watching passengers wrestle carry-ons into the overhead compartments and snagging and flight attendant for a potable liquid, I am tempted to drink my under-four-ounce bottle of contact lens solution in order to get the pill down in time. If you sufficiently dose yourself with say, one to two milligrams of Xanax, you won't care that you are a tube of meat stuffed into a sausage skin, or that you cannot lower your seatback because it has been retrofitted to immobilize Hannibal Lecture.

I didn't drink my contact lens solution. I was patient and waited for takeoff. After the plane leveled out and the seat belt sign was turned off, I walked back to the galley and asked for a cup of water. I'm not nervous about flying so when most passengers are silently making peace with their maker and praying the rosary or thumbing and fore fingering their worry beads, I'm content to study the pitch of the hydraulic system. Because I know if this system starts sounding erratic, and the plane starts shuddering violently or I see smoke issuing from an engine, I'll know to start worrying. No sense getting all worked up over a routine take-off. What you don't know won't hurt you. That the flight control staff in the tower all pissed themselves because your plane came within a hundred feet of colliding with another plane coming in for a landing, is of no consequence to you. Better dumb and unaware than panicking over a near-miss. There was still thousands of miles of land and ocean to worry about if you were so inclined and didn't drink or take the necessary prescription drugs. I waited to return to my seat before taking a Xanax Bar. I didn't want to take the chance of loitering at the galley and having the drug kick in before I found my way back to my seat. It's possible to spend the whole fifteen hour flight confused and disoriented and looking for your assigned seat. My daughter used to have that happen to her. She would still be out of it hours after landing; needing to be guided like a blind woman to baggage claim because of anterograde amnesia. That's the amnesia you can have as a side effect of Xanax where you forget everything after the event – in this case for hours after the plane's landed.

I vaguely remember being asked by my headrest if I wanted something to drink. It was most likely the flight attendant trying to ram me with the serving cart even though I was in the window seat. I don't know what I ordered because the only recollection I have is the warm sensation of wetness spreading in my lap. Either I accepted a drink and carelessly spilled it all over me, or I couldn't make it to the lavatory, or we made an emergency landing in the Bering Straits. I could fucking care less (I formed expressions like that when intoxicated). All manner of embarrassment – which you can only experience if your higher cognitive centers are functioning - passes into oblivion. So it's like these things never happened. It's a free ticket to misbehave. Although a reprieve is not forthcoming in the real world, at least the feelings of guilt and shame can be postponed.

I'm a big guy so the drug wore off hours before landing. I was mildly annoyed that I had missed all the diversions of flying. Which is the same as perks. These are the meager benefits which include mini-bags of peanuts *or* pretzels (not both) and a meal manufactured by Monsanto. I was conscious for breakfast which consisted of Bimbap and tea. Bimbap I discovered is an uninspiring conglomerate of rice and vegetables with a cold fried egg on top. I was told by the passenger sitting next me – who I finally noticed for the first time in 12 hours, and whose soggy shoulder was probably from my drooling on him while passed out – told me it was a staple of the Koreans and that I should have the genuine thing when I get there. It is possible that we bonded during the hours we spent so closely cramped together although fortunately I can't remember anything since this time yesterday. I also noticed, to my surprise, that the flight attendants were all female, Asian, and very attractive. They walked the aisles with room to spare. They could move their hips provocatively without banking a shot, and spoke in little girl voices that sounded like cute Anime cartoon characters. I don't remember having a demonstration of safety procedures and seat belt buckling instructions by such dainty people. Could a change of staff have occurred in mid-flight, like in-flight refueling? Xanax can play tricks with the mind. This is why it's not wise to take it during work – unless your job is as unpleasant as flying. I could tell that I was going to like Korea. If all Korean women were as cute as the flight attendants, I could forgive the food.

Coming into the world of awareness should be undertaken gradually. A hang-over usually accomplishes this, and so does the slowly lifting fog of Xanax stupefaction. I could be pleasant without having a reason to be. I could grin and nod good-morning back to the flight attendants because it came involuntarily. Like we do in imitation of dogs as a sign that we are too weak to defend ourselves against the bigger animal. The one who's thinking and reflexes are quicker than the submissive one's. You don't want to be drawn into a fight when you're high. In addition to a slowing of your reflexes, your inclination to roll on your back for a belly rub can be disastrous. This may explain what happened to Gretchen Whitted when she was attacked by the raccoons.

The sensory dullness produced by a trans-continental flight (Because no oceans were crossed, rather the far north continent including Siberia) provided a mild immunity to the final shake-down through customs. Suffice it to say that I didn't make it through unnoticed by the scrupulous South Koreans. One of my suitcases that dropped from the carousel chute was tagged with what looked like a shape charge. Shackled is more apt a reference than tagged. There was nothing dainty about the device that was attached to my bag. It was the size of a paving brick and was bright yellow, a color that universally signifies caution, even danger - had it been armed with a blinking red light. I noticed how the other passengers at the carousel started to give me a wide berth, collected their bags and darted off before an unseen man in the shadows used his cell phone to detonate my bag. I was tempted to ignore the thing, and walk through customs with a poker face; a blank expression indicating a bluff or travel paralysis. I was kidding myself, because stepping out from the wall paint were two plain clothes security guys who looked like two skinny

Asian kids in baggy civilian clothes. I instinctively shooed them away; pretending they were Korean Jehovah Witnesses trying to hand me The Watchtower. They were polite despite my bad manners; showing me instead of the latest Watchtower edition, badges identifying themselves as customs agents. They demurely escorted me to customs officials in uniform. One smiling customs agent instructed me to open my bag after disarming the sinister device. The Koreans smile a lot, and it seems strange considering the circumstances. These smiles shouldn't be mistaken for cheerful friendliness or submissiveness. Smiles can, and often do signal an impending act of violence. Anyone who's seen Dirty Harry or Charles Bronson movies remembers how these vigilantes of justice would smile evilly before emptying six rounds into the villain. Expressing a smug satisfaction that justice had been served…with a smile. My good humor was however submissive, because I didn't know what I had unwittingly smuggled into the country that could result in a public caning followed by deportation. The customs guys knew, or they wouldn't have tagged me. So I played dumb. Not hard under the circumstances. When I opened my suitcase, two other agents swept in and flanked me. One started probing the contents with a gloved hand. A tiny hand, small enough to retrieve a ring trapped in the elbow bend of a sink drain. I felt fortunate that this was a bag search and not a cavity search. A hand with the deft skill of a magician plucking a coin from behind the ear of a volunteer from the audience produced a pair of brass knuckles, and a Special Forces dagger. Placing a weapon in each hand; appraising each of them and then me with an expression that begged the answer to the unasked question: 'Who are you going to kill while visiting our friendly country? Or aren't there more efficient ways to dispatch an enemy than with a painful beating and a stabbing?' The juried hands weighed the evidence against me. The dagger was placed back in my luggage. However, the knucks remained perched in the upraised palm.

The agent in charge – the spokesman for the trio – finally looked me in the eyes and spoke levelly through a smile indicating no hint of menace. "We do not allow these in the country of South Korea. For what do you use these?"

"Why it's a paper weight. I do a lot of paper work. I like working near an open window. Sometimes a breeze will come up, and I've had a few incidents where my papers…"

"Ah, yes…needed to be taught a lesson?"

"No. Oh, you're joking. That's just a novelty paper weight. I use it only to hold down my papers, and keep things organized."

"What is 'novelty' paper weight? Does it mean also is a weapon? Say a funny weapon that is also for papers to hold down?"

"Why don't you just throw it away? I'll find a rock to use in its place."

"You will use soldier to hold paper down?"

"What are you talking about? No. A rock, a big stone, a heavy object. *And then it dawned on me,,,R.O.C not R.O.C.K. ROC were Korean soldiers. ROC stood for*

Rear Operations Command. These guys were fucking with me. "You know, a heavy object, not a heavy person."

"Of Course. So…we can leave it here for you to pick up. For when you leave country. You like we should hold here for you?"

"No. It's no big thing. You keep it. You might need it for your work…I mean, I'm sure you have a lot of paper work with this job…" My interrogator eyed me once more. Appraising, once again, my dangerousness to the paper work I'd be undertaking while a visitor to South Korea. I got to leave amidst bows and more smiles as I left a little bit lighter for my return trip. I would have to face the five fingers of death without an equalizer. I would be obliged to keep my dagger at the ready. I remind myself that this is no fantasy adventure. My head shrink head hunter may have appeared very cloak and dagger, but he was just an apparatchik for a big corporation that obviously didn't keep a tight rein on its field agents. A tendency toward eccentricity isn't that rare among the over-educated. Particularly likely when the field specialty is akin to rocket science or psychology - present company excluded. Yes, I said, excluded. Mr. Black, I judge him not, was fucking weird. I can't imagine the armed forces decision makers taking him seriously. But then again, they have taken some bad-ass, bad dressers seriously before. They had to. I'm thinking of Omar Kaddafi who looks like an ugly man in drag, and Osama Bin Laden who once posed as Christ at the Holy Land Experience theme park in Orlando. Maybe he didn't, but he could have. For the time being I'll remain cautious and reserve further comment regarding MCI personnel. If during my globetrotting consulting, I disappear under mysterious circumstances, add MCI to the long list of suspects.

I can tell that my brain isn't firing on all cylinders. Jet lag is no fun. Although a common, normal side effect of crossing several time zones, its social consequences are underestimated. In other words you can embarrass yourself royally if say you attend an important board meeting or are asked to give a toast at a dinner party while still fuzzy headed. Although jet lag is not a serious medical problem, and there are a number of aides and remedies for dealing with its minor discomforts, not one reputable source advises the jet lagged traveler how to manage for damage control. First of all, call Jet Lag by its more frightening medial name: Desynchronosis. This sounds like a life threatening disease. It's not, but there are other fatalities that can result such as the premature termination of your employment. I'll explain more about this in awhile. But first, understand that jet lag is a sleep disorder. It's the consequence of alterations to our circadian rhythms. Meaning our body's internal time piece has had its hour hand spun like a roulette wheel. And finding yourself wide awake at two in the morning and wanting scrambled eggs and bacon. You forget the fact that you have been propelled across a revolving globe that is dark on one side and sunlit on the other, and have violated nature's rules for how fast and far homo sapiens should be able to travel as a hunter and gatherer in search of veggies and game. There is a formula you can apply to your routine in preparation for travel in order to mitigate jet lag's effects. Quite frankly, it's too complicated. It would require a supercomputer to crunch the numbers needed to figure your destination time zone in advance, because you are instructed to alter your daily routine beginning three to four weeks in advance of your flight. I can only assume this would work if you reported to your regular job an hour later every day, and left an hour earlier every day for a month. You should be fired just in time to catch your flight. You should therefore prepare to find a new job when you've reached your destination.

There are other aides that are less extreme. Although, their effectiveness is doubtful according to the Jet Lag scientists. Because they are questionably effective, why mention them at all? Besides, I am rarely packed in time to catch the shuttle to the airport, let alone able to plan a month of pampering that's more like slow torture. I'm not wiring my alarm clock to deliver electroshock, and I'm not squeezing protein and carbohydrate goo in measured doses like an astronaut in the confines of a zero gravity, orbiting capsule. I have tried melatonin because it made sense. In fact I've used it for years, against medical advice, because it's one of those hormones that time and age diminish. They say that by the age of thirty we have only 20% of what we had a twenty. I feel that nature shouldn't get lazy and stop producing a hormone as important as melatonin. After all, it's linked to sleep and youth; two things that we're robbed of over the years. I was only stealing back what was mine in the first place. Melatonin is secreted by the pineal gland in darkness, and stops when light hits the eyes. It's the signal our body receives to help us fall asleep at sunset, and rise with the sun. It regulates various body functions, all of which I want to keep. Again, the FDA, who meddle with the distribution of miracle compounds, would have us believe that it might not be good for us. And to use it to stave off jet lag, requires another program of administration that is normally associated with tedious research or nuclear waste disposal. They caution: "the timing of administration needs to be precise and individualized." Yeah? So what is so fucking precise about taking at least five-hundred percent more than the manufacturer recommends, to play it safe (or unsafe depending upon your perspective on dosage), when you need to sleep - especially when it's one a.m. in Oz, and nine o'clock in the morning in Kansas. I am not attributing my age-related insomnia to reckless self experimentation. I have a lot of friends my age who don't sleep well, and they all don't take melatonin. There is - and I wouldn't belabor this subject unnecessarily - one promising remedy in the works. And I have already begun testing it. Viagra! I kid you not. A recent study in hamsters showed that Viagra aided in a fifty-percent faster recovery from shifts in time zones. However, add the overly cautious researchers (who fear the FDA), this has not been tested in humans and is considered an off-label use by the drug's manufactures. Makes perfectly good sense. A long lasting erection - and a little assistance with having one - along with a willing partner or a Vaseline Intensive Care product - always tires me out. I can sleep like a baby after good sex. Even

after sex that's just so-so. I wonder if it works
the same for women. I am curious about the
hamsters. It's possible; I suppose that they might
be employed in some special capacity. I know that
Gerbils have been used for sordid purposes I've
only read about. But this is medicine and certain
things might be legally allowed with a
prescription. The reason I've already tested this
jet lag remedy is something I don't wish to talk
about right now. I tell people that I'm testing a
jet lag medication that offers additional
benefits. And that it has something to do with
keeping you up when you need to be. And letting
you relax and fall asleep afterwards.

Part IV

Camp Casey, Korea and Jet Lag... and the Midget of Toko-ri.

It's two in the afternoon, and the bus has dropped me off at Camp Casey in Dongducheon. Dongducheon is a small city in the province of Gyeonggi, South Korea. Despite it being called a city it is rural by American town and country standards. It is more a city in the sense that Korean's tend to densely pack themselves into villages; leaving the country-side more sparsely inhabited. This gives them room to roam, or to 'Walk the Earth' as Grasshopper used to do in the TV series Kung Fu. Camp Casey is the central landmark in Dongducheon. Military towns have their own distinct character - not necessarily a good character, as in the case here.

There is an intuitive signal that alerts a MCI consultant that another is in close radar range. It's a subliminal signature that can be read from great distances. Long before eye contact can be established. I'm speculating that it might be carried in the air, an olfactory load comprised of exotic molecules that triggers vigilance that contact with the same species is imminent. I don't think its pheromone based because I observed during our group briefing that the mean age of a MCI consultant is about sixty. Production of the good mating pheromone has been exhausted in this age group. Except for me because of the supplements I have been taking thanks to the internet. I am particularly grateful for mail order sites that allow the intrepid human guinea pig to by-bass the FDA and order direct from Chinese and Indian laboratories which produce anti-aging drugs, and other substances of dubious legality. Taking these drugs is not for the squeamish. If you are picky about the animal parts you will eat, or the inorganic excipients used to bind your pills, then don't order. There has been a lot of bad press recently about melamine, lead and Chinese dry wall. If these are substances you can tolerate, go for it. After all, youth is never without its perils. Risk taking and an attitude of invincibility is the hallmark of youthful behavior. Anyway, the scent of MCI consultants, I discover, is more like muscle lineament and day old depends. I remember the German hallenbads when old Germans would swim in the warm waters without having showered first. Wafting on warm air currents suspended above the indoor pools was a veritable fog of atomized pore jam.

Eye contact between MCI personnel stimulates a herd response similar to aged pachyderms. Who from all directions of the compass, have, singly or in small groups, walked hundreds of miles to gather at the bone yard of their ancestors. Our individual travels have originated from every state in the Union. Some consultants have solo assignments. Others are sent in small teams of two to half-a-dozen or more. My rotation in Korea is basically solo.

I am met at the bus depot on post by what at first looks like a small welcoming party. I am still in jet lag where people seem to merge into a crowd of strange faces against a foreign backdrop of Asian stage scenery. I'm easy to identify as I step off the bus. I hope it has less t do with the MCI chemistry thing. I think it has more to do with that *look*: of a traveler scanning the welcome crowd at the airport looking for the driver who's holding up the sign with his name on it. I've never experienced the royal welcome of having the hired limo driver waiting for me at the airport. His mission: to drive me to my five-star hotel as the guest of honor at the annual convention of superstars. I suppose this will do: a young, female major and civilian who look like opposing sides of a 60s war protest rally. The major is mid-thirtyish; looking pretty sexy in a battle dress uniform. She is Hispanic, and I've always been attracted to dark complexioned, brown-eyed women who speak with a Latin accent. Well, I'm attracted to all women of a slender, hour-glass anatomical figure who are under the age of 90. I'm not very particular. The other woman, roughly the age of a late middle aged cougar, looks every bit the flower child of my former hippie days. Although a much withered flower and not exactly a child, she is comely nonetheless. She has apparently reconciled her relationship with the military industrial complex like I have. Selling out is not as shameful as it once was. Everybody does it eventually. I manage to keep my anti-establishment sentiments below the surface. Rarely do I raise my fist in defiance of social injustice. It is foolish, and self-destructive, to do this when the federal government is your employer.

The civilian introduces herself and her uniformed side-kick. This isn't Mutt and Jeff, although a pair who could be cast as these old comic book characters. "Hello, you must be Jack, the new MCIC. *She pronounces this, 'MESICK,' the shorthand acronym for which the military is famous in applying to everything over two words long.* My name's Sedona. This is Major Cora Ramirez."

"Ah, glad to make your acquaintance. Yes, I'm the new MCIC." I'm generally bad at remembering names upon first meeting a person. These two have made it easier than usual. Sedona is not a common name and I've been there - in Arizona – and had my chakra energies aligned by visiting the five vortices scattered throughout the town. Captain Ramirez had her name printed on a Velcro patch over her discretely camouflaged right breast pocket. I think everyone should wear their name on their clothing. It's embarrassing to forget the name of a person you've worked side by side with five years ago, or a former spouse of seven.

Sedona sweeps me up in a bear hug, and I half expect to find a flower in my hair after the brief yet touching greeting. Major Ramirez extends a small hand with delicate fingers. I grasp her hand and squeeze gently though not so gently that she thinks me unfit for hand to hand combat with the North Koreans should hostilities break out while I'm here. I observe her instant attraction to me. She nonverbally communicates this with her dilated pupils and the light blush that colors her cheeks; a blush which looks like glistening apple butter with her olive complexion. This is nature's unmistakable language expressing carnal desire. She corrects this assumption by pointing to my shoe which has landed on her size six-and-a-half combat boot. "Oh, not steel toed anymore," I weakly offer where an apology would have been more appropriate. "No, Jack. Soft suede for desert wear. Breathable panels that help with evaporation when the feet sweat. Supports the ankles, and offers some protection against the bite of sand vipers and camel spiders. But still hurts like hell when stepped on or run over by a tactical vehicle." She describes her footwear like a typical female American shoe worshipper. It's amazing that she can describe a combat boot as if it were an expensive, Italian made shoe with a three-inch stiletto heel. I had hurt this woman to the core of her femaleness. She could suck up the pain like a real soldier, but I had scuffed her boot. I have the sudden urge to re-board the bus and go back to where I came from.

"No big thing, Jack. Just pulling your chain. Sure don't want to start our first meeting off on the wrong foot….wrong foot. Get it?"

"Yes, yes. Maybe I should have stepped on the other one instead." Major Ramirez didn't get it. I should shut up now, because I'm fairly certain that it's the jet lag that's making stupid things come out of my mouth. I have the wherewithal to back up a few paces and focus on nothing or no one in particular. Sedona has been taking in the scene with a detached fascination. And like the peacemaker I took her for, she extracts a handkerchief from between her ample cleavage, and hands it to me. My mind is trying to wrap itself around the meaning of this gesture. Am I to wipe the sweat from my forehead, start crying and dab my tears, or…nooo!…bend down like a cuckolded man or a shoe clerk kneeling at the foot bench - and buff Major Ramirez's boot? I have my pride after all. I am a doctor of philosophy, even though I am called by the pedestrian and too familiar first name. I outrank this mere major. And fuck the invitation from this obsequious civil servant at her side to grovel for favor because I wounded this pint sized warrior in a slight shoe skirmish. I meant her no insult. It was a clumsy accident.

I knelt down and buffed her boot. She smiled in satisfaction. Her dilated pupils and her glistening perspiration denoted genuine attraction. I am attracted to this woman in uniform. I would lay down my life for her in the heat of battle if her life were in danger. Or at least the love not war version of this clichéd script. I underestimated Sedona's gift for unusual diplomacy at a time when a peace offering was nobler than sounding the battle charge.

The numchuk buddies escorted me to my hotel. It was an AFFES-run facility, and a dead-on clone of a Motel 6. I couldn't complain about the accommodations because I was, in a sense - undercover. It is MCI's policy to provide it's consultants with economy class amenities. Nothing too flashy or ostentatious. MCI didn't want to draw attention to itself as a corporate leech sucking down defense dollars like other contractors who charged six-thousand dollars for a toilet. Better to conceal big salaries and fat per diems behind the camouflage of professional senior citizens, wearing clothes from TJ Max and living in a transient hotel. As an agent of a powerful organization with a reach as long as the Far East, I would oblige. Gods knows I wasn't raised in the lap of luxury, so this didn't seem that bad. I only had to pretend I had been sent to prison and approved for the work release program. My escorts didn't carry my bags to my room or offer to tuck me in. I suppose they had to keep up appearances as well. They could only go so far as the booking desk; leaving me by myself to, "unpack and get a little rest."

"You're invited to join us tonight…if you're not too tired. We're going to dinner at one of our favorite restaurants to celebrate a birthday. We understand if you don't feel up to it just yet." How would any normal man react to such an invitation: as a challenge to his endurance and stamina. It doesn't matter that I'm bushed and don't have an ounce of energy to spare. I rise to the challenge.

"Hey, sounds like a good time. Sure. Count me in."

"Super," gleefully chimes Sedona. "You're a real trooper, Jack," says Major Ramirez, with a hint of pride that her command presence might have had something to do with my obedience to the call to party. I shall be happy, I tell myself, to be dragged half unconscious to wherever it is they're taking me. Out of their uniforms they will be two ordinary feminists trying, to my disadvantage…outdo me.

My hotel phone rang at 1800 hours. I had entered the trance state between sleep and wakefulness which I can relate to from scenes of the Night of the Living Dead, aka, zombie. I had passed the last few hours willing myself to unpack; at least the important things like my computer, and oh, yes, a change of clothes and my toiletry kit. The phone snapped me out of my confusion over which item to plug into the receptacle. I had been struggling, undecided, between the computer's power supply and my underwear. I was praying that I wouldn't be led into trouble, or left alone to find my own. I had to blindly trust in the supervision of strangers. I hadn't acted on this kind of faith since college. And that usually didn't work out very well. I answered which wasn't hard because answering the phone is an ingrained habit that most people can and do in their sleep. "Hello honey," I answered. Which didn't sound exactly right since I didn't even address my wife with sugary epithets.

"Honey? Shouldn't we get to know one another better before we get romantically chummy?"

"Oh, sweetheart, it's not you." I could still fake it, which is also an acquired habit. "Is this *ah…shit…*General Sedona?"

"Thanks' for promoting me and enrolling your MCIC colleague in the Officers' Candidate Program. This is Major Ramirez. You can call me Cora. Let's wait awhile before we exchange terms of endearment, okay? Are you alert enough to join us this evening? If so get your tail down here."

I'm glad I didn't have to answer the questions. I liked it that she answered for me, and gave me an order. It made things easier. I understand why men joined the Army. I could see how it could be good training for marriage as well.

"On my way…Cora."

My escorts met me outside the hotel under the covered entry way. They were standing in the gloaming of the setting sun. It seemed as though in the time it took me to exit the double doors and walk the few steps to where they stood, they had become inanimate figures drawn in pencil and shaded with charcoal dust. A curtain of gray velvet closed on the final act of a short daytime skit. I was not in the same time zones as my senses wanted me to believe. I was seriously off my compass and at risk of wandering into a village of savage, anti-imperialist North Koreans. I would have to trust my two guides to steer me clear of the danger zones, and get me safely back to home base. It was my nature to distrust strangers right off the bat. You never knew who the bad guys were.

The ones that would draw you into their confidence and you being naïve, thinking no harm would come to you; end up in Jeffery Daimler's freezer because he didn't look like a cannibal. I seriously didn't think these MCI types would lead me astray or to the butcher's block – unless I gave them cause. I would with great effort try not to antagonize them. Being at the mercy of a dominant woman doesn't intimidate me like it does some men. The idea of being used as a man toy by a pair of dominatrix is kind of exciting so long as they are gentle and keep things playful and light. A night out to dinner and a birthday celebration would probably provide a pleasant social opportunity. I would get to meet some of the people I'd be working with. Of course I expected everyone would be on their best behavior. After all we were professionals selected for our reputations. For our self-discipline and adherence to the codes of decent conduct. Therapists know better than to act irresponsibly in public. Who wants to be greeted by a new therapist who you recognize as the old guy who joined uninvited in the Chippendale troupe's performance at your friend's bachelorette party the week before? So what was I worried about? I was in good hands.

   "Hey, this shit's good. What is it?"

   "It's called soju, Jack," *said Sedona in a voice as sweet as bird song...which struck me as very funny for some reason. I remember her having a deep voice for a woman. A lot like Token Black from the South Park episodes. I laughed and it felt good until I started feeling lightheaded. I was going to pass out if I didn't get my co2 and o2 levels straightened out.* "And you'd better go easy on that stuff. It's not as tame as it seems."

   "It's kind 'a funky tasting, but not bad...exactly. Tastes like rice water strained through a dirty dish rag. Come to think of it; it tastes pretty nasty." I have a dim awareness that this statement doesn't make a whole lot 'a sense, but hell who's paying attention.

164

"Jack, that doesn't make sense." And this is Cora who's drank twice as much as I have. And Sedona…if I hadn't caught pink eye, looks like she's nursing some pink swill from a glass the size of a fish bowl.

"Well, I mean it's an acquired taste. Tastes unfamiliaarr'sss…swhat…i…meannn."

"What was that last thing you just said?" Cora was becoming a nuisance. Why didn't she just mind her own business or excuse herself and go to the ladies room where I'd pay a jucie girl to barricade her in the stall till the next morning? You could get a jucie girl to do just about anything if you'd buy her a twenty-dollar Coke. Not 'almost anything.' Anything. So, I had to be careful what I asked for. I was afraid to act on my urges. I wasn't clear about what they were anyway. If I put one of these provocative Filipina bar girls up to barricading Cora in a bathroom stall, I couldn't be sure how my request would translate. Who'd end up there and what would happen after that filled me with excitement and fear. Mostly excitement and this made me afraid. I was a married man so fear was the predominant feeling. Excitement in our marriage happened rarely; like when we both swooned while watching Brad Pitt and Angelina Jolie make out after trying to kill one another in the movie, Mr. and Mrs. Smith." Our married life was a lot like that. I must be a little out of it to be thinking weird shit like this. Worse, Cora was more capable of such a maneuver, only because she had been in Korea longer, had built up a tolerance to Korean rotgut, and wasn't jet lagged and shit-faced out of her gourd. And by maneuvers, I mean better trained to either have me delivered to a bathroom stall and worked over, or best me in a gun fight. Even the jucie girls can't be trusted. This group I was with was tight with these girls. I sensed their sisterhood pack was strong. I could imagine them working like a pack of she-wolves; defending a shaggy-maned sister from a male intruder with rabid protectiveness. Maybe, Gretchen Witted had something there when she nearly forgave the raccoons who attacked her because, "maybe the mother was trying to protect her young."

Jucie girls are a unique group of sex workers. They are called juicie girls or drinky girls to obscure their more organic occupation. They work as hostesses and bar girls in gijichon villes - red light districts located near military bases - because this is can be their ticket to the good life: meeting an American soldier; getting married; and gaining citizenship. They must have read, The Book of Job(s). Although they should have paid more attention to my admonitions concerning marriage. To their credit, these women have found a job which allows them to do some considerable exploitation of their own.

These clever women and their handlers have devised a flexible citizenship unique to this part of the world. They are illegals that put Mexicans and Haitians to shame. And, like their illegal American counterparts, they flow through local international borders like water through a sieve.

"The main goal of this ethnography is to show how migrant Filipinas make their deployment to South Korea, 'their own,' as migrant women do not merely obey the call of global capital and leave home as commodified labor or sex objects but are also moved by their capacity to aspire, their will to change, and their dreams of flight."

On the Move for Love,
The University of Pennsylvania Press

Jack, always the outspoken misogynist, sees long term relationships, and particularly marriages, as being driven by the political and social economies of desire. I didn't know for the life of me what that meant. I believe I guessed right that it is Jack's way of saying that relationships are undertaken the way venture capitalists build their dreams on the financial investments of dream-deprived insomniacs with money secured under their mattresses. In the case here, men are the light sleepers with money to spend on bigger dreamers. Filipina women have big dreams. Jack has a special place in his heart for women of this persuasion. Unless he's married to one. Jack has always warned men and women to exercise caution when caution is always the least consideration when seeking a mate. 'We should plan in advance, know the pitfalls, and avoid hasty romances, he says.' Never get lazy and ask the man or woman working the cramped work space you share at the McDonalds where you are employed. This is convenience not discretion when it comes to dating. Of course you are working fast food because you are financing your graduate school education. On your way to some fancy boardroom via the scullery route's back roads of second jobs and night shifts. But you only make it to the bedroom with a partner who smells good enough to eat. Not in the lustful manner you might fantasize. Rather because she has absorbed the essence of the deep fat fryer over which she's labored all day. And you, having worked the register all day, smell like money. Now, pay close attention to this next point. Jucie girls generally don't smell like bear grease or vaporized lard. They smell, well…Jucie. Fruit jucie. You still smell like money. It doesn't have to be a lot of money; just enough to buy enough drinks, get pretty damn drunk, and wake up married with "Jucie Girl" tattooed on your ass. Jack admires the resourcefulness of such women who work the system to their advantage. These smart little women don't regret the indiscretion in their choice of men. Like a good job with lots of benefits, the company owner is to be thanked for

168

hiring you and making you a beneficiary of his profits. There you have it: women *and men* driven by the political and social economies of desire.

Jack is shameless. Recommending such blatant usury and social larceny is subject to the heavy fines of major karma. But, as you know, Jack has spared himself and forgiven others of any universal retribution by trashing the whole idea of karma.

"No Cora. I shouldn't dance. Not that steady on my feet right now. In fact, my wife won't even dance with me when I'm sober. But then, I won't dance when I'm completely sober anyway …need some liquid courage. But too much, and I'm helpless. You might even say handicapped….What do they call it? Oh, Yeah, mobility impaired…and deaf too. Music's too loud. Also, did you know that by the third drink the brain's effectively numbed as far back as the auditory nerves…So can't even feel the rhythm…You know… move to the beat because…"

JACK! SHUT UP. NOW, UP ON YOUR FEET AND DANCE WITH ME. THAT'S A DIRECT ORDER SOLDIER! *Fuck. This woman's* taken etiquette lessons from Genghis Khan. This is Cora. The petite soldier who's traded her BDUs and combat boots for a midnight blue dress, fishnet stockings and Prada high heels. What I see is Yosemite Sam in drag; both guns blazing, lead kicking up little dirt devils at my feet. I'm hearing – swear to god I am - *'NOW DANCE PARTNER.'* I vaguely remember hearing that this assignment requires a lot of walking. I can't afford to be maimed and unable to work. I'm thinking all this shit while my body involuntarily jerks and hops around the dance floor. And with a maniac possessed by that Flash Dance steel worker who has me locked in an embrace as inescapable as a boa constrictor's. She's leading. I'm used to it. Donna never surrenders the lead on the dance floor. It's better just to go with it. These are strangers I'll never see again. They're used to seeing spastic white men who can't dance. The men in this place all seem to be okay with acting like fools for some very understanding women who know how to contain their amusement. Just like any team of wise employees who will stifle a laugh or a crude remark when their boss has just farted during a staff meeting. Meanwhile a side show is being performed by two Filipinas and Sedona who have joined the bargirls on stage. They are singing their sad hearts out to a likewise sympathetic audience who judge not, lest they be judged - as foolish adolescent men or bad dancers. Sad or not these girls have a lot of heart. They respect one another and shed the collective tears of oppressed women everywhere. Fortunately they aren't dressed in burkas and haven't undergone any horrible mutilations as far as anybody has seen so far. They aren't inhibited by a jealous husband or a homicidal boyfriend. They can dance and sing, and strive to please everyone; hoping that Mr. Ticket Home is in the audience ready to by her expensive watered down drinks. The man who will play her dating game, beginning with a back alley blow job, and the promise of more 'good time'...with a marriage proposal. It will seem like a good deal to more than a few lonely GIs. The mood this evening is frivolous and gay. There just isn't the tension you'd expect in the Ville on a Friday night. Maybe it's because it not a pay-day week-end, and the bar girls aren't being bullied by the mamma san to, 'pleasie soldier boy.' There isn't any hustle driving the energy this evening. Although the mamma san isn't thrilled with the side show, she knows it's good for business in the long run. Just let the girls play a little. Blow off some steam like boiling water through a whistling kettle. After all they are like little girls playing dress up, and performing their own talent show.

Cora's given me a break from the spin cycle, and has taken me by the hand and planted me next to her at a front row high top. She ordered another pink drink, I heard her call a Strawberry Kettle. The thought of waking up tasting fermented

strawberries rising from a sour gut, elicits a gag
response. But that's Cora's problem, and one I'm
not planning to share by waking up with this storm
trooper wrapped around me like barbed wire, and
pinned to the sheets by her stilettos. I switch
from soju to beer. A Filipina named Brazil is
sitting with us, and is singing along with Tina
Turner's, "Addicted to Love." I had heard Tina
sing it the same year it was released by Robert
Palmer. It was in 1986. I remember the year
because Donna and I had just gotten the AFN
channel in off base housing that year, and the
first program we watched was Music Box, Ltd being
broadcast from England. They were televising Tina
Turner singing the song. Donna sang along with it
while I did a striptease. The lyrics had meaning
back then. I realize just now that switching to
beer was not necessarily a good idea. I was
feeling weepy, and at the same time Cora was
looking better and better. I would exercise
restraint and keep my clothes on. These bar girls,
with no help from Sedona, were massacring the
song. The four girls were doing their own thing;
each singing in a different key and adlibbing the
lyrics. I was tone deaf and couldn't tell if it
was them or me. I am hearing some bazaar shit, but
I tell Cora and Brazil it all sounds kind 'a
groovy. Did I just say, 'groovy?' I was living a
flashback moment and these two chicks were into
me. I'm sounding like the host of Soul Train, and
I also know I'm seriously fucked up. I'm having a
good time by my old college standards. I have my
eyes closed and the girls' wailing to Tina's song
sounds more like four female alley cats in heat. I
can't say for sure if these are Robert Palmer's
lyrics, but the girls aren't expressing any
hesitation with the chorus.

> The lights are on, but you're not home
> your mind is not your own
> your heart beats double time
>
> Your hips gyrate
> another drink is what it takes

You can't sleep, he wants to eat
there's no doubt, he's in way deep
your throat is tight, you can't breathe
he's a well hung cowboy…

You can't be saved
another ride is all you crave
if there's some left for mamma san
you don't mind if he does her too

Whoa, you like to think that you're
immune to the hottie, oh Yeah
It's closer to the truth to say
you can't get enough,
you know you're gonna have to face it,
you're addicted to love

I don't remember Tina ever having mentioned
cowboys or mama san in her version of the song. It
doesn't matter. These women aren't lacking talent.
Their stage performance trumps charades and
Pictionary. There is one little bar girl who has
gyrated herself into painful muscle spasm, but she
doesn't betray the pain she must be in. She's a
trooper. Her grimace is forced into what passes
for Jack Nickelson playing the Joker. Her balance
is death defying. She's hanging ten at the edge of
the stage; her gyrations give her the righting
ability of one of those novelty plastic birds that
you perch on the lip of your cocktail glass. There
she is swaying forward and backward like that
bird. I am truly impressed by this marvel of
female engineering. She is endowed with
counterbalancing tits and ass that are friendly
with gravity. Leonardo De Vinci might have
designed his visionary machines on the
observations of tipsy, well proportioned, dancing,
Filipina bar girls.

At the next refrain of:

> Your lights are on,
> your daddy's not home
> your will is not your own
> your breasts sweat, your hips grind
> another kiss and you'll be mine

I still don't think the lyrics are right…Cora has me on my feet. She locks her arm in mine and we are swaying side-to-side in what reminds me of doing the Electric Slide on a greased bumper car track. I am no longer able to resist this dance bully. I don't have the necessary sobriety - the strength or the balance - to resist. Her last strawberry kettle has topped her tank. It has given her the blush and scented perspiration of a flesh and blood strawberry daiquiri. I'm subliminally aware that I should steer clear of her stilettos. Cora may be holding a grudge about the boot thing. There is both torture and love in her dark eyes. After all, she is Latin I remind myself. This pained, yet sensual expression is what the Spanish painter Luis Royo is famous for capturing. For his forebodingly sensual paintings of women and mechanical life forms. Here with me was a Royo original. I had to prepare myself to be fed to this insatiable sex engine, and emptied out in the morning as useless engine sludge.

"Jack, you're not all that bad for a civilian. You can march the two step like a drill sergeant, and you can handle your soju like an experienced soldier. You know I would take you to my quarters, and teach you a Jodie or two, but hell, I got 'a leave for TDY at 0400 hours. Might consider packing you in my duffle bag. Up for going MIA?"

"As in missing in action? Sounds dangerous. You know, Cora, I think, the soju is talking here, and…."

"Whoa there Jacko. Didn't mean to scare you. Hey, you aren't gay are you?"

"NO. But, close. I'm married."

"Does your wife trust you while you're away?"

"Yes, she does…I think. Meanwhile, Brazil's looking on at this come on as if she's been bumped out of her place in line. These working girls don't take kindly to outsiders hustling their patrons. I get the impression that she will wait for seconds; the way lampreys trail after a shark picking off scraps from a big kill. She isn't going to confront this soldier unless she's prepared to go balls up with this woman.

The women on stage were winding down their act, and drifting back to our group of high tops. I feel slightly less cornered if you consider a pack of hyenas safer company than a solitary, hungry lioness. The women didn't seem to mind that Cora had me cornered. Although Sedona's ears pricked up to our lively dialogue.

"So why not a little to-cha to hold you over? Ease the tensions of travel and all."

"To-cha isn't exactly a dance is it? Like the cha-cha or the two-step."

"Well it sort of is…just done horizontally."

Cora, I'm very flattered, but as I just told you, I'm married. Besides I have to care about a woman to fu… go to bed with her."

"You guys are getting too much into your feminine side. You sound like Kevin Costner talking to Opra. Look Jack I got you figured for a horny guy just like the rest of them, and you are about to turn down a good piece of ass. You're going to regret this in the morning."

"On the contrary, I won't. My wife expects me to be faithful while I'm away."

"You love this woman?"

"Yes. That's what I've been telling you."

"Agh! Love? That is such a form of prejudice."

"I might be drunk, but that doesn't make any sense. I don't think it would make sense if I were completely sober. I don't think we'd be having this conversation if we were both sober. And how in the hell, is love a form of prejudice? "

"Because…it eliminates all other candidates on the basis of you wanting to make things easy. People go after what they need. And love is what they need. You love what makes you feel good, and now you; you go and settle for what's convenient. Now tell me you married this wife of yours because you loved her. Is that right?"

"I don't think I should comment on that right now."

"Alright Mr. Scaredy cat. But you know I'm right. There are probably a million people out there who you could love more, if you ever met them. But you won't meet them. So, you settle for the first one that comes along.

That is discrimination. You should be fined for unfair mating practices."

"I think I'm safe on that count. I don't think that one's in any of the law books."

"I's in my rule book, buster."

"Cora, giving Jack his orientation to the 2nd Infantry Division? Pretty heavy stuff for Jack's first day here. Don't you think?" *Thank god for Sedona's timing. Her off-the-cuff question is enough to snap Cora back to peace time operations, after her assault of make war with love on the new guy in town.*

"Yeah, guess you're right. Jack is kind 'a off balance with everything going on. Aren't you, Jack?"

"Roger that, Cora."

"Hey, let's head over to the Mojo Bar, and see what's happening there," This is Benita, the birthday girl, who I thought was a mute ex-stripper before she spoke up with a suggestion to do more bar hopping. "Heard that the place rocks now. New management or something. And Giji and Fana are dancing there. That's what Sergeant Miller said."

"No, they're working here at the 'Peace." It's their night off. The Mojo's boring. We could get a taxi and head over to the Toko-ri, and check out the entertainment." This is Carina's idea. She was the chick whose hip gyrations gave me vertigo just watching her.

"Gross," pipes in Stephanie. "Fortunately the place has tamed down. I mean in a good way. But it still sucks. That's what I heard. Although, the midget still works there. I'd probably kill that little bitch if I lay eyes on her again."

I was wondering what passed for entertainment in this part of town. So, I ventured to ask. "What's the Toko-ri, and what's with the midget?"

"Oh, don't get Stephanie riled. The midget got stuck to her boyfriend last New Year's. It's kind of a tradition with the Midget of Toko-ri. A soldier will stick the midget. And the midget, the fucking bitch, will hang on all night."

"Carina, do you mean what I think…about, sticking the midget?"

"Yes. It's exactly what I mean. You screw the midget, and she holds like an anchor bolt drilled through drywall. She's outlasted all the other nasties who've worked there."

"Tell Jack about the Dragon Lady," goads Cora. "And the Russian juicie girls who were covered in chocolate and wax."

"I don't think wax is good for you, unless its hundred percent bees wax…"

"Jack, shut up. Tasting wasn't an option. It was the Dragon Lady who stole the show."

"And what was her claim to fame?"

"Well, let's put it delicately: she could do amazing anatomical things with the likes of cylindrical objects, like cigars, and Champaign bottles."

"I think I'd better head back to my hotel. The jet lag's bad enough."

Sedona offers to guide me back to the hotel. I'm relieved that Cora's going to make one last sweep of the Ville, and stay with the party girls to make sure no one gets left behind. Although there would be far more danger to me if that happened. I trust Sedona. It's intuitive. She is high on life, and seems to regard us all with a kind of laughing Buddha attitude of patience and tolerance.

Our long walk back to the hotel would have been unremarkable except for Sedona insisting that I try a local delicacy offered by a street vendor. I was hungry after all the soju I'd drunk. I was still dumb enough to be game for something new and exotic. After all I was in the Far East. Why not have it all in one night.

"Jack, you've got to try these. They're a real delicacy."

"What are they?"

"Silk worm larvae." A large pot sat on a propane burner with what looked like hundreds of cockroaches being boiled alive.

"Nah, I think I'll pass. Besides…the smell…smells like a roach nest."

"Oh, come on. The Korean's would kill for these. You've got to try one."

"Hell, why not. Andrew Zimmern would do it. Right?"

"Who's Andrew Zimmern?"

"I used to watch his TV show; the one where he would eat the strangest things. The show was called, 'Bizarre Foods.' In fact, he'd eat these things and pretend they tasted like chicken."

"Look, I'll buy them, if you eat them. Fair enough?"

"Yeah, sure. I'm game. I'll try anything once."

Sedona forks over 2,000 Yuan, the equivalent of two dollars for a Dixie cup portion of warm, soggy silkworm larvae. The vendor is happy to oblige. He beams with satisfaction that another foreigner has fallen for the Asian delicacy joke. A delicacy is usually a nondescript, organic chunk of offal that no one in their right mind would ever consider putting in their mouth. But I did it anyway. There is no accounting for what a man will do to impress a woman. Or anyone for that matter. Just dare him to run with bulls chasing him down the streets of Pamplona, or to dine on a delicacy of Japanese blow fish at the risk of total paralysis, and he will elbow his way to be first in line. It is why we so readily answer, "I do," when asked to take the vow of love and obedience before a skeptical justice of the peace.

"Sedona, these taste like…agh…I can't quite put my finger on it…I'll try another one. Maybe it's an acquired taste…Ah, no…kind 'a like…umm…

"Not chicken, I take it." This coming from Sedona who is studying my expression. I think she's actually expecting me to roll my eyes, tilt back my head and play ping pong between my cheeks; savoring the rancid aroma of silkworm larvae.

"Maybe chicken road kill, after the maggots have worked it over. Maybe maggot-eating-a-chicken…that's what comes to mind. No, still tastes like boiled roaches. Damn. Do you have any Altoids?"

"You don't like them? The Korean people love them."

"Sedona, I don't see Korean's lining up behind me to order these things. Besides, do you like them, because you can have the rest if you do."

"Nooo. I'm not that crazy about them. Well, I'll have one or two."

"Sedona, you don't seem to be savoring that maggot with any great relish."

"It's been a while. I don't want to waste them. I'll find a local, and offer what's left."

"Why don't you just dump them? No body's going to accept those things from a total stranger. And a white devil stranger at that."

"Oh, that's not true. I'll be right back. I also need to find a rest room."

"Yeah. I'll wait right here." I'm thinking, 'here's your chance to take care of both matters at the same time. Flush them down the nearest toilet.' *Five minutes pass, ten minutes… "Where the hell is she?"*

"Hey, Jack. Sorry. I found someone near the toilets who was really happy to have them. Looked like it made his day!"

"Well, I'm happy for both of you…"

"Are you being sarcastic, Jack. Because if you are, it isn't very nice. These people are poor, and it's a big deal to them for someone to show generosity. They accept an offering in the same manner as it is given…gratefully. They're very Buddhist."

"No, I'm not being sarcastic," I lied. I was still depending on this hippie, love child to get me back to my hotel. Because I have no idea where the hell it is. "I'm happy that you found a rest room, and that you found an appreciative maggot eater, and that your deed was fulfilling to you…in a Buddhist, spiritual sort of way."

"Jack, you're making me sorry that I rescued you from Cora's advances."

"Rescued me? Did I look like I needed rescuing? Do I look like the kind of guy who needs help in that department?"

"Yes."

"Okay. Maybe this one time. Me being a little at a disadvantage and all. Cora is a little aggressive. Not that I mind that in a woman."

"Yes, I'll give her that. But did you say, you admire that in a woman?"

"I don't remember saying 'admire.' I think I said, or meant to say, I don't mind it. As in, it's kind of masculine, and I can relate to her energy and all…"

"Her energy seemed to make you uneasy. Are your sure you're not bull shitting me?"

"No, I'm not…"

"Not what? Not uneasy or not bull shitting me?"

"I'm confused. We shouldn't be having this discussion on a busy sidewalk with all this distraction."

"Shall we continue our talk at your hotel…in your room, or mine?"

"Whaaat?"

"Just kidding with you Jack... See you do get flustered."

"No, a little uneasy."

"See. I was right. Women who come on aggressively do make you uneasy."

"Okay, yes. Anything you say. Can we go back to base now? I'm bushed."

I made it back with Sedona's able guidance. She is a good person; meaning she doesn't expect anything in return for doing a good deed for someone. I consider this a special quality in a person. It seems to me that the majority of the people we meet end up wanting something from us; either in return for some small service they've provided or just begin asking for favors from the jump. And their small favors end up costing us a lot; far in excess of what's ever given in kind. I only knew her for the night on the town, but that was enough to come to appreciate her. She is a person whose true self is not obscured by mirrors and smoke. It doesn't need a disguise. There is no cunning or artifice to conceal.

Sedona was a short timer relative to the short 45 to 60 day rotations we MCICs typically spend on a military installation. Her contract was up two days later, and she was off to some other faraway place to work with yet another group of battle scarred and emotionally wounded active duty military personnel. Fortunately, Cora left before the rising sun flag was hoisted full mast next morning. I can only surmise that she seamlessly ended her vigil over the bar girls in the Ville, and hopped her ride to the air base and was dispatched to her TDY destination. I was relieved that I didn't have to say good bye to her. I admit it. I was afraid I'd be shanghaied in a duffle bag and used god knows how to feed this woman's appetites. She didn't look like a cannibal, but not every creature that dines on the flesh of its own species looks like the Wild Man of Borneo, or walks on all fours and howls at the moon. It's not the bone in the nose that's the giveaway. Look in the freezer, the way newly dating couples sneak a peek into their lover's bathroom medicine cabinets searching for evidence of transmittable diseases. A prescription bottle of Valtrex or a freezer-wrapped leg as long as a moose's that's still wearing a fashionable shoe is well…a dead giveaway. Maybe, I judge Cora harshly, and create abominable fantasies about her. It's my way of dealing with cognitive dissonance; of my equally powerful attraction and fear of her. I can't fight both forces without losing to one of these adversaries. Either way I'm fucked.

Part V

"Power always thinks it has a great soul and vast
views beyond the comprehension of the weak,
And that it is doing God's service when it is
violating all His laws."

- John Adams

The Other Evil Empire

There is an undercurrent of danger and political treachery in foreign countries that share a border with a hostile neighbor. They are as unpredictable as an active fault line overdo for activity. The North Korean military are in a constant state of combat readiness. The way a hungry rattlesnake is when lying low for a desert mouse. Their leader, Kim Jong-Il, other than being a coiffeur's nightmare, is temperamental. A seemingly benign challenge to his totalitarian rule or a frat house hair mussing is cause for execution. Under his Juche ideological government few outsiders ever interfere in the affairs of North Korea. The Juche ideology is rooted in the practice of self-reliance. In the case of North Korea it is taken to extreme measures. For example, a famine that occurred shortly after the collapse of the Soviet Union resulted in the deaths of nearly two million people. The government kept this hush-hush; rather than asking for humanitarian aid from countries outside their borders. For this and other Stalinist-like atrocities and austere pogroms, North Korea has one of the world's worst human rights records. But then again they are the enemy, and therefore the antipathy of Western World holiness and benevolence. The South Korean government is as ready for conflict as their northern brethren. And they have the backing and holy imprimatur of the United States. Skirmishes along the 38th Parallel are notoriously violent and usually go un-reported by the international media. Shortly before I arrived there had been a pitched naval battle with damage to a North Korean warship, and loss of life to crew members of both vessels. C'est la vie, c'est la guerre for the divided nation. My former days as a DOD employee gave me the opportunity to observe the NATO Joint Forces Command at St. Boniface. St. Boniface is the northern most military base snuggled against the 38th Parallel. It was a grim reminder of how tinder dry relations along the border were, and still are. It's as if

they are dry tinder piled too close to a match
about to be struck by an arsonist. Stories of
civilians and soldiers being massacred by
marauding North Korean soldiers are legendary. And
they continue to fuel the feud between radical
political adversaries related by blood and former
empire. We American's have our own history of
internecine conflict to reflect upon. Once upon a
time a country divided into a Union and a
Confederacy resulted in the sacrifice of 625,000
lives to create a Union strong enough to establish
a Juche nation of its own. Ironically, the U.S.
has become the broker of other nation's civil
wars. You would think that a country that had lost
so many men to internal disagreements, would
eschew wholesale national fratricide. As a social
scientist, I have debated the idea: "That man is
innately depraved." My bias vacillates but is
skewed toward agreement. Our humanity is sparing.
Humanitarian motives are driven by practicality.
Such as when the survival of a manageable tribal
group is at stake. The powerful of the species
takes care of the weaker for their usefulness to
the peaceful affairs of the community along with
providing its service-oriented labors. In the act
of depravity – call it war – the strong profit.
And it is better to broker with as few lives of
our own tribe as is possible. It is not, however,
the chief deterrent for continuing a conflict
beyond the established quota of dead and wounded.
It is better, from the perspective presented to
the public that the balance sheet (or body counts)
remains in our favor. It has always been more
important, that the balance sheet of wealth and
added resources is showing its investors a profit.

Here I go being controversial. Well…political. I
take advantage of a lee-way when relating stories
of travel which allows me to express my political
biases. I do it here because I can't when I'm
embedded in the culture of the military. MCI
frowns on us entering into political debate with
our clients no matter how radically different our

views might be. We are expected to be as neutral and impartial as a slug on a muddy path. Even if it is busy with human foot traffic and ground beetles. The risk is to have your most valued beliefs trampled under by the jack boot of ignorance. Besides I know it won't be the reticence forced upon me, or breaking the rules of political silence that'll jeopardize my ticket to travel. I love travel too much to risk a view-point that is only that; a point-of-view on a complex body politic that is fed to us by disinformation specialists backed by the evil genius of a powerful administration. If I honestly admit it to myself; none of it makes a whole lot of sense to begin with. I really don't understand the whole picture.

I am like Jonathan Swift's, Gulliver. In fact I consider myself to have become a marginal character in the affairs of the world. I even write in the style of an earlier literary time. It was customary for the eighteenth century traveler to provide an outline of his life. And construct an historic context that made sense of his experiences at the time. Swift wrote for his time, and I believe for ours as well. He satirized the state of European government and the petty differences between religions. What's so different now? Government is very, very big – like Swift's Brobdingnagians. We are small, very small – like Swift's Lilliputers.

Gulliver and I share a commonality which breeches centuries. Gulliver enjoyed Traveling, and it was his love of Travel that was his downfall. His fate could be my own. I exercise caution in preparing for my next journey; taking care that such a fate does not become a self-fulfilling prophesy. For all of Gulliver's adventures, and all the grand places that they took him, he became a recluse. A man at odds with all humanity. In the end the Yahoos won. The Yahoos are human beings in their basest form. They are far from sentient, although they do possess some semblance of reason which they only use to enhance the vices nature gave them. In our time vice is the corruption of power; power which could otherwise be used for the good of all. These are the men in power that we take for sages and icons of virtue. Men whom he discovered - as we eventually do - are as flawed as we are. The Yahoos still win today. We are deferential to the leadership of the rich and powerful. We willing follow them into the obsolescence they have planned for us- which happens as a slow erosion of our capacity to think for ourselves. Americans are cognitive anorectics starved for information more nutrient then CNN and FOX network. By the age of eighteen most American males have been conditioned to go to war. They will follow their calling which is to aggressively secure the wealth of foreign nations and increase the riches of those in power. I prefer to stay in motion. Once I evaded the draft, and planned a hasty exodus to Canada. Now I travel. Better to be a moving target that is harder to see, and harder to conscript to someone else's cause. I prefer to guard my beliefs behind the popular banner of my socially opprobrious employer - that are not my own. I fear that the fate of the Yahoo awaits me around the bend of my next adventure. The war within may be as simple as keeping one's balance sheet favoring virtue, rather than the abundant natural vices which distract the soul's pursuit.

postscript

Poor Jack is as misguided as ever. His thinking will be his greatest undoing. Jack, however, didn't experience his Lilliputians as the common man he champions like a socialist do-gooder. I know for a fact that he was attacked by little people who could be Lilliput's living descendents. Jack was as helpless as Gulliver when held prisoner after being washed ashore from a shipwreck. The assault of the Lilliputians took place while Jack was debarking from a train at the Soyosan station. He was stormed by a column of tiny South Korean mountaineers. Jack gave me the original account which is far different from the political allegory he derived from it. His personal vices are inherent in the life-style he's chosen. What was he thinking? He is lucky (so far) that his skirmishes with the opposite gender have resulted in his retreat rather than his surrender. However, time and exposure may change this. Although Jack denies this…we'll see. He's never listened to the counsel of others. He is loath to admit that his ability to weave and dodge the fists and kicks of his opponents has slowed with age. So has his virtue.

Dr. Jack Mc Kane's Biographer

Part VI

The Lilliput Mountain Hikers of Korea

My recovery from the night out with the troops - in this case Major Ramirez, Sedona and the Filipinas - was helped by the fact that I had arrived on Thursday. The garrison was deserted Friday due to a training holiday. So, I had time to recuperate. Brian also arrived later that day. He was the new addition to the MCIC team. He was as wasted looking as I was. His raccoon eyes and ragged appearance was due entirely to jet lag. He arrived from San Francisco, and was disappointed that he wasn't able to, "hit the ground running." He felt stymied by the unexpected down-time of several days of inactivity before getting to work. I was thinking: 'There's something seriously wrong with this guy. His body clock is off by a day, and his cuckoo thinks its Junior Bird Man.' I didn't like this guy. How could I be civil toward a man who is the antipathy of my deeply rooted philosophy of personal labor conservation and my reverence for any religious or national holiday that offers time off from work?

Brian's rambunctiousness paid off to our benefit. He suggested a train ride to Mount Soyosan. It is two stations north. So, it's a short trip. Perfect for a Saturday outing. Brian had researched the area like a Fodor's Travel writer. Mount Soyosan is a popular mecca for Korean outdoor types. The mountain park stretches the breadth of two towns, and consists of a series of ridge lines that take about six-and-a-half hours to traverse. It's touted as an easy climb, and no part of it requires technical expertise. Brian read from the brochure: "Old and young visit this popular attraction, and take in the beautiful panorama of the Korean countryside."

This is the ideal time of year to hike it. Autumn in Korea is mild and still warm. The changing color of the leaves would be an added visual treat.

Brian and I boarded the train a few blocks south of Camp Casey's main gate. The ride was enjoyable. The Korean trains are clean and air conditioned. Missing is the graffiti we're so used to seeing on public transportation back home. The station platform is getting crowded by the time our train is due. The train's on time; another pleasant surprise. The passengers scurry in like hurried travelers everywhere. The locals are considerate and two younger men give up their seats to an elderly couple that boards at the next to last stop before we reach Soyosan station. The large group that boards at the same stop is every bit the epitome of the mountaineer. Complete with expensive back packs, boots with soles resembling the treads of giant earth movers, and telescoping trekking poles that double as pogo sticks. This group does not exhibit the neutral Asiatic smile. Their expressions are deadpan, as if they are focused on some distant summit. Their pupils are pin pricks of black, their hands balled into fists, their poles strangled in their grip. I note that they are all sitting in the posture of jockeys waiting for the bell at Churchill Downs.I feel intimidated sitting across from them. Brian shares my concern, and scans the car for an empty pair of seats away from these mountain devils. There aren't any. In fact passengers are standing in the aisles, except for the area in front of the climbers. I'm sure they know something about this group that we don't know. Whatever their knowledge, they are steering clear of what looks to us like trouble.

The train crackles and hisses to a stop. It has slowed from 60 miles an hour to a smooth stop in ten seconds. It's an electric and diesel hybrid. Its anthropomorphic design gives it an organic quality that incorporates twenty first century electrical engineering. It is a modern Frankenstein machine with sleekness and style, minus the scars and off market body parts of Dr. Frankenstein's original. Brian and I have hardly a moment to react; wanting to get up and out of the way before these human drones can buzz past us. Little did we anticipate the rear assault advantage taken by those returning from the mountain and boarding before we have the chance to step onto the platform. As the door slides open, a column of Lilliputians three astride and a block long storms through the doors directly in our path. I've always avoided mob gatherings because I know how unpredictable their behavior can be. I have particularly avoided events like Klan Rallies, world soccer championships, and Stone's concerts. I don't believe anyone would believe how aggressive a mob of mini-mountaineers can be. These little bastards were hunkered down; plowing ahead in formation like a Roman phalanx. All I could make out was a sea of skull caps, narrow shoulders and pointy elbows; moving over us like a tsunami. The wave of slant-eyed munchkins was only waist high, but it was mighty. I can understand how terrifying the hoards of Genghis Khan were. Again I am reminded of the destructive force of ants – as in this case - once more emulated by little people the size of bugs. Some men are more closely related to insects. Perhaps they evolved down a separate path from our simian cousins. Is it possible that our adaptation to the pressures of modern living, and the chemical alterations to our chromosomes has taken some of us down a different evolutionary path? There is a good argument supporting this hypothesis. I have encountered several instances that have made me a believer. I was beginning to feel a strong empathy for my former patient, Gary. He may have been onto a news-breaking scientific discovery if he had published his observations of bikers and their insect metamorphosis. Unfortunately his psychiatric diagnosis compromised his validity. Be that as it may, Brian and I had to fight for our lives to make it to the platform. I know how a football quarterback feels when he's been sacked by the entire opposing team. Brian came out swinging not so much with fisticuffs as with jabbing elbows and sound effects that made him sound like a chuffing locomotive. For a guy I had

taken an instant dislike to, I had developed a new
found respect. If hitting the ground running was
an unflattering characteristic, holding his ground
hitting was an admirable one in my eyes. The
little chink bastards had not defeated us. And I
won't spare the racial epithet because these
militant mountaineers were clearly the enemy. I
suspect they are part of an army of North Korean
soldiers who pour through the underground tunnel
system that breech the 38th Parallel. These tunnels
are still being discovered, and are known to be a
primary route for a planned invasion by North
Korean troops. Those who are currently using this
ingress are the first wave of infiltrators who
come to weaken the defenses of Democracy. I am
happy to be alive, and proud to have Brian as my
battle buddy.

To Edmund Hillary

"Easy my ass. This is a sheer vertical climb, Brian. Are you sure it is the same mountain you read about?"

"Yeah, I'm certain of it. And look at the kids and the old people. They're hauling ass up this slope."

"They're not human. Look at the shit eating grins on their faces. What the hell are they taking? Must be illegal for it to make them act like gamey mountain goats in rutting season."

"Don't go rushing to judgment, Jack. These people grew up here. They've become acclimated to this environment. You're from Florida, a flat-lander, right?"

"Yeah, but that has little to do with it. It's only two-thousand feet above sea level. We're talking about old geezers and elementary school kids racing uphill like lizards chasing flies."

"Well, we can plod along like snails, or we can enter the race. Me, I'm going for the up-hill charge…"

"Okay, okay, Hillary. I can do it. Not a problem. Just admiring the fitness of these people, is all."

"Yeah. But what's Hillary Clinton got to do with me?"

"Not, Clinton, Edmund Hillary. The British climber who reached the summit of K-2. It was a joke, Brian."

"He went missing didn't he? I read somewhere that they didn't discover his remains until years later. You're not afraid you'll die up there are you. I mean it's not that difficult."

"It's a joke. And no, I'm not afraid the climb will kill me. Can't you lighten up a little?" I was back to not liking Brian. He was turning into a pain in the ass. No one is that concrete about everything, unless he's schizophrenic. Which isn't entirely out of the question given the handicaps some of us bring to the profession. I'd have to be careful how I word things with this guy. I was already winded trying to climb, talk and breathe at the same time. I had been focusing on the narrow trail. I was being careful to put one foot in front of the other so as not to lose purchase. I hate heights and the thought of tumbling over the edge and yodeling to my death terrified me. When I braved a glance ahead, Brian was gone.

"HEY, BRIAN...YOU YOU UP AHEAD?" I had the evil wish that Brian had fallen into a ravine. I have no fear of karma, so I feel free to wish all the bad on a person I want. Brian was showing off and he deserved a plunge into the abyss, and nothing existential about it either. No such luck...

"Right here slow poke. Been waiting for you. Take a look at that will you." Brian was pointing and marveling over a temple on a plateau about twenty-five meters ahead. "That's the temple built by Hanyon, a royal prince from the fifteenth century. Story has it that he came to this mountain seeking enlightenment, and while he's here meditating, a Buddhist deity disguised as a beautiful woman tries to seduce him..."

"Lucky him."

"Not at all. You see the deity was tempting his celibacy, without which he couldn't attain nirvana."

"So he turns down this beautiful chic who's offering him a good time, after who knows how long the guy's been without a woman, and he's rewarded with enlightenment? Was that the consolation prize?"

"No that was the big Zambony. It's a big deal to Eastern and Western seekers alike to achieve such a divine state while in human form."

"Yes, I know all that, but the man screwed up in my opinion. Worse, because he set a bad example. And to boot, they build him a shrine extolling the virtue of celibacy. Think how that woman must have felt being turned down like that. Must have damaged her self-esteem; even for a deity."

"Jack, I don't know if your still kidding or not. You like to joke about everything. But, this is serious stuff to these Buddhists, or they wouldn't be flocking here, and lighting candles, and honoring Hanyon and reciting the names of their ancestors."

"You know what I think, Brian?"

"No. And I'm afraid to ask. But I think you're going to tell me anyway…so shoot."

"I think most of them are looking for that deity to take her up on her offer. I won't dare set foot in that temple; because that's the last place I'd be if I were a beautiful woman who got rejected on that very spot where it happened the first time."

Brian didn't say another word. I think he probably saw the truth in what I said. He finally spoke to me again – when I caught up to him for the umpteenth time – about needing water. We were both out. This was a hellacious trek, and we didn't bring enough water. Neither of us expected temperatures in the 80s, or it being a ball buster of a hike that had already taken us five hours with no end in sight. It seemed a long way to the end of the trail, because I think we missed the trail sign directing us back to our starting point. That the signs were written in Hangul characters didn't help.

"I'm out of water, and I'm really parched. You too," he asked?

"Uhh...I'm about to wring out my shirt for something to drink. It's soaked, and it's sucked out every ounce of water from my body. And I don't see anything on this map indicating a water supply."

"Well, maybe if we're lucky we'll run into some hikers up ahead who can spare some."

"I wouldn't count on it. I haven't seen another living soul in the past hour. I'm about to begin foraging for edible berries or plants. Or pray for rain."

"Jack, I can't imagine you praying for anything. Besides you never know how fortune can change. We just might get lucky."

"Well, aren't you the eternal optimist. Luck and fortune! I'll take my chances on the provenance of nature. And, I was just speaking figuratively about praying. I know the folly of such superstitious beliefs."

"You mean to tell me you don't believe in God...you're not a Christian?"

"Look I'm not getting into an argument about religion when I'm just about dying of thirst. I'll believe in god or whatever, if I can have a cup of ice cold water...right now!"

"That's pretty lame. You're not likely to get what you want just like that. And being blasphemous isn't cool with Jesus. You have to have faith, Jack."

"Hey, faith is what you resort to when you've run out of options, and you're fucking desperate. Okay, so I won't count on the hand of god passing me a cup of water, but I'll make my own luck, and pass water."

"Are you talking about pissing, and drinking your...agh, disgusting!"

"I didn't say that. I said that I'll count on my skills as an outdoorsman to survive. I don't intend to die of thirst on some remote mountain in Korea."

"So, you're saying you would drink your own urine if you don't find water."

"I think we'll make it to the base camp before that happens. And I don't know why you're acting like a prude about recycling body fluids in a survival situation."

"It sounds perverse. And, not very healthy either."

"Read the Special Forces Survival Manual. It recommends drinking urine when lost at sea."

"Yeah, I read about that, but it isn't a proven means for slaking thirst, and it doesn't last that long before the urine becomes so concentrated that it even hastens death by dehydration."

"I thought you didn't know anything about the subject, and besides how'd we get on this subject anyway?"

"You brought it up. You said you were going to pass water, and…"

"And…What? Did I actually say I was going to drink my own urine?"

"Not exactly…but, sort of…you implied it."

"I rest my case. But if you want to press the matter – and I'm getting thirstier talking so much – that monk, Hanyon, probably drank his urine, even with that fresh water spring nearby."

"Now, how'd you reach such a far-fetched conclusion?"

"Because I read that holy men at that time practiced urine therapy in the ayurvedic tradition called, 'amaroli.' *They* prescribed urine for numerous cures. There is a religious Sanskrit text called the Damar Tantra which, if I remember accurately, contains over a hundred stanzas citing the benefits of using one's urine. And, a man who would turn down a beautiful woman would be a likely candidate for a urine drinker. Same way he'd turn down a ladle of cold spring water for a dipper of lukewarm piss. And the religion thing of yours, a lot of references in the Quran and the Bible make reference to drinking urine – not that I'm advocating it on the basis of some flimsy biblical interpretations. Let's keep moving or we will be joining the bible's cast of characters."

"I'm not letting you off so easy. I read the Bible, and I don't remember anything about that. And when did you ever read the Bible that thoroughly?"

"I'm moving anyway. And I didn't read the Bible cover-to-cover like some Christian bible thumper. I studied world religions as a minor in college. The urine thing I researched a few years ago when some articles appeared in magazines about some people who drank their urine for alleged health reasons. There was this British actress who claimed it was good for her complexion and skin tone, and she referred to other celebrities she interviewed who cured themselves of various maladies by drinking their recycled water Even J.D. Salinger was reputed to be a urine drinker."

"Who? You mean the author?"

"Yeah, the guy who wrote, "Catcher in the Rye. Weird psych profile regarding him anyway. His protagonist wanting to run around to keep kids playing catch from falling off a cliff and all. Anyway, I've gotten off the subject...which is... I'm THIRSTY AS HELL."

"Apropos, Jack. Hell is hot and has a lake of fire, and that's where you'll end up if you do die of thirst."

"Well, good, because goody, god-fearing you won't be there to piss me off, no pun intended – so it'll be just me and J.D. Salinger having a cold beer with the devil. Unless J.D. orders a cold mug of piss. Which, by the way, is his own damn business if he does."

"And I thought coffee and cigarette breath was nasty."

Any further argument is interrupted by what sounds like talking parrots imitating Valley Girls. It turns out to be a small group of Koreans who had clustered around the next bend to admire the view. They react with amused surprise that two panting white guys are this far down trail. I noticed immediately that their lips were puckered around fruit resembling giant huckleberries. They were extracting the soft inner flesh and juice was dripping off their chins as they leaned forward to avoid making a mess of their clothes. The lustful look I gave the one nearest me caused him to cue the others with a warning glance. One that communicated, 'I've seen their movies, and I know what horrible things American hillbillies are capable of.' Brian, the consummate Baptist missionary that I had begun taking him for, was capable of chastening his lust for food and drink. He bowed obsequiously, and then gestured with a cupped hand that he brought to his lips to communicate the need for water. The group started bowing in unison like those balancing birds on drink glasses. They dug into their backpacks and fanny pouches and removed an assortment of fruits, and rice crackers which they offered in the customary palms-up fashion of generous Buddhist alms giving. I checked myself not to grab the fruit, and gorge myself; and then shake down the bunch for what they had left. I am aware of how our basest instincts will take over in situations where we're suffering deprivation. I showed my gratitude nonetheless, although I still had the urges of a thirsty, hungry grizzly bear stirring within me. Brian again used his Presbyterian political astuteness and good manners to leave

gracefully and move us along in the direction
pointed out by the Alpha midget in the group. The
trail we understood would lead us back to the park
entrance.

"Geez..us. Are your sure they meant this way?
This is like skiing a Black Diamond trail on ice
skates."

"It was your idea to take the switchback, and
descend this old wash. You said it would get us
down the mountain faster. And you're right. We're
nearly doing a controlled fall, and if it weren't
for this boulder field it wouldn't be so bad. So
why are you complaining?"

"I was commenting on the Korean's directions.
It makes logical sense that we would go in this
general direction. Which is downhill of course.
But I never saw a distinct trail except for that
path that ended after a few meters in the
direction they pointed us. I don't trust them is
all."

"Are you always this suspicious of others?
What about their generosity toward us. Heck they
shared their food with us. And they seemed to know
this mountain pretty well- certainly better than
we do."

"You're no doubt acquainted with the Last
Supper. How do you know they didn't just seduce us
with disingenuous kindness with the intent of
sending us to our deaths?"

"They were nice people, Jack. They shared
their few provisions with us…strangers. Can't you
see kindness rather than some dark, ulterior
motive?"

"Of course I can. When it's for real.
Cattlemen fatten their steer, and chicken farmers
increase feeding for plumper chickens before the
slaughter."

"Jack, stop it. You're worrying me with your paranoiac ideas. And you tell me to lighten up!"

"Okay, maybe I'm over doing it a little bit. But you saw what it was like at the train station. There is a cloaking menace in them when they're huddled together like a pack of miniature wolves. Those guys back there could be North Korean agents. And if they are, they would have to terminate any witnesses to their infiltration."

"**JACK, STOP IT RIGHT NOW**. I'll pray that the Lord gives you charity and eases your mind about these people. People who are also God's children, I'll remind you."

"Alright, alright. I'll desist with verbalizing my suspicions, even though it all might be true But only if you don't pray for me; which is the same as saying you can't handle the possibility of me being right, so you'll humor me, but get God to do it for you."

I thought I heard Brian reciting the Lord's Prayer and using my name in there somewhere, but I was too pre-occupied keeping up a rhythm jumping from boulder to boulder like you have to do on the Russian Steppes. One miss-step and you could fall and break your ass in a dozen places. Brian had better put his praying to better use, and get us an angel with the wing span of a Boeing 777 to fly us out of here."

By sheer luck – and no thanks to the 'help' provided by our Soyosan would-be assassins – we reached the trail head where our near-deadly up-hill climb began. I had only suffered some bruises in places that won't show (so long as I keep my tidy- whiteys on), and was able to re-hydrate before my tongue swelled and blackened and I had to start eating dirt. My pride isn't something I'm all that concerned about. But if Brian makes any derogatory remarks about my mountain skills, I'll see to it that he is relocated north of the 38th parallel. I will take him there myself in exchange for the unspoken thanks of everyone back home who knows him.

The rest of the assignment was unremarkable, although that's not entirely true. If I say more, I may find myself in one of our own social re-education programs, otherwise known as the penal system. I'm not paranoid, or inclined toward getting all kinky about government conspiracies. However, I fear the reprisal of my government for criticizing it further. I am a loyal citizen who will never speak badly (in writing) of our government's foreign or domestic policies. I have a healthy fear of Big Government. I don't want to be the poster Domestic Insurgent for inspiring a new era of Mc McCarthyism. I don't want to be forced to recant my beliefs, confess my sins on Opra, or be plagued by the IRS and harassed by the TSA whenever I travel. So, I Pledge Allegiance to whose ever ass I have to kiss, Amen!

Chapter 7

Deutschland Über Alles... Again

"German women, German loyalty,
German wine and German song
Shall retain in the world
Their old beautiful chime
And inspire us to noble deeds
During all of our life.
| *German women, German loyalty,*
German wine and German song! :|"

Second Stanza of the Original
German National Anthem

Let me add to the lyrics what else makes Germany a great nation: beer, breads and pastries! You could conceivably gain five pounds upon arriving at Frankfurt Airport; merely in anticipation of eating and drinking your way through the country. Believe me when I tell you that the body remembers the extra pounds you gained during your previous visits. So, in preparation for your anticipated over-indulgence you are fined a starting penalty by your body's fat regulator. Brown fat cell reproduction is a benign cancer. It doesn't outright kill you. It causes you to swell up beyond belief. I am an avid runner, and work out religiously. I jog through the airport, and don't stop running until I leave the country. I'm not fat like most of the American tourists I see lumbering through customs. We are a country of obese people whose children are now born into this world all looking like Baby Hueys. MCI doesn't have weight requirements for their consultants. This is for several reasons. First, not everyone is interviewed in person. A series of telephone calls usually suffices. So, sight unseen, consultants of all shapes and sizes get hired. The second reason is that it violates some vague set of civil liberties, and therefore employers are not allowed to discriminate on the basis of weight; along with all the other things people get repulsed or homicidal about. Like: color, race, religion, creed, IQ and sexual orientation. I don't care what people look like, or what their beliefs are. I don't appreciate it that the airlines have skinny-sized their seats when fast food restaurants have supersized their meals, and expect me to suffer a middle ages pressing death sandwiched between two large people (aka, lardos) who overflow their armrests.

This gives you some idea then of what the flight to Germany was like. The press of the 'large' crowd is inescapable whether in the air or on the ground. I had been to Korea, the land of Lilliput, and had just left the land of

204

Brobdingnag where the chairs are twelve times bigger than an airplane seat. I had just arrived in Germany, which like the Land of Laputa, used its devotion to music, and mathematics to a non-practical end. That non-practical end was a succession of wars, and as many defeats. However, there is nothing evident in the German psyche that might indicate this. They are a stoic people, whose drive for conquest is still strong. Their last conquest was world economics. They had, up until the beginning of the 90s, been among the strongest nations. They had achieved world market dominance. In 1987, they boasted having the fourth largest GDP in the world; and with only 1.3% of the world's population. They had done incredibly well for a country that was destroyed by two world wars, and had such run-away inflation that it took a wheel barrow full of Reich Marcs to buy a loaf of bread. They were competitive with China. Both nations left the United States struggling to catch up, like the seven year old who chases after his college track star brother who isn't slowing the pace in deference to his age and stride. Not to belabor boring economics, Germany has since lost the race to a nation of Chinese bicycle riders (resembling ants). Before all that happened, the United States, not to be bested by a country of militant financiers, decided to play dirty. The U.S. conspired with the Brits, the French and the Russians (their former Four Powers partners) and called in their markers. The Hooligans of Occupation anted up by helping instigate the collapse of the Berlin Wall, and thereby collapsing the German economy. Although the official historic explanation is that an anti-communist up-rising occurred in the East, and the Russians did not intervene. With the demolition of concrete and barbed wire, sixteen million East Germans were reunited with the West. Like prodigal sons and daughters returning home, they were also dependent upon their well-off West German parents for support. October third is recognized as German Reunification Day. Some people in the West weren't singing, "Deutschland Uber Alles," with much enthusiasm.

So, again, the twice great world power was taught a lesson: Don't fuck with the U.S. of A. Our country is a sore loser when someone beats us at our own game. After World War II, the Marshall Plan loaned billions of dollars to Germany to help rebuild it literally from the ashes of fire bombings, and conventional aerial ordinance. I learned in high school that this was loan money that had to be re-paid to the United States. It was. The Germans made their final payment in 1971. Their dominance was due to the strength of their currency, and their drive for superiority – like the die-hard conquerors that they are still. I vaguely remember reading about the Morgenthau Plan when I took Modern History in college. According to the Morgenthau Plan, the United States took punitive measures against the Germans in addition to dismantling their steel plants. For example, intellectual rights were confiscated; meaning that dozens of German patents, held domestically and abroad, were seized by the government of the United States and applied to further U.S. industries. We know how to make our foes cry, "Uncle…Sam."

So much for history 303. I was back in the beaten, but not defeated Fatherland. For all their recurring debt, and having to carry the rest of the EU by disproportionately backing the Euro, I struggled to stretch my dollars. The dollar isn't worth shit. My father would be outraged. He would say, "We won the war? Why are we kissing Kraut asses? You know they didn't get rid of all them Nazis. They let them run the country after we pulled out. Now they're kick 'n sand in our face." Well, for all his frank provincialism, he was right. But you know, Pop, "All's fair in love and war," even the post-war. I try to stay away from the politics. However, I become invested in the politics of economics when most Americans do. When you can't buy a loaf of bread for less than a wheel barrow full of dollars. Then it's time to sound the clarion, and bring the revolution to the streets. I admit my angst over not having enough spending power. I am a true American; a member of a consumer cult that Capitalism has created. I protest often and out loud – to the annoyance of my family - that we're being conditioned to spend every penny we make. I know our habits of spending disproportionately profit the producers of the goods and services we consume. For this reason, I refuse to watch syndicated TV shows with their blatant product placement gimmicks and the frequent commercial interruptions. If Sarah Palin's, "Joe six-pack" can't afford his beer, look out government. Raw opium isn't the "Opium of the People", the money to support the habit is. And I'm not referring to licit or illicit drugs. If I can't buy the latest Mac, or the HD, 3-D, Widescreen TV, I'm going to be a very unhappy voter come election time. Supply-side economics is the operative term. Admit it, if your political party doesn't continue its crazy spending policies, and lower the barriers for getting what you want, you're going to be jonesing through the next election. And our elected officials don't want that to happen. So they'll gladly *spend* us into double digit inflation and supersize the national debt.

So, I confess that I wasn't being truthful. Saying that I wasn't going to steer this rhetoric into a political argument. I can't help myself. I don't care if *they* come for me, or keep harassing me at the airports. I know I'm in good company with all the other patriots on the No-fly list. I believe that Jesse Ventura and Nelson Mandela share a common cause, though Jesse has not yet paid as high a price. I would like to believe that he is one of the good guys; an old fashion politician with an ax to grind because he wasn't taken seriously as the governor of Wisconsin. At least the old fashion types strove to give the appearance of propriety. Perhaps it's not fair to the neocons and the like who have the media stuck up their ass every trip to the toilet. Along with internet cams hidden in their commodes which provide live streaming to every household computer. I wouldn't be thrilled to share their notoriety or their ignominy. I value my private toilet time too much. I still do my best thinking there, along with catching up on magazine articles of interest. I imagine that Gary thinks likewise, if he ever surfaces again for me to ask.

Being a Teutonophile should inspire the same cautions. The German's have neither succeeded, nor much less ever wanted to control their police. They have been the police state that the United States is now becoming. I have confidence though that the Germans are better at it because they have decades of practice, and I believe manage their social injustices more skillfully. The TSA and Homeland Security as a whole need to perfect their methods, and emulate modern German police tactics. The American lawman icon is portrayed either as a super crime fighter, or a corrupt cop on the take. TSA has more testosterone and anabolic steroid than's required for quelling the minor acts of disobedience they encounter in the security queues. They thrive on knowing that cruelty and humiliation is its own reward. Methods with which higher pay, or patriotism can't compete. Now, here is an example of a large work force whose employees really love what they do for a living. You've got to grant them that. They have genuine job satisfaction. I reserve the right to hate them for it just the same.

I've returned to Germany where I'll take my chances with experienced professionals. I am assured that MCI has special dispensations, akin to diplomatic immunity, whereby the German government allows MCI consultants to operate fairly unobstructed. I am told that it's because MCI's philosophy and political proclivities are consonant with that of the host nation.

I also have to remind myself of my loftier purpose for coming back to work with soldiers and the other members of the armed services. Right now, I'm re-focusing on the mission. Which is to support the wearied, multiply-deployed combatant who the military wants us to help recycle and ready for more combat tourism. I call it combat tourism because soldiers are deployed to foreign countries as temporary visitors, and for many different reasons. These reasons include: peacekeeping, bringing an end to sectarian and inter-tribal hostilities, and providing sustained maintenance during infra-structure building. And, oh, yes, stamping out terrorism, targeting Al Qaida leaders for assassination, and securing oil and mineral rights. No matter where, or to what end, the mission often requires an initial, hostile intervention (i.e., land invasion), and continued vigilance. The amount of time a soldier can remain "downrange" is limited to what a foreigner trained in the skills of war can endure under the most adverse conditions. A year to fifteen months is normal. Unfortunately, it's also enough time to kill a good many young men, and emotionally and physically cripple many more. It's still more or less a visa issued for a combat job stamped with a finite expiration date. Soldiers, marines and other support personnel are temps doing a job on foreign soil. I reckon this implies that we have no intention of leaving behind an occupation force. Unless Halliburton's engineering services – or is it KBR now - counts. Service members are not the ultimate victims of the military establishment's 'good intentions.' The locals are. Like what would happen on Cape Cod where I grew up. In the summers droves of tourists would arrive. They'd come along and muck things up. They'd congest the roads and take over our beaches. They slowed the rest of us down. The combatants are fortunate in that they get to go home when their tours end. Like year-round Cape Codders, the locals will only be truly happy and at peace when the tourists stay away, and the locals no longer have to depend on them to support the economy.

Oh, shit. There I go again. Carrying on a diatribe on a complex issue about which I have very little reliable information. This is why I stick with the job of being a *little helper* who also happens to be an apparatchik of the establishment. At worst, I could become a minor nuisance for my outspoken opinions about my relationship with the military. Nothing more than a sand burr caught on the cuff of a trouser leg. I trust that they won't resort to overkill to remove me. A flick of the thumb and middle finger is all that's necessary; not a flame thrower or a hand grenade.

Part II

Baumholder, Germany

I was happy to be back. To Germany that is. Baumholder wasn't   a familiar town; not one that I remembered having visited during my last tour. But then nothing ever stays the same. Memory doesn't give places that we visited in the distant past an accurate physicality. I found it difficult to tease out familiar landmarks even in the villages where we had lived for several years. This happened last year when Donna and my daughter, Loren, and her family toured the country with me. Granted, Loren was only eight years old in 1989 when we returned to the United States. Yet, Donna and I were no better off at orienteering during our recent visit than was Loren whose memories were based upon the impressions of an eight year old little girl. She had experienced the world as a huge and awe inspiring place. She didn't conceptualize her home as a grid work of named streets and navigation land marks. Donna and I had a hard time seeing the trees for the forest. It was like a Piet Mondrian painting of a familiar place presented as an abstract map on canvas. An acid trip version consisting of vertical and horizontal lines. A geometry that suggested roads and places of interest we had once known like the backs of our hands. Now it was like looking at these same hands and seeing the veins, creases, age spots and scars, and trying to imagine them as before when they were the color of cream and soft to the touch.

There are some places, I suppose, that don't change that much over time. I imagine Baumholder is one of them. I believe this to be true because it is a small village surrounded by Twenty-two thousand acres of woods and training area. It's encapsulated like a wooden barrel held together by metal stays with no room to expand. Meant only to hold what its volume will tolerate. It is its own island population whose boundaries have held its growth in check since 1937. It was the Third Reich who imposed this structure on the area in order to use it for rear armament. The German war machine needed a large training area. Baumholder's varied terrain of forests, fields, hills and valleys made it the ideal location. It has maintained its military importance ever since. It is presently the home of the 170th Infantry Brigade Combat Team. Armored vehicles have the right of way on miles of roads throughout the military training area. The report of field artillery and the sporadic staccato of 50 mm recoilless guns echo like rolling thunder across its hills and valleys. Training schedules for the infantry soldier stationed here can be intense and prolonged, but not always. There are also months on end of boredom when soldiers are confined to the garrison. Soldiers and marines don't do well when their activities are abruptly down geared while still fueled by adrenaline. Duties that had put soldiers in the "zone," were suddenly halted. Imagine a high performance formula race car, forced to a pit stop with its tires removed while the driver continues to floor the accelerator. If the soldier was equipped with a pressure gage his needle would be quivering in the red danger zone. That danger zone unfortunately overlaps with home and family. Marriages have been the chief domestic casualty associated with the extraordinary stressors of military life. The body and mind's appetite for high stim seeks all its chemical and behavioral counterparts in an effort to stave off the withdrawal. It's like crashing after a year-long run on crystal meth. Being a civilian driver cruising idly in the passing lane will get you run over from bumper to grill. The crazy top gun who's left his tread marks of your windshield has taken driver training in Iraq. Where you pass Iraqi drivers by moving them aside by ramming their rear bumper with your armored humvee. You get the picture. Counseling amounts to explaining and normalizing craziness while easing the family out

of painful withdrawal. If you think this is
challenging, you're right. However, not as
challenging as fending off cougars.

Part III

Cougar Pride

    An even greater challenge to my skills is dealing with my MCIC peers. I'm having an easier time treating the post traumatic stress disorders of the soldiers than in dealing with the daily trauma caused by my troubled colleagues. Let me qualify this remark by being specific; it is with my all female group of colleagues who have some issues from which I'm not immune. I will humbly submit that I'm no Casanova when it comes to women. I am not even trying to impress anyone of the opposite sex. What is hard though is being pursued by a bunch of randy cougars, and discouraging their slow advances. You know that slow, crouching movement that a stealthy predator assumes as she advances on her prey. The constant purring, the throaty growl and the pawing will wear down a stronger man than I. I can resist anything but temptation. A cougar is not a pussy cat. The cougar I'm referring to is an older - should I say - mature, seasoned woman who's been encouraged by our permissive society to operate with impunity. Take, for example, this news article I recently came across. I quote it in its entirety. You be the judge of whether or not there is danger lurking out there in the guise of young grannies pumped up on estrogen supplements and sculpted by cosmetic surgery. You be the judge of their motives. If they're seeking equality with men of the same age, look out!

Maryland mom named Miss Cougar East Coast

By TNT News Agency

Last Updated: July 10, 2010

"Dover – A 49-year-old single mother of two is now the leader of the pack after winning the title of Miss Cougar East Coast. Amanda Boser, owner of Edible Arrangements – edibleamanda.com – and a personal trainer in Dover, beat out several other contestants Friday at the pageant held at Rock 'n Tattoo Gallery, where the first annual East Coast Cougar Convention was being held. Its National USA counterpart has been on the prowl since 2008.

"It's interesting," she said of her new title. "I told my 16-year –old son about it. He laughed."

Boser said she never started out with the intention of joining the competition, adding, "It was completely spontaneous. But that's me."

She was having drinks with friends when one of them told her about what was going on at the convention, so she decided to check things out.

The key to winning was convincing the young men at the event to hand over coins – their vote for a contestant.

The outgoing Boser, who has worked as a cocktail waitress in the past, said she found it, "pretty easy" to walk up to tables to make small talk and ask for coins.

She ended up with 49 of them.

Along with bragging rights, Boser gets to attend National Cougar Week in Las Vegas next year and a spot on the National Cougar Cruise in January."

My take on this: Amanda has always been on the wild side. A "cougar" sounds tame considering this lady's talents. I feel sorry for her son. She says, she told him about it and he laughed. Amanda, mother dear, your kid's going to eat shit for your Cougar victory. The laugh is the one you express along with muttering, 'Aw shit, now I'm in for it.' The kid had better know how to fight. The stupid things kids will say about your mother to goad you into a fight is legendary. It all plays on filial piety. Insult somebody's mother and you are asking them to show you their worst. Chides like: 'Your mother's so nasty, I asked her for phone sex and I got an ear infection', is an example of the school house taunt. Even the classicists were aware of how provocative a pointed jab at one's mother could be. Even as far back as Shakespeare. This is from Act IV, Scene II of Titus Andronicus where Aaron taunts his lover's sons:

Demetrius: "Villain, what hast thou done?"
Aaron: "That which thou canst not undo."
Chiron: "Thou hast undone our mother."
Aaron: "Villain, I have done thy mother."

This kid's mother is going to be the subject of a hundred insulting one-liners, innuendos and straight out propositions. It's freaking embarrassing to have a fox; I mean a cougar, for a mother when your friends are all hitting on her. Worse if she fancies veal, or any kid with 49 coins in his piggy bank.

It is open season on the man who ordinarily wouldn't wander from his mate if it weren't for one of these aggressive stay cats jumping in his lap, or wrapping her tail around his pant leg. The way cats do with people who don't like them. Don't misunderstand, I like women. I notice, perhaps too closely at times, when a beautiful woman walks into a room. I know to exercise the three second rule of looking so that looking doesn't become ogling. Three seconds is supposed to represent three inches; approximately the distance from your belt buckle to your genitals. The distance has been changed from six inches to three in recent years. This accounts for style. Jeans are worn low so your boxers show. And six seconds was too long for most men; whose wives or girlfriends had probably walked out on them before the countdown.

216

Time and distance, notwithstanding, you don't go letting your little head start thinking for you. I have always admired a woman who takes the initiative and will ask the man out on a date. This is flattering even if you're married and she doesn't know it because you're not wearing your wedding ring. I don't wear mine for two reasons: my ring finger is fatter than it was when I got married, so it doesn't fit; and secondly I don't need a wedding band to remind myself I'm married. I should use better reasoning when it comes to answering the question, "Are you married?" Answering, "Well, sort of," isn't clear enough. To a cougar this means, 'fair game.' Cougar behavior generally dispenses with innocent flirtation and shy coquettish behavior. It is more forthright and cuts to the chase. And when there are more than one she cat in the pack, look out. Competition among a pride of cougars is nothing short of ruthless. It is almost like the quarry has no say in the matter. He is a trophy to be picked up by the scruff of the neck and carried off at a loping run to the nearest thicket to be cuddled like a prize.

I need to explain something about this awkward situation. The problem is a fundamental one. There are a disproportionate number of females in our profession. The helping professions are inundated with females whose natures make them naturals for the job. They are society's mothers whether they have children of their own or not. They are the nurturers, even though I know mothers who would eat their young if hungry for a midnight snack. I am in a minority. Males are more numerous in the field of psychology, but MCICs are primarily social workers. This is a female dominated group who look like Amish women or nuns, but are mostly Jewish intellectuals from Miami. I am a breath of fresh air to clients who seek a change of viewpoint, or who are allergic to patchouli. Others want a less cluttered office setting that doesn't resemble a Kinkade fairy cottage painting that's decorated in Inspirational poster art and Margaret Keane's, big-eyed children. They are grateful that they don't have to listen to Yanni and Paco Bell being played in the waiting room. Men who want to avoid being repeatedly asked how they feel will gladly schedule with me if they have no choice about having to see a therapist. This is their mistake because I do have an extensive vocabulary and it includes my being able to name the primary emotions which are: sad, glad, mad and excited. It helps that I can apply a pneumonic aid, which is they rhyme. It helps me remember them all. So, having explained all this, here I am surrounded by an older pack of social workers. If there is bad luck in being surrounded by wonton women this is it. They are at an age where, like fresh produce, they are likely to spoil before you get them home. Rude as it may sound, these are women who are past the "use by date." Three out of four were divorced, and seeking a mate to die with. Nobody wants to die alone. I don't mean that philosophically because we all do die alone even though people may be gathered at our bed sides. I mean having someone to call the undertaker if they have been paying attention and notice you haven't moved in a week. The one married woman scheduled to join the group might be safe, because like me she is a committed death-watch observer and isn't looking for a geriatric caretaker. I also figured she would have my back if one of the cougars sprung without warning. She might be able to buy me a moment's time while I run for cover.

It's not very nice to refer to these professional women as cougars – although they meet the criteria. I am sensitive to the fact that this is a sexual epithet, like calling Afghan middle school kids terrorists and Taliban radicals. Little do I realize that I am literally surrounded by the enemy – cougars with common Anglo-American names – and I am in their midst. It's ironic that my work with combatants exhibiting dangerous dyscontrol behavior is mild compared to the quirky

professional interpersonal relationships I
encounter.

Darlene was the first MCIC I met soon after I
arrived at the gasthaus where we are all staying.
She is unmistakably MCI personnel, which is a
formal and polite description. Otherwise she is a
waif. A thin, pale figure that glides rather than
walks, as if spirited around the room inches above
the floor. Her movements remind me of a kid at the
fair standing in the spinning Teacup ride. Her
movement is propelled by some force other than her
own. She's fucking spooky. It's my nickname for
her, but I don't address her as "Spook," but I'm
thinking it as she introduces herself. Her voice
is barely a whisper, and I have to move closer to
hear her, so I can try to read her lips as a
backup. Her breath smells like an open crypt, as
if she had been eating worms. I chalked up my
impressions as the product of double jet lag –
mine and hers. As I said earlier, it plays some
mean tricks on the mind. And I wasn't sure my mind
had cleared after taking all of my Xanax during
the flight over. Darlene exhibited minimal signs
of life. Although, what I took for a glint of
light reflecting off her pupils might have been
beads of anthracite coal. She murmured something
to the effect, "If you're hungry, I have a piece
of limburger cheese in my pocket. I don't mind
sharing." 'No,' seemed like the best reply to
whatever it was she'd just said. I added, "No. The
airline food has spoiled my appetite. I have a
bratwurst in my pocket if I get hungry later." She
cocked her head the way a raven does when curious
about something unfamiliar nearby. Her attention
turned abruptly from me to the two women who
entered the foyer. She turned to me, and pointed
chin up at the pair who came our way. "That's
Grace and Susan. They arrived last week. Be
careful, they're kind 'a weird." A comment which I
took to mean they're probably fairly normal.
Darlene, apparently having become catatonic or
lacking social skills, stood mutely by as Grace

and Susan approached, and introduced themselves. They seemingly ignored Darlene, as though she were my invisible friend. I had the urge to introduce Darlene to them, but didn't risk it. Just in case I *had* imagined Darlene. The women were in good cheer; apparently well rested and adjusted to the time change. Noticing my fatigue, Grace suggested having us all meet for dinner that evening, "that way," she said, "you can unpack and get some rest. If you're up for it, meet us downstairs here in the dining room. Food's pretty good. How's that sound to you?"

"Sounds okay. What's a good time to meet?"

"I guess, around 6:30?" as she looks to Susan for agreement. She still acts like Darlene's not there. Which seems to be the case. "Yes, 6:30's good. Give you time enough to get a little settled?" Susan adds.

"Yeah, good by me. See you all down here at 6:30."

And that was that. Darlene was still standing in the hotel's lobby when the other's dispersed; I assumed to go to their rooms. Darlene took this as her cue to re-enter the present dimension. "Well, good then, see you later for dinner. I told you they were a little weird. Wasn't I right?"

"Can't say that they are. Besides I don't trust my judgment when I'm overly tired. Seemed nice enough...the both of them."

"Hey, what's real anyway? It's all an illusion, right?"

"I can't think that deep right now. What's real is, I'm tired and if I'm dreaming, and going to keep on dreaming until I wake up. Hopefully more rested, and where everyone is normal. Got'a go. See you later."

"Wow, that's heavy. See, you agree with me..."

"Later Darlene."

This is not a good sign. I have been on numerous assignments, and this, by far, is one of the strangest. I know it's just day one, but already it's like having entered the Twilight Zone. For an assignment to begin so…eerily portends no good. There is something overall very unusual about this place. Maybe it's just me and I'm having a jet lag psychotic episode. No, it's not me. I'm certain that it's not. Darlene had creeped me out. It is conceivable that a client impersonating a therapist may have been selected as a consultant by MCI as an oversight. She reminds me of the fictional movie character, Bob Wiley, played by Bill Murray in "What about Bob?" She could just be a case of life imitating art. In this case a work by Edvard Munch, the artist who painted, "The Scream." Maybe I'm exaggerating her behavior. If it is art she is imitating, it's probably finger painting. I withhold any further judgment…of this nut…until I've rested and I'm seeing things more clearly. Still, I'm absolutely convinced, it's not me.

Part IV

1830 Hours...Dining with the Pride

I wish that Siegfried and Roy were here with me among these old wildcats to intercede with stern commands and god forbid - according to this duo - a whip, and a chair. I say this with no disrespect to Roy who was bitten by his tiger, Montecore, back in 2003: this man knows, now, not to trust a creature of wild instinct. At least walk among the jungle beasts wearing a steel neck collar should you trip and fall in its path. Yes, this is the arrogance of a spectator who has the audacity to voice omniscient hindsight from his back row seat at the Mirage. I can't help it. Because that's what I'm thinking as I sit here among the pride. I feel minor relief that they've ordered schnitzel. This should sate their hunger for flesh. I'm fooling myself by thinking I'm safe because they're feeding their visceral appetites. I am no safer in my assessment of the situation, or precognizant of the outcome of a slip and fall followed by an attack, than was poor Roy. You may be thinking that I am over estimating my attractiveness to these women, or perhaps to women in general. I wish! Whether, road kill or freshly prepared beef wellington, meat is meat to a starving animal. They'll eat anything, including their mate if pushed to extremes. My publisher put my photograph on the book cover, so you'll understand what I'm saying. the [first] book of job(s) features a full body shot of my son. He's the chic magnet. Before meeting me, people who'd seen the book cover, would ask, 'Is that you on the cover? What a hunk.' These were *mostly* women asking. I know they wanted to be an author groupie - if there ever were such a thing. I'd lie and tell them, 'yes.' I at least wanted to preserve their fantasies, and moreover buy my book. I should have had Fabio or George Clooney pose for the cover of this one.

Anyway, dinner with three women made me nervous, and…well, flattered. A man is a dumb creature; no brighter when it comes to mating than a male praying mantis or some spiders who are devoured by the female after copulating. I hardly touched my meal of broiled salmon and saltz kartoffeln. They were eyeing me suspiciously. I suspected that being a fish eater didn't meet with their approval. Like Plains Indians who never ate fish or small game because raw buffalo meat was mightier and manlier. "Spook,' hardly said a word, and when she did, it was something entirely irrelevant to the topic of our conversation. Susan and Grace executed their feminine wiles with finesse. Each was a master – or mistress – of the innuendo and double entendre.

I'm a sucker when it comes to mating games. I play like a fool at the casino, with his 'unbeatable system' for beating the house at their game. I engaged them like a mouse armed with nothing more than clever repartee and the ego of Mighty Mouse. "Yes," I said to our commiseration about spouses not being able to join the MCICs on assignment, "My wife can't visit me, but you could conceivably have an affair with a local, and it would pass unnoticed." "Uh huh," they toyed back with me, "Sounds like a good idea." I refused the waitress's offer of another lager, fearing that I'd get myself in trouble with these playful kittens – which I had begun to mistake them for. I withdrew gracefully. "Guten Nacht," I said, and hurried off to my room.

Waking up rested and refreshed is a welcomed feeling. I managed to avoid the MCIC pack this morning. I didn't join the group for breakfast. The extra hour of sleep was more restorative than food. And since my body was operating by its two am internal clock, I wouldn't be hungry for breakfast until this afternoon. Besides, It is safer to be among the warriors than the women.

A new MCIC is due in this afternoon, and I intend to leave the welcoming to those more familiar with the territory. I can only imagine what impact the new arrival will have on the group's dynamics. I was beginning to think we were part of a social experiment devised by MCI to study aberrant civilian behavior. The null hypothesis is: A group of therapists will fare no better than soldiers in combat when exposed to the stress of the military culture in a foreign environment. For the experimental variables, select a group, half of which are confederates of MCI and the rest are therapists in good standing. The confederates will destabilize the balance of professional conduct, and facilitate a collapse of order leading to mutiny or disobedience to authority. You think this is a whacked out idea? If you think so, you've never watched the TV reality series, "Survivor", or "Lost." Well, "Lost," may not fit the genre, but it could easily be our reality. As you know by now, I've worked with some patients whose outlook and their, okay, possibly questionable findings, relating to the depravity of our society's social engineers begs further investigation. If none if this is true, then it will make an interesting movie plot. I want the movie rights. But for now, I'm taking the approach of the cautious "insider," with my senses attuned to potential subterfuge.

Jack is becoming unhinged. Not that the government hasn't subjected unwilling and unwitting human beings to social (and medical) experiments. And, yes, the military, like the prisons, has been a captive population for such nefarious projects. Here is an example. Tuskegee sharecroppers (same as conscripted soldiers) were deliberately untreated for syphilis to observe the disease's progression with and without treatment. This study began in 1932 and ended in 1972. When made known to the public by a whistleblower, it was vigorously defended by the chief physician of the Public Health Service, Dr. John Heller. He commented, in defense of the ethics of the study: "The men's status did not warrant ethical debate.

They were subjects, not patients; clinical material, not sick people." Consider this: In the period following World War II, the revelation of the Holocaust and related Nazi medical abuses brought about changes in international law. Western allies formulated the Nuremberg Code to protect the rights of research subjects. No one appeared to have reevaluated the protocols of the Tuskegee Study according to the new standards. Even though further reform of medical subjects' consent was enacted, it is still possible for U.S. Federal agencies to keep secret their medical experiments on subjects. It can be done by Executive Order. US doctors did a similar, less widely known experiment, on soldiers, prisoners and patients in a mental hospital in Guatemala. This was masterminded by the same group involved in the Tuskegee study. It only came to light in October, 2010. These are just two of many modern atrocities. The point isn't to reveal all of them. The point is: Jack may have a point – though not likely. Perhaps illicit studies of withholding available cures from subjects deliberately infected with STDs aren't the best examples. But the government does have special dispensation when it comes to 'furthering science.' Social experiments are as numerous and as reprehensible. Social experiments didn't always involve inducing drug states or infecting human guinea pigs, some were purely psychological. Researchers Tom Peters and Robert H. Waterman Jr. wrote in 1981 that, "the Milgram experiment and the Stanford prison experiment were frightening in their implications about the danger which lurks in the darker side of human nature." Both induced ordinary people - if you consider college students normal and ordinary – to inflict pain (electric shock) and torture on their peers. It may not be a bad idea for Dr. Jack to be on guard, and not allow himself to be controlled, tortured or eaten by his peers. We should all be advised not to turn your back if trapped in an elevator with a college student.

Though reluctant to do so, I have to cut Dr. Jack some slack. He had some harrowing experiences while in Baumholder. He described a few encounters with MCI field supervisors that seemed suspicious. Suspicious because, the agents were attempting to split the team, by asking for incriminating information concerning their colleagues. This was mischief making which smacked of Republican evangelicals on an inquisition for the government. Yes, Jack's conspiracy notions are rubbing off on me. Jeezus!

Nevertheless, I think Jack turned the bend on his assessment of the new MCIC. He tried to convince me – or convert me to his radical spiritualism – that he and this woman had met before...in another lifetime. And this coming from the cynical atheist. And a scholar no less who vehemently attacks all religious dogma, and challenges any argument which attempts to persuade us that our lives are preordained. Or, that we are destined to act and to feel in predictable ways to our circumstances. And yet he will embrace all things mystical and transpersonal when he can reduce them to scientific, empirically based realities. The kind that is particularly palatable to post-modern thinkers. Dr. Jack is such an old time Catholic. He disputes the strong body of evidence which supports this attribution; like substituting Gautama Buddha for Jesus Christ, and Samanta Bhadra for the Blessed Mother. Creation myths abound. Leave it to Jack and he'll pick a good one. It's all one big, "In the Beginning...there was..." The reincarnation myth is an accomplice to Jack's indiscretion. It comes in handy to justify his infatuation with an honest-to-god knock out whom he takes for a Medieval maiden whose love was unrequited more than nine centuries ago. You'd think that during the intervening nine-hundred years they would have met up sooner and taken care of their unfinished business. But you know Jack; always quick with a comeback. He says to me, "you have to understand that time is not linear in the great cosmos." A soul, according to Jack, "is the part of man which belongs to the formless non-material and timeless worlds." And there are many 'worlds' according to Jack, like the multi-verse he theorizes on about. Worlds linked by wormholes that pierce the folds of the universe and reach back instantly to other times; such that the ancient past and the "Now" are happening simultaneously. And jack's final opus on the soul (how Catholic): it unfolds its spiritual powers in the world and comes to know itself. Perhaps at times propitious to its spiritual development it remembers an attachment to another embodied soul with whom/it there is unfinished business. Holy Shit! And I thought only Dr. Jack Mc Kane could explain the ineffable so knowingly.

Part V

"Revenimus" (We Come Back)

"Revenimus." This is the motto of Scientology's flagship fraternal organization, known as the Sea Organization. You may recall the press some years ago about movie stars, like John Travolta and Tom Cruise, being platinum card members of Scientology. Leave it to founder, L. Ron Hubbard, to cash in on the future - the far, distant future! Members of the organization sign a "billion year" contract to demonstrate their commitment to freeing themselves of past life traumas. I am leery about signing a mortgage contract for thirty years. However, I'd seriously consider a billion year mortgage contract if it would substantially lower my monthly payments. Hubbard is smart to be the lender if it's true that he'll return to his job (via reincarnation) often enough to collect. It will be tough reminding his reincarnated members concerning any binding legal contract they might have incurred prior to their births. I admit I don't understand how the whole thing works. Movie stars can be so gullible.

The origins of a belief in reincarnation is obscure, but may date to the Iron Age. The concept has endured throughout the ages, and a belief in reincarnation is said to be held by adherents of almost all the major religions except Islam and Christianity. Interestingly these two religious groups have killed more people in the name of Allah and Christ than all the others combined. They are smart not to want centuries of victims returning to earth seeking revenge.

Even the most preposterous answers to the mysteries surrounding death and the fears associated with it are eagerly welcomed into our belief system. They become credible when endorsed by the prevailing powers. Particularly when the power is communicated through ritual and ceremony and crafted by society's seers, shamans or divine madmen. Many ancient societies created their mythical power elite to assuage the anxieties of the group, and also to control it. But their power was relegated to just one facet of civil administration; the spiritual domain. Not to be underestimated, it was, and is, an effective instrument of control for those who regulate trade, collect taxes and make war. Those who cause the suffering and hardships must convince its subjugated people that their sacrifices have a higher purpose then furthering the wealth of the ruling class. If I can be convinced that my labors -in the service of others- have a higher purpose, then I will endure it - perhaps even worship it. I will sacrifice my earnings and the generative years of my life to the just causes and enterprises of those in power. If gullible enough to accept that my remuneration will be eternal life and a vacation in heavenly paradise...then, sign me up. If there is no happily ever after to be experienced here on earth, then the promise of a happily here after will have to do. Reincarnation assures the scared-of-dying that things - mainly you - don't have to 'end.' What a comfort it is to really believe that on the other side of the curtain of death is another three act play in which we get to perform. I don't know about you, but I'd like for this to be true.

I've gone on about this in order call Jack on a matter in which he contradicts himself. You see Jack uses cultural sensitivity as an excuse to enable the magical thinking of grown up children. He will humor his patients rather than confront them about their fear based attachments to fantasy. He had better stop being so socially and politically correct in his dealings with people whom he mislabels as having limited imagination, and therefore treats as socially disabled. These homunculi have been nursed on a steady diet of empty nonsense and have been turned into slavering junkies of entertainment passing for information and useless facts passing for knowledge. Who misses the point here, when the conversation going on around you is centered on some team winning the pennant, or who will be the next American Idol, or speculating on the nationality of Angelia Jolie's next adopted orphan.

Modern therapy has sold out to the New World Order, in which everyone is cool as long as they devolve together and conform to the subnormal standards provided by an inferior education and the banal scripting of syndicated news and mainstream entertainment. I would admonish Dr. Jack, if he'd listen, to shift his distrust of government and take responsibility for his role in colluding with them in order to keep people dumb, lazy and happy. When religion in America began losing its grip on the American imagination at the turn of the 21st century, Science and therapy began vying for control. It has become a crap shoot over who will receive the lion's share of what the pious populace will drop in the collection plate. What are you willing to pay for a wrinkle-free complexion, youthful vigor at 60, or a new kidney if yours' fails? What would you pay for salvation (spoken like an ole time preacher)? Brother can you spare a dime?

Okay, okay…I get it. Right? So back to reincarnation. It's a nice idea. Though, I'd like to have a say about what I trade this body in for. And while I'm at it, who my parents will be, the neighborhood where I will live, and with the guarantee of a huge trust that begins paying me at age sixteen when I'm old enough to drive a car. It would stand to reason that I would have to be a real prick in this life to achieve the standard of living I desire in the next. I read that the more selfless that you are and the greater the sacrifices you make in the pursuit of spiritual advancement, the less important material riches become to the avatar. Ideally, you may evolve so spiritually complete that you don't even require a body to travel around in. Just spirit; all pink and fluffy and able to fly without ever having to go through a TSA screening or sit in a cramped *airplane seat. If this be blasphemy, I'll recant on my deathbed. Since I am not gifted with great riches, I may qualify for nirvana by default. Let Dr. Jack have his daydreams. He'll proselytize his Eastern teachings to the needy no matter what anyone else says. You'll see where this magical thinking gets him.*

Dr. Jack Mc Kane's Biographer

Part VI

If love is the answer,
could you rephrase the question?

-Lily Tomlin

Gladly...

-the second book of job(s)

Reunited: Arn Magnusson and Cecile Algotsdotter

*The characters are fictional. They are
portrayed as the romantic characters in a film
based on Jan Guillou's trilogy about the fictional
Swedish Knight, Templar Arn Magnusson. The story
is the typical medieval tale of two lovers who are
separated as their punishment for engaging in a
pre-marital affair. It seems to matter little that
Arn risked his life to defend the royal family
whose cause he helped further. It is the classical
conflict between honor and medieval chastity, and
the passions exemplifying romantic love. The
characters are archetypal. Understanding the power
of archetypes in our lives doesn't help Dr. Jack.
No, leave it to him to become involved with a
woman in whom he (re)discovers this romantic
ideal. It doesn't bode well as such tales go.
Again, leave it to Dr. Jack to add in the reactive
ingredient - reincarnation - to convince him that
this is the real deal, and not a dangerous and
fanciful tale.*

I can't believe it! I know on some deep
intuitive level, that I've met this woman before.
It's not like this happens all the time. It
doesn't. This is a rare phenomenon. I remember
experiencing this way when Donna and I met. Even
Donna felt that way. Although she attributed our
karma to some past master/slave relationship - and
she wasn't the master. So you can imagine where a
past life like that could lead two people. People
tend to shrug off these powerful, chance meetings
and the deep stirrings they cause as, "love at
first sight." No. That's not what's going on right
now. I see the same recognition in her eyes as
well. This is how it's going as I'm being
introduced to Miriam. She has just arrived from
New Mexico. She is a golden haired middle aged
woman with green eyes and lips that form the hint
of a smile. She is enchanting. I have this split
second flashback of this woman standing in a glade

dressed in a fancy surcoat, with a light linen blouse under her tunic. The blouse has slipped over one of her shoulders; exposing skin the color of fresh cream. It is a style I later looked up and learned was the style worn in the sixteenth century by young maidens in this part of the world. I'm not visualizing this scene through the cobwebs of a fuzzy jet lagged brain. I am actually startled by the clarity of the vision. I gather enough presence of mind to welcome her. I engage in some small talk; information about the local weather and the Spartan comforts of the gasthaus. Talk that has nothing to do with what is being subliminally communicated. Our eyes speak independent of our mundane conversation about the weather and the accommodations. As we prepare to go our separate ways, I feel as though I've had a spell cast over me. The sensation is like the clarity and high-tuned buzz you feel when you've just taken a hit off the crack pipe, or have reached terminal velocity during free-fall. I wait for the let down and fatigue that typically follows one of these episodes, but it doesn't happen. I have just pierced the folds of the parallel universe and I am in two places at once; one ancient and the one happening now. I know she feels the same way. I do what any savvy tzadik does when suddenly aware that he's in the presence of the love of his past life. I experience a panic attack.

"Jack," she says with the concern of the White Tara, the female Buddhist deity of compassion, "Are you alright? You look really pale. My dear lad, are you getting sick?"

"No, my Lady, I am fine." *Why am I talking like an Elizabethan courtier? And did she just say, 'My dear lad?'*

"My, aren't we being formal...and old fashioned. Or is it Chaucerian? We're sounding very old English. Strange isn't it?"

"Yes, just as I was thinking. We must be old souls. I read somewhere about people meeting for the first time and behaving as if they were old acquaintances. In fact, I vaguely recall hearing Brian Weiss lecture about it."

"You're talking about the University of Miami professor who did past-life regressions, and wrote a book about his clients' experiences."

"Yes. I read it: 'Many Lives, Many Masters.' Pretty interesting stuff, although Weiss remained somewhat skeptical about the whole idea of reincarnation. I mean, as far as endorsing it as fact."

"Yes, but he presented a pretty strong case didn't he? He reported on his patients' experiences through past-life regression."

"That's the point. He used hypnosis; an instrument of scientific investigation – not proof exactly. I like his work though. He believes that science should do its part in exploring the possibility that there might be something else out there. I mean after we die."

"Don't you? I mean, believe there's something more."

"Well, I'm skeptical…."

"Come on, do you or don't you?"

"I'm not sure. Let's just say that there's plenty going on right here to suggest that there could be a connection between people. Things difficult to dismiss as mere coincidence."

"Like what?"

"Well…us meeting. I couldn't help but notice you had the same reaction I did…when we met…like we've met before…"

"Like we've known each other…maybe for a long time…or a long time ago?"

"I suppose so…"

"What do you mean, you 'suppose so'." It's what you felt too isn't it?"

"Uh…yes. You're right. I did."

"We could be fooling ourselves. Maybe it's just a powerful attraction to each other and we're making something mysterious out of."

"Now who's the skeptic?"

"Just testing you. I really do believe there's more at work here."

"We'd better be careful where we go with this. I'm married to this incredible woman, and she might not understand this attraction if I tried to explain it to her."

"You mean to say she doesn't believe that this sort of thing is possible? And besides, I heard you tell the others that you were, 'sort of married.' I took that to mean…unhappily…like me."

"You too? I don't mean to be so blunt. It isn't that I'm unhappy. I don't know how I feel. Besides, this…whatever it is…is moving way too fast."

"You're right. Let's leave this…us…alone for awhile. Let's just take things slowly…see what happens."

"Yeah. Good idea. So we leave it alone…focus on work. Right?"

"If that's what you want."

"That's what you suggested. I'm just agreeing. I think it's a good idea…you know, not to bring it up, and just wait. See what develops---if anything. Alright?"

"If you say so…"

"Oh, come on…Like we agreed."

You would think that Dr. Jack would know better. He's the scientist after all. Is he so smitten that he's actually buying into, 'haven't I seen you somewhere before,' say, in ancient Saxony. There is a chemical basis for love that makes people crazy. It's a fact: studies have shown that the brain wave activity of those in love resembles those with a mental illness. When we refer to someone as being 'love sick,' they really are; both in the emotional and the physical sense of the word. It isn't only the shortness of breath and rapid heartbeat we're talking about here. The full on attack is accompanied by loss of appetite and an obsession with the object of our infatuation. Jack is counter-intuitively brilliant (nuts). He's added the past life angle; a notion right up there with alien abduction and hearing god talking to you.

I would testify, knowing Jack as well as I do, that he has succumbed to a bone fide case of 'love at first sight.' Which is incidentally a case of lust. I'm not moralizing here. This isn't the one on the list of the seven capital sins. It is the very primal, first stage of human attraction. Religion has always corrupted what is biologically natural; fearing that people might give in to their natural impulses. Unbridled indulgence would keep them from going to church, and make them miss out on being made to feel guilty. Just eating an apple that wasn't theirs was enough to sentence Adam and Eve to wearing sackcloth clothing in the summer, and paying for their free love by having Eve get pregnant and making her suffer the pains of childbirth.

Dr. Jack and Miriam are as vulnerable as Adam and Eve. They are blissfully ignorant of the consequences of their dalliance. But you can't reason with the love-lorn.

Professionals are no smarter than the beasts of the jungle when they are seeking companionship. Jack ought to realize that he is smitten − not by an unrequited medieval love affair − but by a

tsunami of Miriam's estrogen that has just
engulfed his senses and released dangerous levels
of testosterone. This happens as easily to ferrets
as it is doing to Jack and Miriam. I know Jack has
gone and complicated this chemical reaction by
layering all kinds of meaning on it. He's always
lecturing me about intimacy and passion and all
that attachment theory BS. When I try and set him
straight that love's psychometrics - attachment,
caring and intimacy - are convenient constructs
which interfere with more reliable forms of mate
selection, he goes ballistic. He became more
incensed when I offered some sound facts
substantiating that arranged marriages were far
more reliable and ensured healthier clan stability
than capricious pairings based on romantic love. I
argued that I wasn't ruling out a good time, or a
romp in the weeds to increase the labor force of
the clans. I just think it's dishonest to
embellish raw animal passion with a lot of
psychological gobbledygook. When Dr. Jack
pontificates on love theory my eyelids start
drooping, and my libido flat lines. I don't want
to think of love as a cognitive-social-
questionably romantic phenomenon. Jack will find
out soon enough what I mean by the chemistry of
love being mightier than the weak theories of
human bonding. His lust - okay, let's refer to it
as his infatuation phase - will last, oh,
approximately a month or two. This is followed by
the attraction phase. We're talking about more
chemical flooding that will addle his reasoning
abilities. All the hormones involved act like
speed, stimulating the brain's pleasure center,
and causing similar side effects. Side effects
such as increased heart rate, sleep and appetite
loss and intense feelings of excitement. This can
last from a year and a half to three years. This
is fucking dangerous. It's why older men like Jack
can die suddenly from an attack of love.

It I safer to use crystal meth - and pace yourself -, eat well and take a sleeping pill at bedtime. It explains why marriages begin to suffer at the two year mark. Every married couple knows this stage all too well...it signals that the honeymoon's over. The perpetual purgatory of marriage – for those who linger on beyond year two or three - can be explained as yet another dose of chemical toxicity. The love chemists have found that this third stage, the attachment phase, is accounted for by unusually high levels of oxcytocin and vasopressin (trust juices). It's also helps if you own a big screen TV, work long hours and own leg irons and manacles to keep your mate from wandering. I have nothing further to say about reincarnation. If you don't have any of the aforementioned diversions or appliances than I suppose it's likely that you might stumble upon your long-lost lover. I take no offense when Jack calls me a Kinsey laboratory geek who lacks romance, heart and imagination. I know the temptations of the flesh, and I make no excuses for being a carnivorous lover.

There is a bizarre (yes, more bizarre) twist to all of Dr. Jack's speculation regarding the mythic course of his journey. The strangest aspect of it all is in the denouement which follows. I will re-construct the pieces from what Jack told me before he suddenly and inexplicably left his assignment in Baumholder. I should say, vanished. Disappeared in some trick of prestidigitation. Presto chango! There one day; gone the next. Time travel or foul play? My theory is that it is neither. I would wager that Dr. Jack arranged for his disappearance. His motive? To sell his books? This motive may seem absurd, but you've got to know Jack. He would rather be remembered and not be around to collect royalties, then stick around and fade into obscurity or wither away in old age. Although what I reconstruct is a stretch – even for me – his last days are indeed a mystery. It isn't easy for a person to disappear without a trace. We may as well have a micro-chip implanted under our skin with a GPS tracking signal broadcasting our every move. Whether we travel on foot, or by air, or by road, or by rail we leave behind a foot print; a ghostly vestige of our ephemeral presence like Luminol revealing invisible blood stains.

I can recount some details leading up to his...ah, departure. Jack had been keeping me posted daily by email. It's as if he wanted to squeeze as much in as possible before he dematerialized so to speak. Either that or he was finally getting the point that he had missed too many deadlines, and that his publisher was serious about her threats to drop the book project and cancel the contract. Jack would be obligated to refund his puny retainer. Staying in her good graces and keeping the contract meant a lot to him; besides he'd spent the retainer on god knows what. I suspect just as strongly that he succeeded in masterminding a hoax to make the news headlines, and ultimately become a legend. His former patient, Rizzo's, disappearance has always intrigued Dr. Jack. He may, just may have, walked into a trap set by MCI (which I suspect operates as a clandestine branch of the OSD) to discredit his testimony should he be called to testify in the case of Rizzo's abduction. He also knew too much about Rizzo's 'special project.' It stands to reason that relegating Rizzo to the nut squad, erasing his identity and eliminating any credible witnesses would be necessary. Only a powerful government entity could pull off such a sanitary group of disappearances; leaving nary a trace. Not even a drop of occult blood evidence for Luminol to reveal.

Dr. Jack Mc Kane's Biographer

(Who is considering entering the Witness Protection Program)

Part VII

Spy vs. Spy...Still fighting after all these years
First appeared in Mad Magazine, Issue#60, 1961

Spook was the first to spot them. She had
shadowed our group on the hike to the old ruins of
Frauenberg Castle. In her customary habit of
drifting off on her own; only to pop up
unexpectedly several minutes later, she was in a
position to observe the three men standing
together on a copse covered rise above the castle
ruin. Miriam and Susan were with me and about to
explore the deserted court yard, when Spook
sauntered over and pointed a pencil thin index
finger toward the rise behind us and to our left.

"Who are those guys, I wonder. Hey, you think
they're real?"

"Well, I can see them, so I'd say they are,"
I said in the gentle manner a parent would to
assure a child that there were no boogie men, just
damn ugly people.

Susan looking nervous, squinted to focus in
on the trio who had moved deeper into the shadows
of the thicket. Still, Susan could make out what
they were wearing. "Weird get-ups for a warm day
like today. Those guys, can you see them? They're
wearing suits, and dark glasses."

Miriam lacked conviction when she said, "You
know how formal the German's can be. They'll dress
up for a soccer match."

"You mean they dress formally to play soccer.
Wow, that's pretty fancy. You know the American's
should dress up more..."

"Spoo..Darlene. I think Miriam was referring to the spectators. She was exaggerating to make a point."

"Thanks for explaining my remark to Darlene, but it's not necessary. Maybe I did mean it the way Darlene thought."

"You, see Jack, I was right. Hey, but what's real anyway?"

"They seem to be watching us pretty closely," interjected Susan. "I think one of them is checking us out through binoculars."

"Maybe it's a camera lens you're seeing. They're as obsessed with taking pictures as the Japanese." My explanation didn't relax my guard. I didn't like the idea of being watched so intently by strangers…or having my picture taken by some voyeurs. "Maybe I should go and check them out. Ask what they're up to."

"No. Don't do that. Let's move on. Leave them to their bird watching or MCIC watching, or whatever their fancy."

"Okay, Miriam. But if they keep tailing us, I'm going to move around behind them and surprise them. Watch them and see what they're up to."

"Way cool Jack. Like in the movies. Get the jump on them. Turn the tables…"

"Put a cork in it, Darlene. I'm not thinking movie clichés. However, the best defense is an offence."

"Now who's spouting the clichés, Jack? Let's just ignore them and enjoy our hike." Miriam the voice of reason. The peaceful warrior. She's right. I'm thinking ninja thoughts in the German woods. These guys are just doing their own thing. It's the 'whatever' they are up to that bothered me. I'm not the only one who's rationalizing the surreptitious behavior of the trio of the men in suits who are observing our movements.

"Hey, maybe they're an illusion, and we're all sharing a non-ordinary reality. I read about groups all sharing the same vision. It's a powerful mind thing…"

"Spoo…Darlene. Why don't you go talk to them? Explain to them they're an hallucination, and that they should disappear."

"Jack, I think you're kidding me, right? You know, if we're all imagining them they can still hurt us. What's real is what we create. If we create them and they're hostile, well, you never know…maybe we should all close our eyes and make them go away."

Before I could figure out what Spook had just said, she was off again. I noticed that the mystery men had also moved on or were better hidden. Maybe Spook had the right idea. Being schizoid offered more possibilities to a situation than could be imagined by the rest of us. She could make things she didn't like go away, like *she* did when things got tense.

Miriam and I left Susan to rest on a stone bench while we climbed a crumbling stone walkway to the castle ruin. From the court yard at the top we could see a vast green sward spread out below us. It was why these old fortifications were perched so high in the hills. They offered a vantage from which the medieval guards could see an enemy approaching from miles away. The labor that was involved to construct these structures required hundreds of men and artisans and took years, often decades, to finish. The spirit of the past which inhabited these ancient places is palpable. You can feel a presence as if the ghosts of the Saxons still resided here, and continued to carry on their commerce, wage their wars and live their lives as they had eight hundred years ago. I became aware that Miriam was studying my face with a look of bewilderment, as if trying to remember where she'd met me before. Before we met several days ago… maybe long before that. I've seen that look in the eyes of old people who were wracking their memory in an effort to recollect an event that had occurred in their childhood. I was stunned by her intensity.

She didn't speak. She was utterly absorbed as if in deep thought or far away, yet still linked to me in some way. Her behavior was freaking me out, and I tried to avert her gaze.

"Miriam. What is it? You okay? You look like you've seen a ghost."

"I think I may have, or I am…close your eyes, and be very quiet and very, very still…watch and tell me what you see."

I didn't question her. I just did what she asked…

I see a man and a woman. I'm the man. I'm wearing an armor breastplate. It surprises me that I know it is called a cuirass. I'm attempting to dismantle it. I'm tired, hurt, and the armor's weighing me down. There is a woman dancing in the field. Her eyes are closed and she does not notice me approach. Her hair is swirling like golden strands of spun gossamer. Her garments are flowing with her graceful movements as she turns in a gyring fashion; her arms out-stretched like a ballet dancer. She doesn't yet see me. I'm almost close enough to touch her. I don't want to startle her, but I need her help. The ties of the breastplate are along my spine, and beyond my reach. My hip is on fire with pain. I look at my right hip and I see the broken shaft of an arrow. It's buried deep, and I think it's penetrated my pelvic bone. The arrow has pierced the fauld which is supposed to protect my waist and hips. There is a thin rivulet of blood running the length of my right leg. It has soaked the armored sabaton that covers my foot. I feel lightheaded, and can no longer stand and bear the weight on my right side. The lady sees me. She is shocked to see that a man has come up on her, and that he is in shambles from a battle in which he did not fare well. She is angry with herself that she wasn't on her guard against this intrusion. Her mortification is

*brief. Her attention becomes focused on my wounds
and the shattered aspect of my visage. She
approaches me tentatively; with both cautiousness
and compassion. She supports my arm which has
grown slack and hangs by my side. I feel as though
the sky is a pressing stone intent on crushing me
beneath its weight. I go down on my knees, making
every effort to remain up-right. I see a lovely
face that must be the angel of heaven come to take
me to my Savior. An awful darkness engulfs me and
I feel cold as if buried beneath an avalanche of
snow. And then…there is nothing.*

"Now what happens? Go on."

"There's nothing else. Every thing's dark."

"Keep your eyes closed. Mine are closed too.
Just watch…"

I'm off-balanced with what's just happened.
With what I saw, or more like it, had just
experienced. The vision sent a shock through me as
if I had been jolted by a thousand joules of
current through my heart. I really didn't want to
repeat the experience, but I am intrigued at the
same time. I am curious as to why this is
happening to me. And what role Miriam plays. It
seems as though she acts as a catalyst for a
powerful psycho-chemical reaction that has me
boiling with old and familiar images and feelings.
I shut my mind off, and…

*I am an old man. There is the vestige of a
younger man still in love with this wizened face
looking down at me. Her face is a map of wrinkles
like a tea strained map pointing the way to a
buried treasure. Her eyes are a deep green; still
youthful in their emerald clarity. They are both
beautiful and sad. I am listening to her tale. She
is telling me a story – of us – so that I will
take the memories to the life beyond this one. I
must be dying because I am weak; deeply weary with
a cold I feel in my bones. I'm not able to speak
or rise from this hard pallet on which I lie*

supine with advancing rigor. I can communicate with her only with my eyes. I feel a rising panic like seeing a far off tidal wave moving toward me gathering great speed and I unable to move. She calms my panic with a stroke of her hand as she brushes my cheek and hushes me in a gentle, soothing way.

'You came into my life with little spirit left in you from wounds suffered in battle. You nearly died. I and my Lord's surgeon nursed you back to this life. My lord – my husband then - was not pleased with the attention I gave you, because I believe he knew the future of our instant bond. When finally you bedded me in the forest glade amidst the lupine and the green grass, our passion only grew. It came to pass that we could not conceal our admiration for each other. My husband's spies saw us climb the glacis; my hand in yours. Although I lied and told my lord it was for support as the embankment was steep and my foothold unsure, he punished me and banished you from our lands. The scars on my back are from the lashes administered by the nuns while my lord watched. Not another word of you was spoken. I knew not where you had gone or if you still lived. I surely believed that my lord's huntsmen had killed you and left you for the wolves. And here you lie in this castle chamber dying, and I am here again by your side - this time to say goodbye. My lord has been gone for many years and I searched for you all this time. I do not regret that I have found you at last, and I do not grieve the lost years without you, although I will mourn your passing. We will meet again, my love. May the gods unite us again, and bless our love to last. Goodbye my dying knight…'

I am embarrassed that tears are running down my cheeks when I open my eyes. Miriam is full of sadness as well. She takes both of my hands in hers. She tells me what she saw, and it was the same as what I had experienced. We walked back in silence to the bench where we had left Susan. She looked as us as we approached like a little sister sent to spy on her older sibling. A tattle-tale who would tell mother that big sister was not where she told her she would be.

"You two look as though you've seen a ghost."

"If you only knew," I began. But speaking of ghosts, Darleen materialized from out of the blue. "Darleen, how do you do that?"

"Do what, Jack?"

"Just show up out of nowhere."

"You know, no where's someplace somewhere. I heard Susan mention ghosts. Have you seen any? You know, they could be real." I must be losing it. Darleen is beginning to make sense to me.

"I saw you and Miriam from up there." She points to a high ridge above us not far from where we last saw the suspicious trio. "You looked kind 'a strange. Not real solid. Sort of filmy, gauzy. But oh, well, what's real anyway?"

"Darleen, will you stop saying that…about what's real and what's not. And what is filmy and gauzy supposed to mean?" Although I really wasn't sure I wanted to know.

"I don't know if I can explain it if I can't say what looks real when it's hard to tell to begin with."

"Okay then. Just tell me what you saw."

"You remember Star Trek?"

"Yes. Who doesn't. What does Star Trek have to do with what you saw?"

"You remember when ship's engineer, Scotty, would beam the crew someplace outside the Enterprise?"

"Yes, from the transporter room. Go on…"

"Just before they would be transported they got kind of fuzzy, remember? Their molecules were being converted to an Rf analog of the radio frequency band. Then they would be re-assembled at their destination." I was stunned by Darleen's explanation. So were Susan and Miriam who had been tolerating Darleen as one would with an odd cousin with Tourette's.

"Um, that's a pretty interesting explanation. I get the fuzzy transporter room part, but where'd you come up with the physics theory?"

"My friend Mr. Rizzo told me about it. He's pretty smart that way."

"Rizzo…Rizzo who? What's he look like?"

"I don't remember. I mean I knew it, but I forgot."

"What do you mean, you knew it, but forgot? When did you forget?"

"Ah, just now. I almost had it. You know, on the tip of my tongue. And then I got this headache, and I forgot what I was talking about. What did you ask me?"

"I asked you what Mr. Rizzo looked like."

"Mr. Rizzo who? What are you talking about?"

"When did you see Mr. Rizzo last, and don't ask, 'Who's Mr. Rizzo'?"

"Shhh…Up there." She points to the rise where she had been wandering a short time ago. "Up there with his friends. Who knows if they're real?"

"Well Darleen, let's pretend everything's real for the moment. And you were up on that hill top, and there were some men standing there. What did they say or do?"

"They didn't say or do anything…just stood there…"

"Then what happened exactly?"

"Well, nothing…except I told them not to point that thing at me."

"Darleen, please be coherent. What 'thing' did they point at you?"

"I'm trying to think. I think it was…what's his name…Mr. Rizzo. He pointed a phaser at me and said, 'This won't hurt. Stand still.'"

"Darleen, are you still on the Star Trek kick. Phaser? Like in the episodes where a phaser is a ray gun or some sort of weapon?"

"I don't know for sure. They didn't call it that. It looked like the phasers the crew used on Star Trek, but maybe bigger."

"And what happened after that?"

"I don't remember…really! Next thing I knew I was back here talking to you…wait. I think that they were watching you and Miriam from the trees up there…and they were pointing that thing…the phaser…at you guys. Every time I try to remember…my head hurts. Jack, do you think what I saw was real?"

"Darleen, I'm beginning to believe it was. And the thought scares me. By the way, this Mr. Rizzo, is he a skinny guy who flaps his hands like a penguin when he talks. Maybe a little high strung?"

"He was…I'm trying to remember…on the thin side. I don't remember much else. Does anyone have any Tylenol?"

"I do, Darleen," said Susan coming to her rescue. "Jack, can't you see, Darleen's upset? Let's head back to the hotel. This place is getting to us. It's probably nothing, but those men have us all freaked out."

"I'm going up there to have a look around. I'm going to find those guys and confront them. I'm going to ask them why they've been spying on us."

"They're gone Jack." Darleen just said this with a certainty that surprised me.

"And how do you know that for certain?"

"Because my head doesn't hurt anymore."

"That's because Susan just gave you Tylenol."

"No. I haven't even taken them yet. I know when they're gone. I just know it. Don't ask me how…I just do. And they'll point the phaser at you too. Up close this time. It's worse up close."

"Jezzus…alright let's leave. I don't know who freaks me out more; the men in the suits or Darleen."

The ride back to the hotel was uneventful. No one seemed to want to bring up what had happened back at the ruins. I was glad for the silence. It was rare for this group to not to have uttered a peep during their waking hours. It was a loquacious bunch who was always showing off with what they knew about such-and-such a thing: the latest hot topic in international politics; the latest therapeutic breakthrough; what Dr. Oz was advising women to do about their waning libidos…and so on. I was deep in thought over what had transpired between Miriam and me. More so because what I saw felt so real. The clarity of the vision - of us in the glade, the sight of my wounds and even the pain I felt - unfolded as if it had happened in the present moment. I was also troubled by Darleen's mention of a Mr. Rizzo. It couldn't be the same person as my patient back in the states. The missing one. But, how many Rizzos could there be? Rizzo was my patient's first name. Darleen had implied it was a last name. But then again, Darleen's grasp of things is well, slippery. I had to think if I had told the group about Rizzo, and she had borrowed the name to fill in her reality gaps. It gave me pause nonetheless; something   to think about - or worry about. I made up my mind without sharing my intentions with my colleagues, that I'd go back to the site tomorrow and check things out closer. The old Frauenberg ruin is enveloped in an energy field that may explain the strange phenomenon we experienced. Such places actually exist throughout the world. Energy trines and grids roughly matching the latitudinal and longitudinal plats used to illustrate the globe. They not only serve as a cartographer's mapping technique but also designate the flow of magnetic forces originating from the North pole. Ancients and modern peoples alike have had a strong affinity for places of power. They felt and sensed them. They built their temples, and monuments on these energy centers. The great cities and early civilizations sprung from these geocentric anomalies. So, why not here, at a site selected centuries before. Chosen not only for its strategic location high in the hills from where an approaching enemy force could be seen for miles, but also for the power that radiated from its center. It was a state of mind as well as a place inked on a tattered map of animal hide. The authority of kings and the medicine of the shamans were more potent for it. It may be a far-fetched notion when I propose that it might be serving a modern and far more sinister purpose. That Rizzo may in some way be connected. And that he, in the service of the government's psych ops tricksters, may play a part in this nasty business. That business being an experiment in mind control. After all, the perfect subjects can be found here: soldiers and civilians stationed far from home shores. Unwitting subjects forced to be the guinea pigs of a nefarious government experiment. It was all coming together. Rizzo's appearance may not be a coincidence. He and I have a history, and not to a good one made in ideal circumstances. His business with the men in suits was decidedly dark and sinister. The agency that had been gunning for Rizzo probably wasn't involved with the Nature Conservancy or the Sierra Club. Our government's relationship with the Germans is likewise historically dark and sinister. I should have listened to my father concerning his misgivings about our treatment of the Nazis at the end of the war. The Nuremberg Trials were a farce he would say; "Just a circus act to put the spotlight on the crazies that couldn't be trusted to keep their mouths shut if we hired 'em to do our dirty work." He'd quip,

"They'd be giving themselves away raising their arm up in a Heil Hitler salute every time one farted." He would rattle on about how the Americans had hired some of the best torturers and mad doctors they could find among the Nazi war criminals. They had to be old as dirt, but they or their off-spring were still carrying on their dirty work.

Later that evening we gathered for dinner in the dining room of the gasthaus. We were unusually silent; not really enjoying the schnitzels and spatzle we had ordered. It wasn't the meal that was blah. It was us. At one point while trying to make small talk, Susan announced that she wanted to have my baby. I think she surprised herself with the comment. I did my best to ignore the offer, but thanked her for nominating me as the donor. I had to set the record straight, and confide to her that I had had a vasectomy twenty-five years ago, and I didn't think it was the reversible kind. I still don't know why she said what she did. I don't know why I was so polite about declining the offer, and felt obliged to offer a medical explanation that sounded like an apology. Miriam rolled her eyes in disbelief. Darleen looked at her with daggers in her coal black eyes as if entering the competition for donor recipient. I asked for a to-go container for the uneaten portion of my dinner, and left the cougars to their grumbling.

So this is what the group had come to. From cohesion to non-coherence. There was definitely something affecting the mental stability of each and every one of us. Surely, Darleen had a head start on us, but I could see we were catching up with her. I was worried because I was beginning to understand her, and had begun paying closer attention to her cryptic statements. She knew a Rizzo, and it was too uncanny that it could be someone different with the same unusual name. I don't remember having talked to this group about my patient, Rizzo. I don't talk about my patients as if they were abstract case studies or

medical subjects of the Tuskegee study. I was
feeling strange about this entire Baumholder gig.
Too many strange and inexplicable happenings.

Part VIII

Dénouement....

According to witnesses, Jack left the
gasthaus around nine a.m. He ate breakfast alone
said the breakfast server. He told her he was
going off to explore a ruin. She mentioned that he
alluded to seeking the medieval zeitgeist. The
German server never could decipher Jack's German
phrases. She interpreted his fanciful German
phraseology to denote an expedition to a local
museum. The MCICs knew otherwise. They understood
Jack's reference to mean he was going to the
Frauenberg castle ruin to probe the mysteries of
his and the team's experiences there the day
before.

Jack didn't return that day. He didn't return
at all. MCI made like it was Jack's decision to
terminate his assignment. The team members felt
that MCI was being intentionally vague about the
circumstances surrounding their colleague's
precipitous absence. To MCI, Dr. Jack had simply
abandoned his assignment without giving notice. To
his team, he was MIA.

You would think that an American citizen's
unexplained disappearance from a foreign duty
station, would grab national or international
attention. Dr. Jack's disappearance didn't. Most
strange, is the fact that his wife, Donna Mc Kane,
hadn't seen him in the weeks since he vanished.
She acted, said her children, as if she had no
recollection of him. Investigators attributed
Donna's reaction to either shock, or to early
dementia. The latter was speculated because she
acted confused and disoriented. She kept insisting
that she was notified by a man speaking on Jack's
behalf that her husband was on a mission for them.
His whereabouts, they had added, was classified.
The man who allegedly reported this to her, had
come to her home. Donna described him as being

very official looking. He showed her a federal badge from some department or other, and insisted that she swear an oath of secrecy. She kept rambling on, and added that he checked her eyes with an ophthalmoscope and took her finger prints. According to her story, they needed physical scanning data in order to prepare visitation documents should Dr. Jack's handlers allow her to visit him. She kept complaining that the scope they used to examine her eyes, had given her a terrible headache. It was concluded by investigators that Ms. Mc Kane's far-fetched story about the visit was a symptom of severe depression. The wild conjecturing one might expect from a distraught wife who's been abandoned by her husband. A man who is known for his global meanderings and a proclivity for unusual adventures. His friends weren't surprised either. They remember Dr. Jack often remarking that he dreamt of living an anonymous life; secluded and off the grid. So, his disappearance, whereabouts unknown, came as no surprise to anyone. Ms. Mc Kane wasn't going to cry about it either.

As I said, Dr. Jack's vanishing act had the desired effect. His absence was becoming the stuff of urban legends. There were more theories than plausible explanations. Although at first, I had accused Jack of pulling off a publicity stunt, I'm not so sure anymore. For a man with no 'public' following this doesn't seem reasonable or fair to his memory. True, he left me to finish his biography with little solid evidence of a life beyond chapter 7. As you have no doubt concluded long ago, I have always been dubious about his stories, and skeptical of his interpretation of the events he shared with me. His absence for so long (six months now), makes me wonder: Were there government agencies at work here? Did Jack get himself involved in a social or psychological experiment; not necessarily voluntarily. His predilection for working with unusually bizarre

clients and aligning himself with occult
scientific ideologies may have made him a prime
candidate for their sordid purposes.

I became infected with a curiosity about the
matter of Jack's disappearance and the
circumstances surrounding it. I say infected
because having worked so closely with Jack on this
writing project; his paranoia was bound to rub off
on me. As the old saying goes, "just because
you're paranoid, doesn't mean there isn't somebody
out to get you."

I'm not being an Islamic extremist when I say
the U.S. is the Evil Empire. Or "Satanic" as they
might ineloquently phrase it. It isn't un-American
to criticize our country - specifically our
federal government. It is un-American not too, or
at least protest against too much government
control. You don't have to be a Republican to
caution against this either. Creating factions and
labeling them is in itself a form of distortion
manufactured by the disinformation pundits who
compose public policy. The point I'm trying to
make is this: there are, not might be, acts
perpetrated against us by sociopaths who operate
with the imprimatur of the Executive Branch of
government. The military establishment is
preeminent among them. I am not alluding to a
fictional Orwellian Ministry. I am pointing the
finger at our government's Intelligence agencies.
The most diabolical human experiments have been
either contracted or carried out by the black ops
agencies within the military. Baumholder, I have
good reason to believe, is a test installation.
There are strategic and operational reasons that
make this group particularly useful as test
subjects. Infantry troops are the soldier ants of
the Marine Corps and the United States Army. They
are both vital and expendable assets; no less or
no more than a missile-equipped drone or an
expensive round of hardened ordinance. If the
military war gamers of the real world of armed
insurgence can produce a hybrid warrior - part man
and part machine, and minus the emotions of fear,

and perfected in the skills of combat, then our nation commands the world's best fighting machine. With little training, a novice in the art of war can be readied in a few weeks to become an invincible warrior. It can all happen through the scientific sorcery of electronic stimulation and robotic engineering. Like any virtual reality tool all that's required are twenty-something specially trained gamers sitting at a console controlling an Iron Man hybrid. These hybrids can be readied, mass-assembled and deployed anywhere on the planet. I know for a fact that it is happening. This isn't fantasy or science fiction. The inventions inspired by Leonardo De Vinci and Jules Verne that came to fruition centuries after their conception. The pace of new technologies has accelerated at warp speed.

No, Dr. Jack has not become a hybrid warrior suited in Kevlar armor. His role or use is uncertain. I'm not making an elaborate case to sanction his disappearance. I am suggesting that he may have played a part. A minor part, perhaps, but one that exacted a heavy price. I decided not to borrow anything from Jesse Ventura's investigations of secret government plots. I found my own. So, Jesse, eat your heart out. Here is what I found out about the military's unscrupulous activities that they had been carrying out in Baumholder during Dr. Jack's time there. To lend credibility to the disturbing information I uncovered, I am citing an article from a reliable source. The facts presented here are accurately quoted. Its relationship to what really happened to Dr. Jack Mc Kane is purely speculative. It doesn't mean it didn't happen this way. Your guess is as good as mine. Well, maybe it isn't. Do your own checking and see what you find. Here's some information to peak your curiosity, and shake up your apathy.

Mind Control: Patent

Check out this US patent by going to the
United States Patent and Trademark Office website,
and search for patent number 3,951,134. I've saved
you the trouble of booting up your computer, and
performing the search. By all means, check this
out yourself if you have any doubt concerning its
validity. Here is the patent information:

United States Patent: 3,951,134

Malech

April 20, 1976

Apparatus and method for remotely monitoring and
altering brain waves

Abstract

Apparatus for and method of sensing brain waves at
a position remote from a subject whereby
electromagnetic signals of different frequencies
are simultaneously transmitted to the brain of the
subject in which the signals interfere with one
another to yield a waveform which is modulated by
the subject's brain waves. The interference
waveform which is representative of the brain wave
activity is re-transmitted by the brain to a
receiver where it is demodulated and amplified.
The demodulated waveform is then displayed for
visual viewing and routed to a computer for
further processing and analysis. The demodulated
waveform also can be used to produce a
compensating signal which is transmitted back to

the brain to effect a desired change in electrical activity therein.

Inventors: Malech; Robert G. (Plainview, NY)
Assignee: Dorne & Margolin Inc. (Bohemia, NY)
Appl. No.494518
Filed: August 5, 1974

BACKGROUND OF THE INVENTION

Medical science has found brain waves to be a useful barometer of organic functions. Measurements of electrical activity in the brain have been instrumental in detecting physical and psychic disorder, measuring stress, determining sleep patterns, and monitoring body metabolism.

The present art for measurement of brain waves employs electroencephalographs including probes with sensors which are attached to the skull of the subject under study at points proximate to the regions of the brain being monitored. Electrical contact between the sensors and apparatus employed to process the detected brain waves is maintained by a plurality of wires extending from the sensors to the apparatus. The necessity for physically attaching the measuring apparatus to the subject imposes several limitations on the measurement process. The subject may experience discomfort, particularly if the measurements are to be made over extended periods of time. His bodily movements are restricted and he is generally confined to the immediate vicinity of the measuring apparatus. Furthermore, measurements cannot be made while the subject is conscious without his awareness. The comprehensiveness of the measurements is also limited since the finite number of probes employed to monitor local regions of brain wave activity do not permit observation of the total brain wave profile in a single test.

SUMMARY OF THE INVENTION

It is therefore an object of the invention to remotely monitor electrical activity in the entire brain or selected local regions thereof with a single measurement.

Another object is the monitoring of a subject's brain wave activity through transmission and reception of electromagnetic waves.

Still another object is to monitor brain wave activity from a position remote from the subject.

A further object is to provide a method and apparatus for affecting brain wave activity by transmitting electromagnetic signals thereto.

The technology behind these applications has significantly advanced since it was proposed in 1976. If you're wondering what became of this patent, I'll show you.

Here is the good: "Navigation helmet creates sound maps for the blind" (actual quote from DARPA article).

Here is the...well, not so good: "DARPA wants to Install Transcranial Ultrasonic Mind Control Devices in Soldiers' Helmets."

Popular Science Article

Posted 09/09/2010 by Clay Dillow

"DARPA has been trying to crawl inside the minds of soldiers for a while now, but a new ultrasound technology could let them get deeper inside than ever. Working under a DARPA grant, a researcher at

Arizona State is developing transcranial pulsed ultrasound *technology that could be implanted in troops' battle helmets, allowing soldiers to manipulate brain functions to boost alertness, relieve stress, or even reduce the effects of traumatic brain injury.*

Manipulating the brain to enhance war fighting capabilities and maintain mental acuity on the battlefield has long been a topic of interest for DARPA and various military research labs, but the technology to do so remains limited. Deep brain stimulation (DBS), for instance, requires surgically implanted electrodes to stimulate neural tissues, while less-invasive methods like transcranial magnetic stimulation (TMS) possess limited reach and low spatial resolution.

*But Dr. William J. Tyler, an assistant professor of life sciences at ASU, writes on the DoD's "*Armed With Science*" blog: "To overcome the above limitations, my laboratory has engineered a novel technology which implements transcranial pulsed ultrasound to remotely and directly stimulate brain circuits without requiring surgery. Further, we have shown this ultrasonic neuromodulation approach confers a spatial resolution approximately five times greater than TMS and can exert its effects upon subcortical brain circuits deep within the brain."*

Tyler's technology, packaged in a war fighter's helmet, would allow soldiers to flip a switch to stimulate different regions of their brains, helping them relieve battle stress when it's time to get some rest, or to boost alertness during long periods without sleep.

Grunts could even relieve pain from injuries or wounds without resorting to pharmaceutical drugs. More importantly, in the periods after brain trauma ultrasound technology could reduce swelling and metabolic damage that is often the root cause of lasting brain damage.

There doesn't seem to be a medical treatment to heal the sick that doesn't have a darker side used to cause harm. Take nuclear power for instance. Harnessing the atom to produce electricity and produce diagnostic imaging devices is both awesome and wondrous. This same element when manipulated by man to enter a state of rapid instability is a weapon capable of destroying civilizations. It's disillusioning realizing that we are creatures running on an operating system governed by binomial code like a primitive computer. Our choices Reduced to a simplified dichotomy of right and wrong, good and evil and black and white. We operate like an oscillating crystal keeping time and counting down our inevitable destruction. So, for every good we invent, there is an entity whose goal is to pervert the good and turn it to evil. I would recommend that you inspect your hat the next time to doff it. One final note regarding the sinister inventions funded by the defense industry. And that is to call attention to another *innovation* I stumbled upon while checking out DARP's brain child (pun intended). It concerns a new patent application for an aerosol dispersant intended for use as an altitude sickness remedy. Why altitude medicine? Well, for one reason: to instantly acclimate ground troops once they've arrived in the mountainous regions of Afghanistan. Losing combatants to attitude sickness is an inconvenience to the combat team and the mission. It might sound like a reasonable treatment if it didn't sound like a concoction brewed from the contents of a goddamned Gilbert Chemistry set on steroids. I thought I had been directed to the website by a server error because of its intimidating research title:

Mixed S-nitrosylated polymerized bovine hemoglobin species moderate hemodynamic effects in acute hypoxic rats

The findings and conclusions in this article have not been formally disseminated by the Food and Drug Administration and should not be construed to represent any agency determination or policy.

Sources of funding: This work supported by the Defense Advanced Research Projects

Agency (DARPA) and the U.S. Army Research Office (ARO), contract number W911NF-

06-1-0318, and in part by the NIH NSRA Training grant 5-T32-HL07171 (David Irwin)

Mothers and fathers may want to reconsider if they are encouraging their son's and daughter's to enlist. Dr. Jack didn't enlist but he may have been shanghaied in the old British naval custom. Yes, a far out scientific explanation cloaked in military Black Ops secrecy is the stuff of Stargate, The Matrix and conspiracy theory. No one would conceive of the notion that Jack simply passed through a time warp and vanished. That he still shares these present moments with us – in another time. Imagine that he is roaming the hills and forests that he traveled with his colleagues months before. Imagine he is wandering the trails and glades searching for Cecile. Longing for her embrace, and the chance to elope with her to a distant kingdom that's beyond the cruel lord's reach.

Too maudlin and romantic, don't you think? My bet is on mind control and abduction by government agents because he got in their way. If I ever see or hear from Jack again, I'll let you know. Although if he returns, I wouldn't believe a thing he tells me about where he's been.

Epilogue

So, here it is: The End. Although, a premature ending to a story with no Jack Mc Kane around to sum things up. No Jack to leave behind his unconventional, parting words of wisdom. I had actually been looking forward to hearing his conclusions to his life-long dissertation on attaining job satisfaction and achieving employment bliss. I can't rightfully say whether he found it or not. I gathered from his description of work with MCI that he had found its closest equivalent; a job that embodied the ideal of working little and getting paid for it. The job afforded him the opportunity to travel to exotic places and share interesting customs. He got the chance to meet unusual people who were not necessarily patients but could have benefitted from taking major psychotropic medications. As a consultant for MCI Jack was in his element and at his finest moment. It is befitting perhaps that he should leave the world of job markets and stock markets, and disappear into the mist of time or microwave-induced forgetfulness (courtesy of DARPAs gyrotron treatments). It is plausible that Dr. Jack Mc Kane is employed in their service as an agent charged with carrying out their experiments. Jack's moral fabric wasn't made of wire mesh or rip-proof cotton twill. Jack could be persuaded to do just about anything if he could be convinced there was magic in it. Helmets that produced unlimited access to one's pleasure center, or made one fearless in the face of cougars would excite his interest. He would buy-in in an instant. He would even wear one, because Jack, no follower of haut couture or Foo-Foo fashion trends, would see it for its intrinsic value: an instrument of subjective - though artificially produced - job satisfaction, relationship fulfillment and instant nirvana...at the flip of a switch. Jack Mc Kane's high school, senior yearbook described him as, "Most likely to succeed as a scientist working for the Russians."

That was when Russia was our enemy; before it disbanded its vast republic and became our fair weather friends. I've probably known all along that Dr. Jack would eventually sell out. He was a man looking for the easy road to success and the most expedient course to riches and fame. Though he may not have made it in the fullest context of his dreams, he may have found enough of it to settle his bets, hold on to what remained of his meager winnings, and grateful to be able to leave the game table flush. Happy enough for his relative good fortune.

Jack. If you are reading this, good luck and god speed (whatever that means). And stay the hell away, and don't you ever point that thing at me.

Dr. Jack Mc Kane's Autobiographer

In Closing...

"Imagine that the problem has never been physical, that it is not biodiversity, it is not the ozone layer, it is not the greenhouse effect, the whales, the old-growth forest, the loss of jobs, the crack in the ghetto, the abortions, the tongue in the mouth, the diseases stacking everywhere as love goes on unconcerned. Imagine the problem is not some syndrome of our society that can be solved by commissions or laws or a redistribution of what we call wealth. Imagine that it goes deeper, right to the core of what we call our civilization and that no one outside of ourselves can effect real change, that our civilization, our governments are sick and that we are mentally ill and spiritually dead and that all our issues and crises are symptoms of this deeper sickness.... Imagine that the problem is not that we are powerless or that we are victims but that we have lost the fire and belief and courage to act."

Blood Orchid - An unnatural History of America, by Charles Bowden, published in 1995

www.ingramcontent.com/pod-product-compliance
Lightning Source LLC
Chambersburg PA
CBHW020616260626
47157CB00003B/1041